Tanya is a mother of three who lives with her two youngest children and husband in regional New South Wales. She has worked as an educator for over twenty years and is currently employed as a liaison officer and placement coordinator at a local university. Tanya enjoys writing novels in her spare time and to date has written four books, *The Awakening and The Purge* (from the Triune Trilogy series) as well as two unrelated novels: *The Fall of Shadows* and *The Underside of Humanity*. She is currently completing the third book from the Triune Trilogy, *The Affliction*, with the aim of finishing it by the end of the year. With many more novels to write, Tanya aspires to work full-time as a writer in the future.

This book is dedicated to my beautiful children, Josh, Kaileigh and Callum, who have supported me throughout my journey as a writer and been a constant source of inspiration. Everything I have ever done has been for you and I hope that by seeing me follow my dreams, you will never be afraid to do the same. Many a wonderous things have been discovered down a previously unexplored path.

Tanya Schiller-Hartnett

THE PURGE

Book Two of the Triune Trilogy

AUSTIN MACAULEY PUBLISHERS™
LONDON • CAMBRIDGE • NEW YORK • SHARJAH

Copyright © Tanya Schiller-Hartnett 2022

The right of Tanya Schiller-Hartnett to be identified as author of this work has been asserted by the author in accordance with section 77 and 78 of the Copyright, Designs and Patents Act 1988.

All rights reserved. No part of this publication may be reproduced, stored in a retrieval system, or transmitted in any form or by any means, electronic, mechanical, photocopying, recording, or otherwise, without the prior permission of the publishers.

Any person who commits any unauthorized act in relation to this publication may be liable to criminal prosecution and civil claims for damages.

This is a work of fiction. Names, characters, businesses, places, events, locales, and incidents are either the products of the author's imagination or used in a fictitious manner. Any resemblance to actual persons, living or dead, or actual events is purely coincidental.

A CIP catalogue record for this title is available from the British Library.

ISBN 9781398427693 (Paperback)
ISBN 9781788780254 (ePub e-book)

www.austinmacauley.com

First Published 2022
Austin Macauley Publishers Ltd®
1 Canada Square
Canary Wharf
London
E14 5AA

There have been many people over the years who have helped me achieve my dream of publishing a book either by reading my manuscripts or providing advice, and I am so grateful to them all, but two people need special mention. First, I need to thank my aunty, Joan Schiller, who introduced me to the horror genre as a teen; instilling in me a great love for all that is supernatural and macabre. It is because of her that I started to write all those years ago. Second, I need to thank my husband of seventeen years, Paul, who never once told me I was wasting my time with writing and who has endured endless conversations about possible characters and plots as it all came together. Without his support, I would not have dedicated so many hours to writing and I feel this is what has allowed me to develop as a writer.

Chapter 1

The large wolf's heart kept a steady rhythm as it casually loped down the mountain pass; its ensuing pack keeping pace directly behind him. The air was filled with a myriad of scents that escaped the soft damp earth and wafted through the trees, alerting the pack to the presence of foraging creatures scampering across the forest floor. The bright moon overhead illuminated the forest and the pack, ignoring the animal scents, moved into the trees, keeping to the shadows for cover. Sniffing the air, the Alpha wolf snarled at the pack and they instinctively dodged a concealed trap that had been hidden beneath a clump of undergrowth; a pungent human scent betraying its presence. They continued on, moving silently as they padded towards a wooden signpost. The Alpha wolf suddenly stopped and sniffed the air; its eyes glowing bright red as it identified the source. It turned to face its pack and howled; the long, deep sound echoing down through the valley below and into the narrow suburban street ahead of them.

****

Paige Newman tied back her long blonde hair and dove into the tepid waters of her family's backyard pool, emerging in front of her boyfriend, Corey. Playfully spitting water through her teeth, she dodged his attempts to splash her and swam to the far side of the pool. Reaching for her water bottle at the pool's edge, she casually turned to watch Corey as he climbed out of the pool. His smooth skin shimmered in the light as he positioned himself to do a back flip into the pool. Grinning playfully, he flashed his backside at her before performing a perfect backflip into the centre, splashing Paige as she giggled in delight.

He swam towards her, his blue eyes sparkling with mischief as he dove under the water and tried to remove her bikini top.

'Stop it, Corey, can't we just swim for once?' she admonished, giving him a playful shove as he resurfaced.

'There will be time for that later. Right now, swimming is the last thing on my mind,' Corey replied, pulling her in for a kiss.

Returning his kiss hungrily, Paige wrapped her legs around his waist, relishing the warm feeling that flushed her skin.

Sensing her excitement, Paige's Labrador dog, Rufus, began to run alongside the pool, wagging his tail and barking in excitement.

'Rufus! Shut up, you stupid dog!' Paige yelled, laughing as the dog licked her face.

'Shit, Rufus, you are the worst wingman ever!' Corey joked, splashing water at the persistent canine.

A long loud howl suddenly reverberated through the forest nearby, sending Rufus scuttling into his kennel. It was the kind of howl she would have described as spine chilling if she had ever needed to explain it to anyone. It hung in the air with such heaviness and menace that it instantly put her at unease.

'What the hell was that?' enquired Corey as he pulled away from her.

'I have no idea, and I don't particularly want to find out either,' Paige replied, pulling herself out of the water. She didn't feel right in the stomach and her skin prickled with fear.

'Where are you going? We've only just got in and your olds won't be back for another hour,' Corey protested.

'I don't care, I don't want to stay out here anymore. Let's go back inside,' she said, hastily picking up her towel and wrapping it around her.

Corey shook his head in frustration. 'Gees, could you be any more boring if you tried? Don't you like me anymore?' he said hauling himself out of the pool.

'I'm scared, okay! I have never heard anything like that before and I want to go back inside where it is safe. Look at poor Rufus, he is terrified,' she explained, trying to console the whimpering dog.

Corey came up behind her and hugged her. 'It was probably only a wolf. You don't need to be afraid of anything around me. I'll always keep you safe,' he soothed, stroking her hair.

'You better, especially if you want me to put out,' she teased, turning to face him.

A bloodcurdling scream rang out from her neighbour's house and Paige's face blanched with fear. She ran for the back door and fumbled with the handle, banging the door in frustration.

'Shit, Corey! The door is locked, it won't open!' she said fearfully.

'It's okay, we can climb up onto the roof and get in through your window. I do it all the time remember!' he replied, leading her to the side of the house.

The sound of smashing glass emanated from inside the house and Paige jumped back in terror.

'There's someone inside!' she whispered, her body trembling uncontrollably.

'Quick, let's hide in the cubby,' Corey suggested, as he guided her up the rope ladder into her brother's treehouse. Hastily pulling up the ladder, they retreated to the far wall of the wooden structure and huddled in the corner.

The smashing sounds ceased inside the house and Corey crawled over to the cubby entrance, peering anxiously out over the backyard. The rear light suddenly switched off, cloaking the backyard in soft moonlight. The pool below shimmered, its surface so still and serene, it resembled a perfect sheet of glass. Corey scanned the pool side, eager to locate the backpack he had left on a deckchair beside it.

'Wait here, Paige. I need to get to my phone from my pack so I can call the police,' he whispered, prying her arms from his waist.

'No, you can't leave me! Don't leave me up here by myself! Corey, please!' she begged, firmly gripping his arms.

'I have to get down there, I'll only take a minute, I promise,' he said reassuringly, wrenching away from her and dropping the rope ladder.

He climbed down and jumped the final rung, landing softly on the grass below. He waited cautiously, listening for any sounds from within the house. A distant scream startled him, and he looked around in fear, his heart pounding like a drum within his chest. As adrenaline surged through his veins, he sprinted to his backpack and slung it across his shoulder before turning back towards the treehouse.

Rufus began to growl and bark loudly from within his kennel, sending shivers down Corey's spine. He froze as he suddenly heard a sound behind him and felt hot breath on the nape of his neck. Slowly spinning around, he gasped as he came face to face with a naked man. The man's amber-coloured eyes drilled into his own and he stood transfixed, unable to move under his intense gaze. The man opened his mouth, revealing a row of sharp fangs that appeared to grow in length before his very eyes.

A loud shot rang out and the man cried out, grabbing at his side in shock before staggering off around the side of the house.

'Are you okay, son?' boomed a voice from over the back fence.

Corey turned to face his rescuer and nodded slowly. 'I think so,' he said breathlessly before collapsing to his knees in shock.

'Uncle Doug!' screeched Paige as she stuck her head out of the treehouse. Quickly descending down the rope ladder, she rushed to open the back gate.

'Oh, Uncle Doug, I was so scared! I thought that man was going to kill us both!' she said, sobbing in his arms.

'You are both very lucky I happened to be out hunting tonight. I was checking on some traps in the forest behind you when I heard the howl,' he replied. 'Where are Johnny and Rhonda?' he enquired, looking towards the darkened house.

'Mum and Dad took Gus to his baseball presentation, but they should be back soon,' Paige replied, wiping tears away with the back of her hand.

'Well, it is a good thing that they weren't home, or we could be dealing with a lot more than a smashed-up house,' Doug surmised.

Corey stood shakily and walked over to Doug and Paige.

'What was wrong with that man?' he enquired. Paige noted his whole body was beginning to shake and all colour had drained from his face.

'That was no man, son, that was a werewolf,' replied Doug, slapping him on the shoulder and walking towards the house.

****

Anya Chemarov slapped an armful of files down on her desk and sighed in frustration as she looked around her new office. It was considerably smaller than her previous one at the Rockdale Police Department and the dark-brown carpet and textured walls gave it a sickly, claustrophobic feel. Dated posters and flyers plastered the cork board behind her desk next to a small, curtain-less window. A rendered cement wall from the building next door obscured her only possible view from the third floor and blocked any natural light from entering. Her sole light source, a dusty fluorescent light, flickered spasmodically overhead, its incessant buzzing threatening to end her sanity with each passing hour. By her estimations, the office had not received a makeover since the early eighties and the only assurance that Anya had not inadvertently stepped back in time was the modern BENQ computer that dominated her laminate desk.

Anya walked around to the back of her desk and took a seat on the swivel chair, cringing as it shifted under her weight and lurched to one side. She logged on to her computer, deliberately ignoring the blinking light on the answering machine to her left. *It will only be that jerk-off again,* she thought as she tapped away at the keyboard and searched through the Police Department database.

She had been transferred to The Westmont Police department a few days prior and her partner, John Goodwin had persisted in calling her, claiming he needed to speak with her in person. Anya assumed he wanted to apologise and had told him where he could stick his attempt at an apology, but he remained adamant that he needed to meet with her. The phone sounded again loudly, startling Anya and she let it ring a few times before picking up.

'Hello, Detective Chemarov speaking,' she answered unenthusiastically.

'Anya, please don't hang up! I need to...' a male voice sounded on the other end.

Anya quickly slammed the phone back into its cradle and swore loudly. She grabbed at her head in frustration before pulling the phone cord out of the wall and returning to the screen in front of her.

Her secretary knocked and walked in with a coffee in her hand, placing it on the desk. She picked up the disconnected phone cord and shot a look of disapproval in Anya's direction.

'Save the lecture, Penny, I couldn't give a fuck what you think anyway,' said Anya, reaching for the steaming mug. 'Thanks for the coffee, now if you haven't got anything else useful to add to my already shitty day, please kindly leave,' she added dismissively.

Penny tutted indignantly and walked towards the door. 'No wonder, nobody likes you,' she muttered before slamming the door behind her.

Anya shrugged with indifference. *No skin off my teeth*, she thought, taking another sip of the coffee. Since her arrival at The Westmont Police Department, she had sensed equal measures of both curiosity and hostility among her new colleagues, particularly the female officers. News had travelled fast about the disgraced detective who had been suspected of having an unprofessional dalliance with a suspect and her female colleagues were not discreet in showing their contempt. The same could not be said for her male colleagues who, it appeared, mistook her alleged dalliance as proof of her moral decline and readiness to sleep with anyone willing. Anya's vituperative tongue soon dissuaded their advances and they, for the most part, were now keeping a healthy, yet ever hopeful distance.

A sharp rap sounded on her door and Anya looked up to see John standing in her doorway. 'For fuck's sake, John! Can't you take a hint?' Anya sniped angrily.

'Anya, I wish you would check your bloody messages, I have been trying to get a hold of you since yesterday afternoon!' John admonished, walking towards her. 'Nice office!' he added patronisingly.

'What the fuck do you want from me? You have ruined my career, not to mention my reputation and you expect me to accept your apology! I don't ever want to speak to you again!' Anya fumed.

'Anya, shut up and listen to me,' John demanded, standing over her desk. 'I am not here to apologise!'

Anya glared at him indignantly and opened her mouth to speak, but John held his hand up dismissively.

'Anya, for once, just listen instead of trying to tear my head off,' he implored, waiting for her silence before continuing.

'The autopsy reports have come in from the Smythe blaze. Wakehurst was not one of the victims. The bodies were identified as twenty-five-year-old Connor James and fifty-three-year-old Melinda Smythe.' Anya stood up from her desk and stared at John in disbelief.

'Ash is not dead?' she asked incredulously.

John shook his head. 'Not to my knowledge, Anya. Although we now must question why his bike was at the scene and the fact that Connor was already dead before the fire,' he replied.

'You think Ash may have killed him and Melinda? Why would he have done that?' implored Anya.

John shrugged his shoulders. 'There is speculation that perhaps he staged his own death to get away clean and tried to make it look like a tragic accident. Although he must have known that eventually the body would have been identified,' John theorised.

Anya's mind reeled with the news and she turned her back on John, not wanting him to see the tears of relief that pricked at her eyes. She had cried a lifetime of tears for Ashton Wakehurst when she had presumed him dead, and she had tried hard to put him out of her mind with each passing day. This latest revelation had brought all her feelings back to the surface and she felt a fresh wave of emotion course through her. Hugging her arms to her chest, she turned back to face John.

'Do you have any other theories as to Ash's involvement?' Anya enquired. 'I don't believe he is capable of killing anyone, let alone someone he cared about.'

'It has crossed my mind that perhaps he has been set up and is being held somewhere against his will. Most likely by Logan Smythe. At any rate, we need to find him to clear this up and to do that, I will need your help,' John replied.

'Why would you seek me out, John? It was you that sent me to this shit hole and got me taken off the case. There is no point in asking me for help as my judgement is apparently clouded in my lust for Ash!' she replied sarcastically.

'Look, Anya, I know you still have feelings for him, that probably won't change anytime soon, but I need you reinstated. You know more about these unsolved murder cases than anybody else and the bodies are still piling up. We have had a dozen more murders since last week and numerous calls regarding supposed werewolf sightings. This whole town has gone bat-shit crazy and I need your help, and so does Wakehurst,' he pleaded. 'If anyone can find him, it will be you.'

Anya remained silent, pensively biting her lip.

'We have had an anonymous tip off about a possible hide out for Smythe and his friends up in the mountains,' John continued. 'I want you by my side when we take them down.'

'What about Harry, does he support my reinstatement?' the Chief of Police had made his disappointment with her very clear and had not even considered her side of the story before suspending her. That had hurt more than the suspension itself as Harry was like a father to her.

'I have already requested that you are put back on the case and he has agreed,' John explained.

Anya sighed and threw her hands up in the air.

'Okay. I will help you, but only for Ash's sake,' she replied. 'Besides, this place is doing my head in!' she added, grabbing her files and walking out the door.

****

Matt groaned in pain as Logan inspected his gunshot wound. 'Who did this to you?' he enquired, pouring water on the wound.

'Some fucking farmer, I don't know. I didn't see him,' Matt replied. 'Why isn't it healing?' he implored, writhing on the table.

'I don't think he was an ordinary farmer, Matt. Hold still, this is going to hurt,' Logan said as Alex and Will held Matt down.

Matt screamed out while Logan dug out a single shotgun pellet from his side. He struggled against Will and Alex's firm grips, as Logan continued to dig for more pellets, not stopping until he had extracted all nine from his mangled flesh. Once finished, Logan flushed out his wound and applied a gauze to his side, patting him affectionately on his head.

'All done. Hopefully it will heal up quickly now,' Logan said eying the offending pellets.

Matt's eyes were glazed over in pain, but he mustered a smile in Logan's direction. 'Thank fuck for that. I thought I was going to cry there for a minute,' he joked.

'I have never seen you cry the whole time I have known you. Don't turn into a pussy now,' Logan laughed. He walked over to the kitchen window and held a pellet up to the light.

'These pellets are not made from lead,' he stated as vapour began to form around the pellet. It burnt his finger and he dropped it onto the sink.

Will approached Logan and examined his fingertips before picking up the pellet with a pair of tweezers. 'I think it's made from iron,' he said curiously. 'How could iron burn your finger?' he added.

'It gave off a vapour before it started to burn,' Logan explained.

'Then it must have something inside it. Silver perhaps?' Will suggested.

'Not silver, mercury,' Alex said coughing violently and pointing to the pellets on the table. The eight pellets were each shrouded in a wispy vapour that was quickly filling the small room.

'We all need to get out now!' Logan yelled, grabbing Matt and dragging him out the door.

Once safely outside, the group coughed and spluttered as Matt retched onto a patch of grass alongside the house. Will grabbed Logan's arm and spun him around to face him.

'If you hadn't got those pellets out when you did, Matt would be dead right now,' he announced.

'I know. And now we have a big problem. Someone out there is making mercury bullets that could kill us. That man was no simple farmer. We need to find him before this happens again and fast!' Logan replied gesturing to the large camp site that spread around the perimeter of his cabin.

'Especially now that there are so many of us all in the one place,' he added.

****

Evelyn Giuliano dried the last of the dishes and stowed them safely away in the cupboard overhead. The sun was setting in the mountain beyond her friend, Leila Merrin's house and she looked out the window to see Ash sitting by the hot tub, silhouetted by the sinking sun. He had been forced to endure so much; not only the murder of his girlfriend, Rana, at the hands of his own brother, Logan Smythe, but also the embodiment of an ancient Triune spirit. He knew that he may have to kill Logan to vanquish the evil Nequam entity that surged within him and threatened humanity on a global scale. In addition to all that, he had also nearly killed his grandmother, Lillian Russell, during her botched attempt to sacrifice him. It was a huge burden for such young shoulders, and she worried he was on the brink of giving up altogether.

Leila entered the kitchen and took a blood bag from the fridge, deftly opening the bags port and drinking down its burgundy-coloured contents.

'Have you spoken with Ash today?' Evelyn asked Leila once she had finished feeding.

'No, he hasn't spoken with me at all. In fact, I have hardly seen him,' she replied.

'He worries me, Leila. He internalises everything and without Rana, he won't open up to anybody,' Evelyn fretted.

'I know and there is a good chance the Triune will resurface again if Ash gives up control. He may even try to finish off Lillian if that happens. Have you tried talking with him?' Leila questioned.

Evelyn nodded. 'He just shuts me out. I don't know if he is emotionally strong enough to deal with anything at present, he is so conflicted with his feelings of loss for Rana and Logan,' she explained.

Ash had been very quiet since their encounter with his twin brother, Logan on the mountainside a few days prior. Evelyn wasn't sure if it was guilt for nearly killing Lillian Russell or his hatred towards his brother that was consuming him. Lillian had been rushed to hospital in a coma after losing three and a half pints of her blood after her attempt to sacrifice Ash. She had inadvertently awakened the Triune spirit inside him, and he had almost killed her instead.

While a blood transfusion had saved her life, she was yet to awaken from her comatose state. Doctors were baffled as to why she had nearly bled to death but attributed her condition to injuries she sustained during the cave in. Only those who had been present in the cave that night knew the real story. The Triune had made Lillian almost bleed to death with just one word uttered from his lips. If Evelyn hadn't stopped him, he would have succeeded. A mystic gold chain clasped firmly around his neck was all that prevented Ash from losing control and the fragile balance that existed between the need for revenge and maintaining his humanity was taking a toll on his sanity.

'What about his feelings for you?' Leila said, interrupting her thoughts, 'I know he can be a bit distant at times, but he does seem to be letting you get a little closer.'

'Sometimes I think that, but more often than not, he is belligerent towards me as though he resents me coming back for him,' Evelyn said sadly.

'Give him time, Evelyn, he will come around eventually. At least he calls you Mum now,' Leila reasoned.

'When he is not angry with me, he does. Unfortunately, he seems to be angry most days now,' Evelyn observed.

Leila smiled reassuringly and touched Evelyn on her shoulder. 'Go and talk with him. It will be good for both of you to get a few things off your chest,' she coaxed, and Evelyn nodded, heading out the door.

****

Ash watched the sun slowly descending behind the mountain and took a deep breath, relishing the silence around him. He could hear the muted discussion taking place inside between his mother and Leila and knew that he was the topic of their conversation once again. That was all they seemed to do lately, and it was not helping his current state of melancholy. Picking up the guitar by his side, he began to lightly strum, finding instant comfort with the familiar feel of the strings beneath his fingertips.

The events over the past few weeks had unnerved him a great deal and he felt he was losing the fight to stay in control of his own body and consciousness. The Triune, now Awakened, lingered just below the surface, only subdued by the presence of the gold chain around his neck. He touched the chain, feeling it pulsate beneath his fingers. At times, he had been tempted to tear it off his neck and allow the Triune to take over, extinguishing the tumultuous surge of emotions that tormented him daily.

Hearing soft footsteps approaching, he turned as his mother took a seat alongside him and placed her hand on his leg.

'How are you feeling today, Ash?' she asked, fixing her warm blue eyes on his.

Ash looked away, his attention focusing on the darkening horizon in the distance.

'I don't really know, Mum. Everything is just bubbling below the surface and I feel like I am about to lose my grip on reality. I can't keep existing like this,' he said, shooting Evelyn a desperate look.

'It will get better with time, Ash, I promise. You have endured things that no one should ever have to go through. You are strong, my dear son, stronger than you will ever know,' Evelyn soothed.

'I wish I shared your optimism. I am honestly struggling to find a reason to keep on existing,' he said sadly. 'Especially now that Rana is gone.'

'You need to keep fighting, Ash. Rockdale needs you more than ever,' Evelyn affirmed. 'We all need you if we are going to survive what is yet to come.'

'Everyone in Rockdale thinks I am a murderer!' he replied, angrily throwing a stone across the yard.

'Then go to the station and explain what happened. You have witnesses, Ash. Leila and I are both prepared to give statements. Speak with Detective Chemarov, she will listen to you,' Evelyn suggested.

Ash nodded. 'Yeah, maybe. I don't trust her partner, but I might be able to appeal to her good judgement,' he replied. 'Besides, I can't stay hidden forever.'

Ash looked across at his mother as she struggled to hold back her tears; her brow furrowed with obvious concern. Reaching for her hand, he squeezed it gently.

'I will try and fight this, Mum. For Rana and for you,' he asserted.

'What about Logan, Ash? Are you going to fight for him too? Despite what you may think, he is an innocent victim in all of this as well,' reasoned Evelyn.

Ash shook his head stubbornly.

'I can't promise anything with him. I picture what he did to Rana and I want to hurt him so bad,' he said, angrily lobbing another stone into the back fence. 'But then I think of everything we have been through over the years and all the times he has had my back and it kills me to harbour such resentment towards him. What the hell am I supposed to do?'

'I don't have the answer to that question right now, Ash, but I know you have to try and help him if you can. The Nequam has a strong hold over him, but we will find a way to free him. We will find a way to free you both,' Evelyn replied.

'Well, whatever we decide to do, we had better act soon. I can feel the Nequam calling me from somewhere up in the mountains and it is getting stronger. I have to find it and send it back to where it came from and unless you can find another alternative for vanquishing the Nequam, without hurting Logan, I won't have a choice but to end him as well,' he said rising from his seat. 'And that is something I never want to do,' he added before slinging his guitar over his shoulder and walking back into the house.

****

As the sun set, casting shadows over the clearing, Logan walked amongst the campfires that dotted around his uncle's cabin. The smell of wood smoke wafted around the makeshift camps as he individually greeted the newest arrivals. With Matt's help, he had amassed a small army of newly blooded werewolves and they now waited en masse for his instructions.

The scent of a female caught his interest and Logan looked over to his right, locking eyes with an attractive, dark-haired woman as she leant against a tree trunk. At last count, only three females were amongst the population of fifty plus werewolves that congregated on Mount Westmont and this particular female was the newest addition. Female werewolves were very rare as few could handle the transformation from biped to quadruped, a problem that Logan had discovered himself by accident.

He recalled the morning, two months prior that he had taken Amity, the newest staff member at BJ's, on a ride to the waterfall. He had borrowed Ash's motorbike and driven her to the "Cathedral Cavern", with every intention of having sex with her. She had also been keen, but during the throes of passion, the Nequam had surfaced and he lost control, biting her deeply on the shoulder. Amity had screamed and run off into the cavern, stumbling around in the dark until she succumbed to her blood loss. Logan had waited nearby for two hours before she awoke and began the transformation into a werewolf. Her limbs had twisted and turned as she screamed in agony, breaking in an attempt to align. The end result was a hunched, whimpering creature that pleaded with him to die through weeping eyes. He had killed her and hidden her body away, deep within the caves, certain that no one would ever find her.

Logan's mind wandered back to the female werewolf in his camp. She had long dark hair and deep blue eyes that stared back at him without the slightest hint of fear. The piercing in her nose glinted as she shook her hair and began to walk towards him, her tight leather pants creaking as she approached. Logan stood still and watched while she circled him; touching his arm suggestively as she made her way around to face him.

'Hi, I don't believe we have met,' Logan said, reaching out to touch a blue streak of hair on her otherwise raven head.

She smiled seductively, running her tongue over her full lips. 'I don't believe we have either, although I do know all about you,' she replied.

'Is that so? What do you know about me?'

'I know that you are the most powerful werewolf here,' she replied. 'And I also know that you don't currently have a girlfriend.'

'You are right on both accounts, but if you knew me as well as you think you do, you would also know that I don't have any need for a girlfriend,' Logan said, turning away from her.

'That's only because you have never met anyone like me before, someone who could be your equal,' she declared.

Logan laughed and turned back to face her, his eyes glowing red. 'I don't have any equals. You will do well to remember that,' he chided before turning back to the others.

'I always get what I want, Logan. You will do well to remember that!' she yelled after him.

Logan shook his head and kept walking back towards the cabin. Will was standing on the porch, a bemused look on his face.

'I see you have met the enchanting Alexa Bartour. She is an exquisite creature, wouldn't you agree?' Will teased.

'Exquisite, yes, but I wouldn't say she is enchanting. Where did she come in from? I haven't seen her before,' Logan probed.

'She hails from Westmont. I don't know who blooded her. She has been asking for you since she came in this morning.'

'Well, she finally found me. I hope I was worth the wait,' Logan looked back towards the tree line where she had been standing, but she was now gone.

'She seemed fairly happy judging from the exchange,' Will teased, slapping him on the back.

'Is everyone accounted for now?' Logan said, abruptly changing the subject.

'Most of them are here already. When are our special guests arriving?' Will enquired, throwing several rabbit traps over his shoulder.

'Just before dawn.'

Logan bent down to examine one of the traps. 'How many of these did you find in the root cellar?'

'Eleven in total. I will get a few of the guys to help me set them up around the perimeter. Maybe Alexa could be persuaded to come for a walk with me. I could test her out for you first.'

'I wouldn't recommend it, Will. By the looks of her, you might wake up with one of those traps attached to your cock,' Logan laughed.

'Yep, I think you might be right about that. Duly noted! I will see you once I am done,' Will replied, walking towards a group of nearby men.

Logan turned towards the cabin door and opened it, feeling a sudden jolt as the Nequam stirred within him. *Not now!* he thought desperately, leaning on the doorframe for support.

He will come for us and you must be ready! the Nequam's voice screamed in his ear, causing Logan to cry out in pain.

'I know, I know, but we still have time to catch him!' Logan grimaced.

He must be killed! the voice screamed.

'No. I can reach him! I just need more time to bring him around,' Logan pleaded.

There is no more time! If he is not a member of my pack by the next New Moon, I will kill him and then I will kill you! the Nequam warned, finally releasing his internal grip.

Logan fell to the ground, breathing hard as Alex raced over. Logan held out his hand to stop Alex and slowly rose to his feet.

'We have to trap Ash. If we don't, the Nequam will kill him,' Logan despaired.

'We need to find him first,' Alex replied.

'We won't need to find him. He will come to us. Of that, I am certain. First, we need to make our special guests feel welcome.'

****

The roller door clunked as it slowly made its descent behind Anya's car, blocking out the sounds of the busy traffic outside. Anya's modern, one-bedroom apartment stood in the centre of town, nestled between a row of identical buildings. Each apartment boasted a small, yet private front yard enclosed by a wrought iron gabled fence and a security gate. Anya had resided in her apartment for the past few years and enjoyed the solitude and safety it provided. Her neighbours, mostly professionals like her, tended to keep to themselves and this was an arrangement that suited Anya perfectly.

Anya switched off the engine and swung her legs out of the car, reaching back inside for her handbag. A scraping noise startled her, and she looked around to find Ash standing at the rear of her car. Her heart skipped a beat as she reached for her gun and instinctively pulled it on him.

'What the hell are you doing in my garage?' she demanded.

Ash held his hands up submissively and began to walk towards her.

'Detective, please hear me out. I'm sorry I had to speak to you here, but I didn't want to make a statement at the station. Not with everyone looking for me and thinking the worst,' he reasoned.

'Stay where you are!' Anya ordered, and he came to a halt alongside her rear passenger door.

'Anya, I am not here to hurt you. I just need to talk to you about everything that has been happening. There are some things you need to know,' Ash replied.

Anya, with her gun still trained on him, spun him around to face the car and patted him down one-handed. She felt the firm muscles on his backside flex beneath her hand and heard his sharp intake of breath as her fingers brushed along his inner thigh. Willing her hands to stop shaking, she finished her inspection and backed away from him.

'You should not have come here, Ash. My partner already thinks we are involved somehow. I nearly lost my job because of the bullshit allegations he made about us,' she retorted angrily, bringing him back around to face her.

'What allegations?' Ash enquired curiously.

'He told the Chief of Police that you and I were having a steamy affair,' she replied, lowering her gun.

Ash nodded thoughtfully and leaned back against the side of the car. 'Why would he have thought that?' he replied suggestively.

Anya's face began to redden, and she turned away, quickly changing the subject.

'So, what is so important that you felt the need to break into my home to speak with me?' she said.

'Well, technically, I didn't really break in, I only ducked under your roller door.'

'You entered my property without my permission, Ash, so at the very least, you are trespassing. Besides, you scared the shit out of me. Why didn't you just call me to arrange a meeting?' Anya replied.

Ash shrugged dismissively. 'I guess I didn't want to give you the opportunity to have the police lying in wait for me,' he replied.

'You honestly thought I would set an ambush for you? I have been the only one in your corner since the very start. I know you are not a murderer, Ash, I wouldn't still be standing here talking to you if I suspected you were. Besides, your mum and one of her friends came to the station this afternoon and explained what happened to you. You are in the clear now.'

'I know you must still have some questions yourself as to why every crime scene seems to have a direct link to me. That is why I am here. I am ready to explain everything, but I think you are going to want to sit down for what I have to say,' Ash explained, running his hands nervously through his hair.

Anya stared at him and nodded, holstering her gun and picking up her handbag. 'You had better come inside then. I didn't have any better plans tonight anyway,' she said, opening her interior door and ushering him into her laundry.

Chapter 2

The cupboard door shut silently behind her as the girl crawled into the tiny space and hugged her knees to her chest. Outside in the hallway, sounds of breaking glass and her mother's screams echoed throughout the house. The young girl covered her ears and desperately tried to control her sobs as the fighting continued unabated.

When the noises finally stopped, the girl burst from her hiding place and ran into the kitchen to find her mother lying face down across the table, her dress hitched up around her waist. Her father turned to face the girl as he heard her approach, his face bloodied with scratches and his eyes wild with fury.

'Do you want a turn too? Like mother, like daughter,' he slurred, spitting at her feet.

'No, Ben, leave her alone,' her mother's feeble voice begged from behind him.

'Shut your fucking mouth, slut!' he reeled on her, 'She needs to be taught a lesson,' he added, grabbing the girl's arm and pulling her towards him.

The girl struggled, and he slapped her hard across her face, causing her to cry out. She began to sob as he roughly pushed her towards the table and ripped her dress.

'Now be a good girl and shut the fuck up while Daddy has his fun,' he said trying to pull her pants down.

'NO! GET OFF ME!' the girl screamed desperately. The room began to shake, and the knives rattled loudly in the knife block.

'You'll do as you are told young lady, you know what happens to Mummy when she...' her father stopped short as a knife dislodged from the block and hurtled across the room, lodging itself in his left eye. He immediately slumped to the ground, the impact of his face against the tiled floor pushing the embedded knife further into his eye with a sickening crunch.

'You will NEVER touch me or my mother again, you piece of shit!' the girl spat, kicking him in the head. Her mother screamed and crawled over to the lifeless body of her husband, her hands slipping in the sticky blood that pooled on the floor beneath him.

'Lillian! What have you done?' she screamed.

'Something you should have done years ago, Mother,' the girl coolly replied, walking back to her room.

****

The EEG monitor spiked as Lillian Russell's brain activity fluctuated, alerting the attention of a nearby nurse. She examined the woman, lifting her eye lids and gently poking her feet with a needle, but the woman didn't respond. 'That's strange,' she said out loud to her colleague, who appeared equally puzzled.

'According to the brain activity we have just recorded, she should be awake,' the first nurse observed.

'She must be dreaming. I haven't seen so much as a muscle twitch from this one. She doesn't look like she will be awake anytime soon,' the second nurse surmised as she replaced her chart.

The first nurse nodded and they both exited the room, heading for the cafeteria for their first coffee of the day. After a few minutes, the EEG monitor spiked again, and Lillian's eyelids fluttered before she returned to her deep slumber.

****

'So, are you going to tell me where you have been for the past few days? There has been a state-wide man hunt for you since your disappearance,' Anya declared, passing Ash a glass of water.

The pair were seated in Anya's living room with a glass coffee table conveniently situated between them, keeping Ash, at what Anya considered, a respectable distance. She studied him thoughtfully as he sat across from her, his hands absent-mindedly playing with the glass she had offered him. She hadn't seen him for two weeks and it looked as though he hadn't shaved or slept in that whole time. His dishevelment made him look even sexier and she found it difficult to stop herself from openly staring at him. His voice broke her temporary trance and she folded her legs underneath her as she settled onto the sofa.

'You probably won't believe most of what I am about to tell you, but it is the truth,' Ash said earnestly.

'Try me. After everything that has been happening of late, I am definitely learning to keep an open mind.'

She listened intently as Ash explained everything that had expired at the Smythe's house and Lillian Russell's involvement in his abduction. When he was finished, she calmly unfolded her legs and perched herself on the edge of the sofa.

'Your mum hadn't mentioned a ritual sacrifice in her statement. Why would Lillian do something like that?' she asked sceptically, 'Is she supposed to be a witch or something?'

'Because she thought she could take my powers if she killed me,' Ash stated matter-of-factly.

Anya snorted and inadvertently spat her drink out on the floor. 'Powers? Who do you think you are, fucking Merlin?'

'It's not a joke, Anya. There are things about me that… Look, I don't even know where to begin in explaining it to you, but I am not who or what you think I am,' he said quietly.

'Ash, I know there is something you have been keeping from me. I can sense you have a secret and my instincts tell me that it is something dangerous, but I know that intrinsically, you are a good man. I feel safe around you and I can't explain why,' Anya replied.

Ash stared down at his feet. 'Can I trust you, Anya?' he said.

'Of course, you can, Ash.'

'Promise me you won't freak out or try to shoot me. I want to show you something,' Ash said walking to the sofa and kneeling in front of her. She nodded trustingly as he placed his hands on her face and closed his eyes. '*Recordabitur enim omnium,*' he whispered into her ear.

She gasped and threw her head back with a jolt, her eyes wide in terror. Ash removed his hands and stepped away from her.

'What did you just do to me?' she said desperately, stumbling to her feet and edging away from him.

'I gave you back your memories. The ones that I stole from you to keep my secret,' he replied.

She stared at him in disbelief, her mouth opening and closing as she struggled to find the right words.

'I have all of your memories. I saw everything that has happened to you, not just the things you made me forget,' she announced.

'Because I compelled you to forget, the only way I could give them back to you was to transfer my own. You now know I have been telling the truth about everything, especially the existence of werewolves,' Ash replied.

'Not just werewolves, Ash! Vampires too!' she said shaking her head. 'I think you should go. I need some time to process all of this and I don't think I can be around you at the moment. Please leave,' she said coolly, gesturing to the door.

Ash nodded and made his way towards the entrance way. As he opened the door, he turned around to face her.

'You know where to find me if you change your mind. You are linked to me, Anya and I will always look out for you, whether you like it or not,' he stated before walking out the door. 'Oh, and I need you to release my bike form the impound,' he added before shutting the door.

Once he was gone, Anya broke down and cried, banging her fist into the sofa.

'Why can't I ever catch a break? First, I get engaged to a philandering bastard and now I fall for a fucking hybrid werewolf, witch, vampire or whatever the fuck he is. Anya, you sure can pick them!' she chided herself, burying her head under the cushions.

****

Anya sat on the edge of Commissioner Willis's desk absentmindedly chewing the end of her pen as John, Harry and the commissioner scanned an aerial map that was spread out on the table before them. The commissioner motioned to her and she begrudgingly made her way over to them, wedging herself between John and Harry.

'We will strike at 4 am. The areas that John has highlighted are our rendezvous points. The team will not be progressing past this point until everyone is in position,' the commissioner ordered.

Anya took a closer look at the map, trailing her finger along the contour lines around the targeted cabin.

'Correct me if I am wrong, but shouldn't we have men approaching from behind, not just in front?' Anya challenged.

'The terrain there is not ideal as it is quite steep. I don't want to risk our people tripping over and breaking limbs. We need to stick to the safest vantage points, here and here,' he said pointing to the map.

'I still think we should be spreading ourselves out more. We have only twenty-four officers and no one knows for sure how many people are holed up there or what weapons they may have,' Anya persisted.

'Don't worry your pretty little head, Anya, we have considered all angles,' the commissioner replied patronisingly.

A sharp rap sounded and Jasmine, the commissioner's private secretary, poked her head around the door.

'I am sorry to interrupt commissioner, but I have an urgent phone call for Detective Chemarov,' she explained.

'Can it wait, Jasmine? We haven't quite finished here yet,' the commissioner replied irritably.

'It is Ash Wakehurst and he was very insistent that he speak with Detective Chemarov. He says it is an emergency and that she will want to hear him out,' she insisted.

John instantly bristled and shot Anya an accusatory glance.

'I will speak with him now commissioner if that's okay. I can't stay for much longer anyway and I am confident I am up to speed with where I need to be during the raid,' she replied, picking up her handbag.

'Wait, Anya, I think I should hear him out too. I assume he has some information on Smythe,' said John.

'I am sorry, Detective Goodwin, he has insisted that he will only speak with Detective Chemarov,' Jasmine explained.

'That figures,' John replied curtly.

'You stay here, John, we need to go over these plans some more. I am sure that Anya can handle a phone call on her own,' the commissioner ordered.

Anya smiled sweetly at the commissioner before heading out the door.

****

Will Saunders stretched out across the double bed, basking in the afterglow of their love making as his girlfriend, Morgan Russell lay alongside him. Resting her head on his heaving chest, she ran her fingers up and down the length of his arm before interlocking her hand in his.

'It is so nice to be able to sleep with you in a bed for a change,' she said, smiling up at him.

'Personally, it never bothered me where we made out, but this sure does beat the back seat of your Datsun,' he replied, kissing her hand. 'I hope we weren't loud enough to wake up any of the girls,' he added with a grin. Morgan's mansion was shared with what remained of her grandmother's coven and with plenty of space, there hadn't been a need to evict any of them just yet.

'I really don't care if we did,' Morgan replied seductively. 'They are lucky I am still allowing them to even stay here.'

'Do you think Lillian will ever come back? I mean, if she wakes up eventually?' Will enquired. He hoped that the evil bitch would never wake up but didn't want to voice his opinions in front of Morgan. Afterall, Lillian was still her mother no matter how badly she had treated her in the past.

'If she does wake up, I think she will have a new residence by the name of Lincoln State Penitentiary,' Morgan replied.

Will nodded and sat up, pulling Morgan into his arms. He kissed her tenderly as he ran his hands up her slender back and twirled her long dark hair in his fingers. He couldn't believe his luck that someone as beautiful as Morgan had wanted to be with him, especially considering he was a werewolf. It had never bothered her what he was, and he certainly wasn't concerned that she was a witch. The revelation that she was also Ash's aunt, while initially a shock, had also not dampened his feelings for her. To him, she was the perfect woman and it was going to be hard to leave her side.

'I have to get back, Morgan. Something big is going down in a few hours and I need to be there,' he said, reluctantly pulling away and sitting on the edge of the bed.

'Will, I don't feel good about you following Logan's every command. He could get you killed one of these days.'

'You don't understand, Morgan, I don't have a choice. The Nequam controls me as much as it does Logan. If I don't follow orders, it will cause me unimaginable pain. I tried to resist once, but it was pure agony, like someone was tearing the veins out of my body. I don't ever want to feel pain like that again,' Will explained, pulling on his clothes.

'Then we need to find a way to get rid of the Nequam.'

'There is no way to get rid of it. We just have to accept that this is how things are going to be with us. We are lucky that we are even allowed to see each other at all,' Will replied.

'I just want to wake up with you every morning and spend my days with you like a regular couple. Is that too much to ask?' she replied, standing up and wrapping her arms around his neck. 'I have fallen for you, Will Saunders, and I don't want to share you with the Nequam.'

Kissing her deeply, Will lifted her up and pulled her into a strong embrace as she wrapped her slender legs around his waist.

'What did I ever do to deserve someone as wonderful as you,' he said with a grin, finally pulling away and sitting her on the edge of the bed. He pocketed his mobile phone and began to make his way to the door.

'Let's run away together, Will. We can move to another state where the Nequam can't reach you and we can be together,' Morgan replied, her blue eyes brimming with tears.

'It's just a pipedream, Morgan, there is no running away from this. The Nequam would pursue me to the ends of the earth, you know it would. I can only keep you safe if I serve it and that means doing whatever Logan tells me to do. I am sorry that I can't be what you want me to be, but it is going to have to be good enough as it is all I can offer.'

'I don't know that it will ever be good enough, Will. I am so sick of worrying about you and wondering when or even if, I will see you again.'

She had turned her back to him; her shoulders sagging in defeat.

'Morgan, I don't want to leave you like this. Look at me,' Will said softly.

She shook her head and climbed back into the bed, pulling the covers over her. 'Just go Will. Go and be Logan's puppet on a string. I don't want any part of it anymore.'

Will pulled the door shut behind him. The sounds of her sobbing near broke his heart and for the briefest of moments, he considered defying the Nequam and returning to Morgan's embrace. He shook his head knowing it could never happen and continued down the stairs.

****

Ash held his phone to his ear as he paced the carpark, his frustration levels rising with each passing minute. A monotone, robotic voice assured him that his call would soon be attended to and that he should continue to hold the line. After five minutes of the repeated message, he was contemplating hanging up when Anya's voice finally rang out.

'Ash, what do you want?' she asked coolly.

'Firstly, thanks for getting my bike back, I didn't think you would be able to release it that quick, especially with all the bureaucracy bullshit that usually takes place,' he stated.

'Get to the point, Ash. What did you really call me for?'

'I have been trying to call your cell for the past ten minutes. Anya, I know that something big is going to happen tonight. I don't know where, but I know it will end in innocent human lives being lost. I have a feeling it has something to do with the raid you are all talking about.'

'My phone has been turned off. Ash, how did you know about the raid...? Wait, of course you would know, you probably read my mind earlier,' she challenged.

'Look, this is not a time for jokes, Anya. Yes, I do know about the raid, but only because I am standing in the carpark outside your building and I can hear everything you guys are planning. I have werewolf senses, remember?'

'Ash! You have been listening in? Do you have any idea how many privacy laws you have just violated? You can't just listen in on people's conversations!' she replied indignantly.

'Anya, you need to get them to call it off. My instincts are telling me that wherever this raid is taking place, Logan and his men know you are coming. I can feel it. You have to trust me on this,' he pleaded.

'Ash, I don't have the authority to shut it down. I have already questioned their positioning of the SWAT team, but they won't take me seriously.'

'Then don't go. Promise me you will stay away,' he whispered into the phone.

'Ash, I can't...' she began.

'Promise me!' he insisted.

'Okay, okay! I won't go. I will tell John that I am not feeling well. I'll think of something.'

Ash audibly sighed with relief and the phone went silent.

'Ash? Are you still there?'

'Yeah, I'm here,' he replied. 'I can hear your heart beating. Why is it beating so fast?'

'Ash, I cannot tell you how creepy that sounds. Look, I have to go. I'll talk to you tomorrow,' she said, hanging up the phone.

Ash cursed and put his phone away, before walking towards his bike and riding away.

****

The line of black SUV's headed up the mountain pass in a single file, snaking through the winding road in one fluid motion. Anya stared out the window at the dark tree shapes that flashed past, her mind deep in thought. She had lied to Ash when she had promised not to go on the raid. Even though she now knew what he was, the logical side of her simply could not accept his crazy story. When he had given her back the memories she had lost once compelled, the images that flooded her brain were still not clear. She had seen his eyes change and his teeth grow into fangs, but each image appeared like a faded polaroid in her mind. She remembered when he had bitten her in the maintenance shed and the sensation she had felt made her flush at the memory.

'I want you to stick with me, Anya,' John declared, suddenly interrupting her thoughts.

'I can look after myself, John, I hardly need your protection,' she replied stiffly.

'These men are dangerous criminals and we cannot underestimate what they are capable of.'

'I don't underestimate anyone. That is why I always carry this,' Anya replied, gesturing to the butt of her concealed side arm.

'Hopefully, you won't need to use it. We will hang back until the SWAT team has secured the site.'

John pulled the vehicle to the left and followed the lead car ahead of him into a small rest area. Bringing the car to a halt, he switched off the engine and opened his door.

'Are you coming?' he enquired as Anya remained in her seat, her eyes on the dark forest beside them.

'Something doesn't feel right,' she stated, reluctantly unbuckling her seat belt. 'It is so impossibly dark out there and we are going in blind. Do we even know for sure how many suspects there are?'

'Our intelligence has suggested we may encounter a dozen or more armed men, but we are counting on the element of surprise to surround and disarm them.'

'So, that would explain why no helicopters have been deployed although, I would feel safer with some air support and the odd spotlight from above,' Anya reasoned.

'They would give us away before we had a chance to get in to place. The ground team is equipped with night vision goggles and we can use our torches when we need to,' John explained as they walked towards the gathered SWAT team.

Commissioner Willis stood in front to address the men and woman that waited patiently for their orders.

'We are all set to proceed. Delta team will do the reconnaissance and establish a perimeter. Alpha team, you will go in second and radio back once you are in position. The rest of you will wait for radio instruction from the half-way point. There is to be no gunfire unless you are under-fire yourselves. Proceed with caution!' the commissioner ordered as the first team set off quickly into the forest.

Anya looked over at John and anxiously bit her lip, her hands trembled slightly as her fear levels rose.

'You look nervous, Detective,' observed the commissioner as he approached her.

'I just don't think this is a good plan. What if they are prepared for us? We could be walking into an ambush.'

'Detective Chemarov, I have twenty-four of the best trained men and woman that the police force has to offer, and they will do their duty. Believe me, the suspects will all be in cuffs before you even lay eyes on the cabin,' the commissioner replied.

'I hope you are right, Commissioner, I don't want to be out here for any longer than necessary. This place gives me the creeps,' she said, adjusting her bullet proof vest before following John into the darkness.

****

Logan impatiently walked the length of the cabin porch, repeatedly glancing at his watch.

'We should have heard something by now,' he stated, scanning the darkness.

'They'll be here any minute now, Logan,' Matt reassured just as a figure emerged from the trees.

Logan stiffened but relaxed when Will came into view and began to remove his clothes.

'They're coming!' he shouted urgently, 'We need to go now.'

Logan followed suit and let out a deep howl to alert the others as they waited in their designated hiding spots.

'Let's go and say hi!' he said before quickly transforming and bounding off towards the tree line.

****

Anya moved silently between the trees, shadowing John as he trod carefully ahead of her. He held his hand up and they stopped, allowing several SWAT team members to pass them by.

'What are we waiting for, John?' she asked impatiently.

'We need to wait for further instructions from the Delta team. They know what they are doing, let's just wait for them to do their jobs,' he replied.

Anya's walkie crackled, and a voice sounded. *'Delta team is in position. Alpha team, what is your location?'*

A loud howl sounded from deep within the forest and Anya jumped, clinging onto John's arm.

'Alpha team is in position. No sign of...' the voice was cut short and an ear-piercing scream split the night air. Gunfire rang out ahead of them and between the muzzle flashes, Anya

saw large shapes moving at speed through the forest around them.

'What the hell is going on?' Anya whispered, pulling her sidearm out and fearfully scanning the trees.

More screams sounded, and Anya and John broke into a run, heading towards the location of the SWAT teams. Anguished cries of pain sounded to her right and Anya changed direction, stumbling upon a man with his foot stuck in a rabbit trap. She bent down to help free him but was yanked to her feet by John and steered back in the direction she had come.

'We have to help him, John!' Anya shouted, struggling to break free of his firm grip.

'No! We must stick to the path! We can help him later,' he insisted, pushing her in front of him.

The walkie crackled again, and a panicked voice shouted over the air waves, '*We are under attack! Retreat, retreat!*'

Anya stopped suddenly as a feeling of unease overwhelmed her. A dark shape loomed into view ahead and a large wolf stepped onto the path. Its grey fur was matted with blood and its eyes stared at her hungrily. Anya held her breath, her heart pounding violently within her chest as the wolf began to transform. It snarled and whimpered before quickly straightening out; its fur replaced by smooth skin and its jaw reverting to a human shape. A stunning woman now stood in front of Anya, unashamed in her nakedness as she tossed her blood soaked, raven hair.

'What the fuck are you?' Anya whispered, backing up slowly. Her back came into contact with John's chest and she spun around. He was staring at the woman, his eyes glowing a deep amber colour as he met her gaze.

Anya stared at John in disbelief. 'You are both werewolves, like Ash?' she remarked, feeling her body tremble all over.

'You knew about Wakehurst?' John replied, curiously.

'Yes, he told me, but I still didn't believe him, not entirely,' Anya replied struggling to break free.

'Look around you Anya. If seeing is believing, then you are definitely in for a treat!' John remarked.

Anya fearfully scanned the forest around her. The clouds had moved away from the moon and it now shone, illuminating the dark shapes that ran through the trees and the bodies of mutilated officers that lay strewn on the ground. Anya panicked and turned to run back towards the cars. She tripped suddenly and fell hard to the ground, her hands landing in a sticky pool of blood. She screamed as she found herself staring into the lifeless face of Commissioner Willis. His jaw hung open at an impossible angle and his left eye protruded from its socket, staring at her in shock.

She retched violently before John dragged her to her feet and half carried her to Logan's cabin.

****

A large wolf moved stealthily through the trees, careful not to stray from the animal tracks that wove their way through the thick undergrowth. Will had scattered traps throughout the forest, each heavily scented with urine to alert the wolves of their presence. The humans, however, were not able to detect the traps and many were now floundering and screaming in their efforts to escape.

Painful cries ahead alerted him to another trapped human and the wolf darted from behind a bush to find a petrified man, desperately trying to free his mutilated foot. The man spotted him and drew his weapon, aimlessly firing into the space around him. The wolf snarled and leapt at him, tearing his head clean off his shoulders. The man's severed head rolled clumsily under a nearby bush as the headless body slumped to the ground with a heavy thud.

Satisfied that no one was still alive, the wolf resumed his bipedal, human form and strode back towards the cabin. He passed Will and Matt as they stood over another body, both of them breathing heavily as they wiped the blood from their faces and chests. A voice called out and Logan turned to see Detective Goodwin and Alexa walking towards him with a terrified woman.

'Ah, Detective Goodwin. It is good to see you again,' said Logan, shaking his hand enthusiastically.

Will threw Logan's clothes to him and he began to pull on his jeans.

'You two know each other?' Anya questioned incredulously, trying to avert her gaze from the naked men in front of her.

'Logan, this is the woman I was telling you about, Detective Anya Chemarov,' John said pushing her into Logan's chest.

Logan grinned and held her face with his hands. 'I see. Very pretty! I can see why you want to keep this one,' Logan replied, letting go of her face.

'Keep me? What the hell are you talking about?' Anya said.

'Dear Anya, you have been promised to our mutual friend, John, in return for information regarding your attempt at a raid tonight,' Logan smirked.

Anya reeled on John, pushing him on his chest. 'You caused all of this? You had our own people slaughtered for this murderous bastard? Why would you do that?'

'For the ultimate prize, Anya. You!' John replied smugly.

'You will NEVER have me!' Anya raged, slapping him hard across his face.

Logan laughed loudly and began to walk away.

'Looks like you might have your hands full, Detective. Have fun with that little vixen,' he joked, 'I am going to have some fun with my own,' he added as Alexa sidled up to him and linked her arm in his.

Anya tried to run, but John quickly grabbed her and with the butt of his gun, knocked her unconscious. He caught her before she fell to the ground and stood, stroking her hair affectionately.

'Sorry Anya, but you and I have a hot date that has been a long time coming,' he stated before slinging her limp body over his shoulder and making his way back to the main road where his car was waiting for him.

****

Ash paced his living room and threw his phone down onto his couch in frustration. He had tried to call Anya numerous times, but she wasn't picking up. He couldn't shake the feeling of unease that swept over him and he knew something was very wrong. She was in trouble and she needed him. The Nequam was active, he could feel his evil energy as images of pain and terror flashed through his mind. He didn't know where it was hiding only that it was unleashing hell on innocent people and Anya was in grave danger.

His hands reached up to the chain around his neck and he took a deep breath as it vibrated reassuringly between his fingers. He grappled with his desire to rip the chain from his neck and allow the Triune spirit to resume control, but he knew he couldn't relinquish his will, not if it meant hurting more people. The bloodied face of his grandmother still haunted him each time he closed his eyes and he knew it would be a long time before he could forgive himself. Evelyn had done her best to console him, trying to convince him that if he hadn't allowed the Triune to take over, his grandmother would have killed him. Despite this, Ash still struggled to accept what he had done and refused to lose control again. If he was going to defeat the Nequam, he was going to do it while he still had full control of his faculties.

His thoughts wandered back to Anya and the promise she had made to stay out of the raiding party. Ash had overheard most of the conversation regarding the raid, but no mention was made of the rendezvous point. He knew it was a residence of some sort, judging by the conversation and it was possibly in the mountains, but Ash was not aware of any permanent dwellings on the mountainside. There was only one access road up the mountain, and this coupled with the inhospitable terrain left little opportunity for homes to be established.

Ash suddenly stopped his pacing. 'You fucking idiot!' he swore out loud as he rushed out of the room to his study. He pulled open the drawers on his desk and rummaged through them until he found a dog-eared photo. A teenaged Logan beamed out of the picture as he stood over the carcass of a deer that he had shot. Logan held his rifle proudly while Ash had stood behind the camera and taken the photo in front of his uncle's cabin. It all made sense and he chided himself for not having thought of it earlier. Logan was hiding out at the cabin and the SWAT team were walking into a trap. Ash threw his jacket on and grabbed the keys to his bike, racing out the door. He revved his bike and took off at speed, the back wheels spinning in protest as Ash exited his driveway and headed towards the mountain.

The sun was rising slowly over the mountains as Ash pulled the bike up behind a line of SWAT vehicles parked on the side of the road. He cautiously made his way to the front of the rear vehicle, a black armoured truck. The driver's side door was slightly ajar, and Ash carefully swung it open further. The driver was slumped at the wheel, his arms limp at his side with a firearm still clasped in his hand. Ash reached in and pulled the man's head back, his fangs instinctively protracting at the sight of the deep gash across the man's throat. The wound was relatively fresh, perhaps only an hour old.

Ash smelt the air around him, picking up a familiar but unexpected scent. 'Detective Goodwin?' he said in puzzlement. Ash reached over for the dead man's arm and bit into the flesh of his wrist. He gagged at the taste of the congealing blood but continued to drink as the man's last living memories flooded through his mind. Ash pulled away and retched violently, wiping his face with his sleeve as he knelt on the ground. *Goodwin is a werewolf and he has Anya*! he thought, quickly getting to his feet and racing to his bike.

Chapter 3

Evelyn sipped her cup of tea before placing it back on the dainty saucer and frowning across the table at her friend.

'We need to act fast, Giana. I fear I am going to lose them both if we don't find that spell soon,' she despaired. Giana Rossellini had been searching for a spell that could help them purge both entities from her boys without harming either of them. If they didn't succeed, they would be helpless to stop the prophecy from taking place and destroying everything and everyone they knew.

'I am working as fast as I can Evelyn. I have scoured every book and scroll I have, and I haven't found anything remotely suggesting that a spell even exists. You may have to accept that there is nothing you or I can do to stop this prophecy from taking place,' Giana replied.

Evelyn pushed her chair back and stood up stiffly, her face rigid with frustration. She stole a glance at Leila who stood, leaning against the door frame, her face equally drawn in worry.

'I won't sit back and do nothing. There has to be something we can do to help them both,' Evelyn snapped, banging her hand on the kitchen table. 'The answer is somewhere in the caves. I can feel it in my bones. I am going back tomorrow, and I am not leaving until I find something to help us,' she added with determination.

'The caves have been blocked off. After the tremors, the council ordered that they be sealed up permanently. I'm sorry, Evelyn, but there is no way in now,' Leila soothed, placing her hand on Evelyn's arm.

'There might be a way,' Giana said, animatedly rising to her feet. 'You said that Lillian used a spell to restore the Cathedral Cavern. I think I may be able to find a spell to revert it back.'

Evelyn stared at her friend in disbelief. 'That's it, Giana! The walls of the cavern were heavily inscripted before Lillian restored them. The spell has got to be there!'

'If the spell exists, Evelyn. Please don't get your hopes up, it might amount to nothing. Besides, I will need to find the right spell to revert it back first,' Giana warned.

'The answer is there, I know it!'

Evelyn hugged and kissed her friend, her eyes filled with renewed hope.

'If it is there, we will do our best to find it,' Giana replied. 'But for now, I best get to work finding that reversion spell,' she added, heading upstairs.

****

Doug Newman threw a worn leather book to his niece, Paige before settling into his comfortable armchair. The leather chair squeaked beneath his weight as he pulled the lever on the side and it reclined with a jolt. Stretching his legs out, he relished the feeling of weightlessness as his tired and swollen feet nestled into the soft fabric.

Paige glanced at her uncle momentarily before sitting on the floor with her legs crossed and her back propped up against the sofa. She slowly flicked through the pages of the leather-bound book. Each page contained her uncle's nearly illegible scrawl below coloured photos of different people. She stopped as she came across a picture of a man she knew and held the book up to her uncle.

'Hey, this is my math's teacher,' she declared.

'Not anymore, Paige, he has been turned,' Doug replied, closing his eyes.

'How do you know he is a werewolf, Uncle? I mean, you can't really tell just by looking at them,' she implored.

'I can't explain it, Paige, but I just get a feeling about certain people. I have always been able to sense supernatural beings, ever since I was a little boy. I drove my parents crazy with my constant stories about ghosts, vampires and witches. I am sure they thought I was insane,' he explained.

Paige nodded and was quiet for a moment before continuing. 'The feeling that you get, is it like a tingling sensation?' she said softly.

Doug opened his eyes and quickly sat upright. 'You feel it too?' he asked incredulously.

'I think so. It is like a flush of heat spreading across my chest and then my stomach tingles like a low volt of electricity is running through it. I have been feeling it a lot lately, particularly when I am passing strangers in the street,' she replied, pulling herself up from the floor and standing in front of Doug.

'You have the gift, Paige! You are a Custodian like me,' he marvelled, holding her face in his hands.

'A Custodian? You mean like someone who protects something?'

'Not something, someone. Paige, you and I have the ability to sense anything inhuman and protect the people around us,' Doug replied enthusiastically. He shook his head in disbelief. 'I can't believe you are a Custodian! This is fantastic news. I will need to teach you everything I know; how to hunt, how to trap and most of all, how to kill!'

Paige held her hands up in the air. 'Whoa there, Uncle Doug. I am only seventeen. I can't go around killing people! Besides, isn't it impossible to kill supernatural beings anyway?'

'Not when you have these,' Doug declared, pulling his jacket open and handing Paige a large bullet. 'It's a prototype. That one is filled with mercury pellets that will only react when it comes into contact with a werewolf. It will incapacitate him immediately and as the iron casing breaks down, the mercury inside enters the bloodstream as a vapour. This one will usually take thirty minutes to kill the werewolf, but we are close to creating faster acting bullets that kill on impact,' Doug added, pulling a dagger out of his back pocket. 'This here baby is for vampires, but I don't see too many of them around that need putting down. They are mostly peaceful.'

Paige looked at her uncle in shock. 'You have killed before, haven't you.'

Doug nodded and shrugged. 'I only kill when I have to Paige and lately, I have had to kill plenty of times. There is evil all around us, I am sure you can sense it too. It is my job to protect as many people as I can and with your help, we might actually have a chance. Come, I want to show you something.' He grabbed her hand and began walking towards the back yard.

Paige followed him in silence as he led her down the back stairs to the root cellar. It had always been off limits and she now felt a flutter of excitement at the thought of seeing what was inside. Flinging open the doors, Doug gestured for her to follow as he disappeared into the darkness below. Paige trod carefully, pinching her nose as the smell of dank mustiness reached her nostrils. Doug flicked on a nearby light switch and the room was instantly illuminated, revealing a large cage in the back corner. Paige grabbed at her stomach as she felt the usual tingling sensation sweep through its depths. She peered into the cage to see a half-naked man curled up in the corner in the foetal position. His eyes stared at her hungrily and he lunged, just stopping short of the cage barrier; hindered by a silver collar chained around his neck.

'Paige, I'd like you to meet my buddy, Sean. Sean is helping me with some very important research, aren't you buddy?' Doug said, loading his gun.

'Go fuck yourself,' snarled Sean, pulling at his chain.

'Now, that is not a very polite way to speak around a young lady, Sean. I think you and I are going to need to have a little talk about manners. But first, it is time for you to have your daily nap,' Doug said, shooting him in the neck with a tranquiliser dart. Sean groaned and hit the ground with a loud thud.

'It's time for your first lesson, Paige; getting to know your enemy,' he said, grinning as he opened the cage and pulled the inert man onto a nearby table, shackling his hands and feet.

'Put some safety glasses on. Things are about to get messy,' he added before firing up a circular saw.

****

Searing pain ripped through her abdomen with each passing contraction and the young woman screamed in agony. Whilst her doctor gently probed her swollen belly, a nurse applied pressure to a gaping stab wound below her left breast. The woman had presented at the hospital in early labour after both she and her husband had been attacked in an alley way.

'We need to get this baby out now. The placenta has been ruptured,' the female doctor announced, before placing her fingers inside her and feeling the baby's head.

'You need to push now, Serena, the head is about to crown,' the doctor urged the screaming woman.

Serena grunted and began to bear down, pushing her legs against the women that held them apart. She screamed as the baby's head emerged and fell back onto the bed. The doctor audibly gasped and looked at the two other women in shock.

'What's wrong?' the young woman demanded breathlessly as another wave of agony tore through her.

'Nothing, Serena, just keep pushing,' the doctor exclaimed, her focus shifting back to the unborn babe.

Serena pushed once more, and the baby slid out onto the bed sheet between her bloodied legs. The doctor backed away, shaking her head and crossing herself, as the nurses quickly left the room.

Serena leant forward and reached for the slimy form, holding it to her chest. It mewled feebly, its mouth opening and closing like a fish as it filled its lungs with air. She stared into the face of her newborn baby girl, her heart filling with love for the helpless infant that searched for her nipple. Serena's tears ran down her cheeks as the tiny baby latched onto her breast, her tears splashing on to the prominent gash that partially covered her left cheek. Assuring her that she could have a few moments alone with her new daughter, before she headed upstairs to surgery, the doctor promptly left the room.

Moments later, a dark-haired woman entered and gently took the infant from her.

'Oh, Serena, she has been touched by the Goddess herself. Such a beautiful child. It is too bad you won't get to see the remarkable woman she will become,' she soothed, humming a lullaby as she rocked the sleepy baby.

Serena looked at her in confusion and tried to sit upright, her tear-stained face suddenly blanching as she began to choke. Frantically grabbing at her throat, her eyes began to bulge as she struggled to breathe. As life finally left her, she slumped back on the bed, her head lolling sideways as a large tarantula crawled out of her open mouth and disappeared under the bed.

'There, there, sweet baby, your Mumma might be gone now, but you will never be alone,' she soothed, placing the baby back in her mother's arms. Pricking the top of her finger with a scalpel, she placed her hand over the baby's cut and watched as a single drop of her blood dripped onto the baby's face.

'In aeternum meus es tu,' she whispered, stroking her little face lovingly. 'You and I will meet again when you will

take your place at my side as is your destiny,' she added before exiting the room.

The melodic beeping of machines filled the small ICU ward as Bernard stealthily entered, pulling the door shut behind him. Lillian lay on the bed, her face as pale as the white sheet beneath her and her long hair splayed across her pillow.

'My love! What has he done to you?' Bernard lamented as he picked up her hand and stroked it fondly. He felt her thumb twitch slightly beneath his touch.

'Can you hear me, Lillian?' he whispered, touching her face. Her eyelids fluttered slightly, but she remained perfectly still.

'If you can hear me, twitch your thumb again,' he said excitedly, grabbing her hand firmly.

He felt the slightest sensation as her thumb twitched and the cardio machine's beeping began to intensify.

'Sir! What are you doing in here?' a stern voice interrupted. 'You need to leave now before I call Security.'

'There is no need to do that, I was just leaving anyway,' Bernard replied, walking towards her.

'She will be coming with me though,' he said, snapping the nurse's neck before she could say another word.

He returned to the bed and ripped the electrodes from Lillian's body, detaching her from the myriad of machines that monitored her vitals.

'I will keep you safe, my love and they will all pay for what they have done to you. They will pay with their lives,' he said before gently picking her up and carrying her out the door.

****

Anya roused from her forced slumber to the sound of water dripping overhead and the humming of a nearby hot water tank. She moaned softly and attempted to sit up, pain instantly shooting through her head. Holding her head in her hands, she willed her eyes to adjust to the darkness around her, barely making out the objects and furniture that shared the small space she found herself in. She instinctively reached for her phone, but to her dismay, she realised it had been taken, along with her gun and CB radio.

The room smelled musty and she screwed her nose up as she fumbled in the dark around the mattress, staggering in an attempt to stand upright. A sharp jolt to her ankle impeded her and she fell back awkwardly, hitting her head on the stone wall behind her. Rubbing her head, she reached down and felt the cold surface of a chain that was shackled to her right ankle. Panic rose from within her as she followed the chains length to what she assumed was a pipe fitting on the wall. She pulled at it frantically, but it wouldn't budge. Her attempt at freeing her ankle proved equally futile and she slumped back on the mattress in defeat, sobbing in frustration.

An overhead light suddenly flickered and came on, illuminating the basement space around her. Shelves of boxes and cleaning supplies adorned one side of the room, whilst a large hot water heater and boiler occupied the adjacent wall. She heard the sound of a door creaking open and looked across the room to a set of six wooden steps leading upstairs. John appeared on the top step and began to make his descent whilst balancing a tray of food.

'Ah, I see you are finally awake. I must have hit you too hard, you have been out for hours,' John replied placing the tray on the floor next to the mattress.

'Stay the fuck away from me!' Anya seethed through clenched teeth, backing further against the wall.

'Anya, why the hostility? I saved your life,' John declared, reaching out to touch her hair.

Anya flinched beneath his touch and pushed him away.

'You didn't save my life! You are the reason an entire SWAT team lie dead on that mountain. You are a fucking traitor to your own people!' she stormed.

John laughed and shook his head.

'My people? I don't have any loyalties to people anymore. I was chosen, Anya. I was chosen and given the most incredible gift. The gift of strength and power beyond my wildest dreams,' he replied. 'This attack was only the beginning. The next wave will take place soon and all of Rockdale will be brought to its knees. You are one of the lucky ones, Anya. You will be safe by my side and all you need to do is submit to me. You might not like it at first, but you will soon get used to it. Hell, you might even grow to like me,' he said reaching for her.

Anya screamed, and John grabbed her firmly, placing his hand over her mouth as she struggled beneath his grip.

'Listen here, you ungrateful bitch. You would have been killed along with the rest of your team if it wasn't for me. I spared you and now you owe me,' he sneered, stroking her hair.

Anya glared at him and clawed at his face, drawing blood as her long nails came into contact with his cheek. He pulled away from her and laughed as the scratch marks instantly healed.

'I thought you might still have some fight in you. That is why I came prepared,' John said pulling out a roll of gaffer tape. Anya's eyes widened in fear and she lashed out at him again. John grabbed her flailing arms with one hand and punched her hard in the face. Her eyes glazed over, and she struggled to stay conscious as blood poured from her nose. Moaning in pain, she slumped back onto the mattress. John quickly taped her hands together and began to unbutton her shirt.

'I didn't want it to be like this, Anya, I was hoping you would be a bit more receptive to me. It doesn't concern me though as, either way, I will still have you,' he said as he tore the bullet proof vest from her, exposing her flat stomach. 'I have wanted you from the day I met you. You have cock-teased me at every opportunity with your super tight skirts and perky tits,' he added, groping at her white lacy bra.

Anya sobbed and flinched at his touch.

'John, please don't do this,' she pleaded. 'This is not who you are!'

'It is now, Anya. I can do whatever I want. Who is going to stop me?' he laughed as he began to unzip his fly.

'I will,' boomed a loud voice as Ash leapt down the steps and punched him square in the face, knocking him into the shelves. 'Keep your dirty fucking hands off her!'

John snarled at him and protracted his teeth and claws. 'Come and get me, pretty boy!' he challenged.

Ash quickly moved towards him and punched him again, sending him flying into the concrete wall. As John tried to stand up, Ash kicked him hard in the ribs and grabbed him by the head, bringing his knee up to his chin. John fell backwards into the corner and slowly pulled himself to his feet, dusting the cobwebs and dust from his shirt. He reached into a nearby box of washing powder and flung it in Ash's face before lunging at him. Momentarily blinded, Ash was caught off balance and knocked to the ground.

'I have been waiting for this moment, Wakehurst! I doubt Anya will still have the hots for you after I have finished messing up that pretty face,' John sneered, straddling his torso and protracting his claws. He slashed at him, but only found air as Ash quickly moved out from under him and brought his elbow up to connect with the side of his face. John cried out and staggered away from Ash, holding his jaw. He took off his torn shirt and sneered at Ash.

'It is time someone put you down, Wakehurst. Your brother should have done it ages ago. Let's see how you go fighting me in my werewolf form,' he said, spitting blood at Ash's feet. John tried to transform, but upon realising his efforts were futile, he backed away, glaring at Ash.

'I can't transform! What the hell have you done to me?' demanded John as Ash began to walk towards him.

'It is what I am about to do to you that you need to be most concerned with,' replied Ash as he grabbed John by the head and began to squeeze with both hands.

John screamed as his skull fractured instantly and the bones in his face each cracked under the crushing force. His screams were replaced by a low gurgling sound as Ash twisted his misshapen head and ripped it off his body, like a ripened tomato from its stalk. Dropping John's head onto the dusty floorboards, he turned to Anya. She was cowering on the mattress, her eyes wide as saucers as she covered her bloodied nose with her hand. Ash rushed to her and held her face in his hands, stroking her hair. 'Are you okay? Did he... did he do anything to you?' he said breathlessly as he freed her hands.

Anya shook her head and flung her arms around his neck, sobbing uncontrollably into his shoulder. After a few moments, she stopped and looked up at him, her eyes red and puffy.

'I'm sorry I didn't listen to you, Ash. You tried to warn me and...'

'Shh, it's okay,' Ash interrupted, placing his finger on her lips. 'You weren't to know that Goodwin was leading you all into a trap. He wasn't the one I was worried about. I didn't know he was a werewolf either, he must have only been turned recently.'

'Everyone is dead, Ash. There were so many werewolves and they just tore everyone apart. Logan allowed me to live as a gift to John for his part in planning the ambush. John was going to rape me, Ash and then do God knows what with me,' she said as fresh tears welled in her eyes. 'If you hadn't found me when you did, I wouldn't have been able to stop him!'

'It's okay, Anya, he has been stopped. Permanently,' Ash said glancing at the lifeless body across the room.

Anya nodded and wiped her face clean with a napkin from the upturned food tray near the bed. Fumbling with her torn blouse, Ash watched her with unfeigned interest; his heart quickening at the sight of blood dotted across her lacy bra. Her breasts jostled as she struggled to button up her blouse and Ash looked away, suddenly embarrassed by his lust for her in her current vulnerable state. He had never wanted a woman more than at that very moment and it took everything he had to keep his composure.

He switched his attention to her chained ankle, and she gasped involuntarily as he touched the exposed skin beneath the chain. Her ankle was bruised and swollen from her earlier attempts to escape and Ash knew it was going to hurt her even more when he tried to free her. His eyes met hers and he held her gaze as he quickly snapped the chain around her ankle. She cried out in pain and he gently lifted her foot and held it in his hands. *'Non magis dolorem,'* he whispered, blowing softly on her ankle before placing it back on the mattress. Anya stared at him open mouthed and reached down to her foot. 'What did you do? It doesn't hurt at all anymore,' she said in astonishment.

'I took your pain away. I can do the same for your nose if you'll let me,' he said.

Anya suddenly leaned forward and brushed her lips against his briefly before pulling back. Ash quickly looked away in embarrassment and stood up.

'Oh God, I am so sorry, Ash! I shouldn't have done that, not with you losing Rana so recently,' she said. 'I am such an idiot!'

'It's alright, Anya, I didn't mean to react like that, you just caught me off guard,' he said. 'I do still have feelings for Rana, I don't think that will ever change. I just feel a bit guilty because I also have feelings for you.'

Anya smiled and reached for his hand, pulling him back onto the edge of the bed.

'I understand how conflicted you must feel, especially after losing Rana, but this whole terrible experience has taught me something. Life is too short, and I am not going to waste another minute denying my feelings for you. I have wanted you from the second I laid eyes on you at the diner. When I thought you were dead, my whole world ended, and I have never felt so much pain at the thought of never seeing you again and of never knowing what it feels like to be in your arms.'

'Do you still feel that way knowing what I am and what I am capable of?' Ash replied.

She nodded. 'I don't care anymore. I think I have fallen for you, Ash Wakehurst.'

Ash reached out to touch her hair, tucking it behind her ear. 'Perhaps we could try that kiss again?' he said, pulling her towards him. Her heart rate quickened, and she tilted her head in anticipation as he lowered his mouth to meet hers. He kissed her tenderly at first, tentatively running his tongue along the inside of her lip and sending shockwaves throughout her entire body. She brought her hands up to the back of his head and pulled him in closer still, relishing the taste of his mouth and the firmness of his lips as they rhythmically moved in sync with hers. Switching positions, she winced as her nose bumped his and she reluctantly pulled away.

'Ow! That really hurt. I think I should have let you fix that first,' she said, laughing as she rubbed her nose.

'I aim to please,' Ash replied, repeating the healing ritual on her nose. She reached out to touch his face, running her hands across the stubble on his jawline.

'Thank-you, Ash. That was exactly what I needed, and I am not just referring to the incredible nose job you just gave me,' she said with a grin. 'How can someone as amazing as you have the same blood running through your veins as that monster lying on the floor?'

A look of hurt crossed Ash's face and he pulled away from her.

'I may have the same blood as him, but I am in no way comparable to the monster he became,' he replied, handing Anya her shoes. 'I won't ever let that happen.'

'I didn't mean it like that, Ash. I don't see you as a monster. You don't have an evil bone in your body,' she said stepping into her shoes.

Ash nodded and smiled weakly.

'It's okay, you just touched on a sore point. Forget about it. Let's get out of here. Would you like me to drop you off at the station? I had already tipped them off about the SWAT team attack, but they will be keen to know that you are alright,' he said, taking her hand in his.

'No. I think it would be best if they still thought I was dead. I can't trust anyone there at the moment. Who knows who else Logan has corrupted? I can't go home either, that will be the first place they will look when they can't find my body,' she said sadly. 'I don't want to be alone tonight, Ash. Can you stay with me? We could check into a motel out of town?' she suggested.

'Are you sure that is what you want, Anya? You have been through a lot and I am concerned you might not be thinking straight in your current state,' Ash replied.

'I have never been so sure about anything in my entire life, Ash Wakehurst,' Anya declared, tracing her finger across his chest. 'Right now, you are the one person I feel safe with.'

Ash put his arm around her protectively and began to guide her towards the steps. As they passed John's body, Anya kicked John's bloodied pulp of a head into the wall. Noticing Ash's bemused look, she shrugged. 'What? That asshole fucking deserved it,' she stated before striding ahead of Ash and scaling the stairs.

****

Anya sat up in the bath, lathering herself with the complimentary lavender soap and shampoo that the cheap motel had provided. Ash had taken her to the quaint, Mountain Retreat Motel, twenty miles north of Rockdale and they had signed in under false names. It was now ten o'clock at night and Ash had left her to find some food for them both while she had a much-needed bath. She rinsed the shampoo from her hair and lay back into the bath, audibly sighing as the warm water enveloped her tired and battered body. She closed her eyes and listened as the motel television blared from the next room.

'Breaking news just in has revealed that twenty-four members of a SWAT team in the Nebraskan town of Rockdale, have been reported missing. Two homicide detectives and the Commissioner of Police are also named among the missing team as they attempted to bring in a group of suspects. The men, believed to have been led by Rockdale local, twenty-five-year-old, Logan Smythe, have also been implicated in the murder of twenty-one college girls and numerous other local unsolved killings. Smythe's group of thugs has once again eluded police and their whereabouts are still unknown. Chief of Police, Harry Medcalfe has pleaded with locals to remain vigilant and report any sightings of the men. Meanwhile the search continues for the missing officers. Our thoughts are with their families and we pray for their safe return.
This is Rowena Frazer for CPC News.'

The sound of the front door opening, momentarily startled her and she instinctively reached for a towel.

Ash poked his head around the corner. 'Everything all good in here? I found you some food. I hope you like tacos,' he announced waving a takeaway bag in front of his face.

'I would eat just about anything right now, I am starving!' she replied, pulling herself up from the bath and wrapping the towel around her. Ash stared at her, the corner of his mouth turning up as he watched her appreciatively. She shot him a look of reproach and grinning, he backed out of the bathroom and closed the door. Anya quickly dried herself and wrapped her wet hair up in a towel before putting on a robe and heading into the bedroom. Ash was lying back on the bed with his hands behind his head and he sat up quickly as she walked in.

'That is a good look for you, Chemarov,' he teased. She smirked at him and made her way straight to the takeaway he had left on the table.

'Oh, my God! This tastes divine!' she said through mouthfuls of food, her eyes closed in apparent ecstasy. 'Did you eat already?' she asked, watching him as he removed his shoes and shirt.

'Nah, I'm good. I am just going to have a shower. I am glad you are enjoying the taco's,' he said before stepping into the bathroom. Anya returned to her meal as the sound of the shower running echoed from the bathroom. She took a bite from the second taco and then stopped short, hitting her forehead with the palm of her hand.

You idiot! She chided herself. *He needs blood, not fucking Tacos*!

She stood up from the table and pushed the chair in, making her way back to the bathroom. The door was open, and she could see Ash's silhouette through the steam as he washed himself in the shower cubicle. She tentatively opened the shower door and cleared her throat loudly. He had his back to her, but he twisted around to look at her.

'Can you still eat regular food or is it strictly a liquid diet for you from now on,' Anya said, taking another bite from her taco.

'I can still eat food, but it won't sustain me like blood does. It just allows me to blend in with the rest of the population,' he replied.

'When was the last time you had a feed, Ash? I mean a real feed?' she asked, eyeing his toned backside lasciviously.

'Yesterday morning, I think. It's okay Anya, I don't need blood as regularly as people need food,' he said, lathering his hair.

'But it makes you stronger, right? And it allows you to heal much faster?' Anya persisted.

'Yeah, it does. That's why I use blood bags although, I need to be careful where I get them from. You can't keep taking blood from the same hospitals. You're bound to be noticed if you are not smart,' he said. 'I use frozen blood bags mostly, as Leila has a good supply, but I can feed straight from the source if I am careful,' he answered.

'I imagine that fresh blood would taste a lot better than the reheated variety,' Anya said.

'Yeah, definitely. It's like comparing a bottle of Dom Perignon to cask wine. They will both get you drunk in the end, but the champagne won't leave a horrible taste in your mouth,' he replied, rinsing off his hair. 'Fresh blood is not easy to get, not unless you want to draw attention to yourself and I don't particularly need that right now. Don't worry about me, Anya, I can go a few days without a feed,' he said, rinsing off his hair.

Anya nodded and turned around, stepping back into the main room. She had only gone a few steps before she stopped; the images of the night Ash had fed from her in the maintenance shed, flashing through her mind. Hugging her arms to her chest, she felt her skin tingle and flush at the memory. It had felt so impossibly good, the moment he had bitten into her throat and drunk from her veins. She had felt his breath quicken with anticipation as his hands had wandered up her waist and across her chest, finally stopping at the base of her neck. The sensation of his mouth against her delicate skin had flooded her with a longing she had never before experienced, and she had not wanted him to stop.

Anya pulled the towel off her head and shook out her wet hair, letting it spread across her shoulders. 'Fuck it!' she said as she quickly walked back into the bathroom and stepped into the shower with Ash. He didn't have time to register his shock before Anya grabbed him and pressed her lips to his.

Returning her kiss, he pushed her up against the tiled wall; his hands intertwined in her long hair as his tongue slowly explored her mouth. 'Mmm… You taste like tacos,' he said, licking his lips.

'Shut up, Wakehurst,' Anya replied, pulling her now drenched robe off and letting it drop to the floor.

He stepped back to admire her body; a grin forming at the corner of his mouth as he reached for her.

'You are the most beautiful fucking thing I have ever seen,' he said, running his hand over the curve of her breast and taking her left nipple into his mouth.

Anya felt her knees buckle and she moaned as he expertly teased each nipple in turn with his firm tongue; sending delicious sensations throughout her entire body. His breath felt hot against her tender skin as he traced his tongue back up over her shoulder blade and along the length of her throat. It was the most exhilarating feeling and she melted into him like putty as his tongue continued to tease her. She could feel the sharp edge of his teeth against her throat and she knew he wanted her as much as she wanted him. She wanted him so badly, she literally ached with desire. As Ash moved his hands down her slender back and grabbed her backside, she ground her hips into him with an urgency that surprised them both; moaning loudly as he moved in unison with her. Her heart thudded in her chest so fast, she thought it would explode and she knew she wouldn't last much longer.

'I want you to bite me, Ash,' she whispered breathlessly in his ear. 'Feed from me.'

'Are you sure that is what you want? What if I lose control?' he replied as his fangs involuntarily protracted.

'I want you to lose control. I know you won't hurt me,' she said, wrapping her legs around his waist and guiding him deep inside her. She moaned loudly, and Ash's breathing quickened as he slowly began to move his hips in time with hers. Holding her hands above her head, he gained momentum and she cried out, throwing her head back in ecstasy. The pleasurable sensations that tore through her body were maddening, but she wasn't ready to let go just yet. She wanted to feel the sensation of him biting her again and she didn't have to wait long.

Ash ran his fangs across her neck and sunk them deep into her carotid artery, gasping at the sweet taste of her warm blood as it slid down his throat. Her blood triggered an instant reaction throughout his body, stimulating every nerve and resulting in a powerful orgasm that took his breath away.

Anya cried out, her body shuddering as waves of pleasure rippled through her. Her body went limp in his arms and he continued to drink from her; slowly moving his hips against hers as he enjoyed the last moments of their orgasmic union. He finally stopped and placed his hand on the tiles behind her head, gently kissing her neck around the site of the two small puncture wounds he had left. The wound still bled slightly and the sight of Anya's blood trickling down between her cleavage, stirred him once more.

She opened her eyes and wrapped her arms around him, kissing him deeply.

'Seriously, Wakehurst, you could go again after all that?' she whispered in his ear.

He laughed and pressed his nose onto hers before kissing her forehead.

'I didn't hurt you, did I?' he said, pushing a stray hair from her face.

'No, you didn't. That was absolutely incredible,' she said, smiling as she untangled her legs from around his waist. 'I don't think I am going to be able to walk for a while though, my legs are like jelly.'

Ash turned off the shower and effortlessly picked her up, laughing as she squealed in mock protest.

'Now, we can't have that. I need you fully recovered for round two,' he said, grinning as he carried her to the bedroom.

****

Logan stirred in his sleep and rolled over to the warm body beside him, spooning her like a perfect jigsaw piece. Alexa reached for his hand and held it against her stomach as she nestled back into him.

'Good morning my lover,' she said, reaching her head back and kissing him tenderly.

'Mm…' Logan mumbled groggily as he buried his face in her hair, his hands wandering over her lower stomach and down between her thighs. 'What time is it?' he whispered, feeling himself stir as she moaned quietly.

'It's nearly noon,' she replied breathlessly, slowly grinding against him.

'Shit, Alexa!' Logan swore, sitting upright. 'We should have left ages ago. We can't still be here when the authorities come looking for their men,' he added, reaching for his clothes.

'Relax, Logan. Everyone moved out hours ago. The bodies have all been disposed of and Will has blocked the only way in, and it will take them a few hours to get through now. Come back to bed,' she replied, running her hands up his back.

'Why didn't anyone wake me?' Logan asked, ignoring her and pulling on his jeans.

'You needed to rest, Logan. You said so yourself that you hadn't been sleeping well of late and Will and I agreed that a sleep in would do you good,' Alexa reasoned, pulling herself over to his side of the bed.

Logan turned to look at her and nodded in defeat.

'Yeah, I guess I did need a sleep,' he said. 'Not that we did much sleeping.'

He stood up and walked over to a large duffel bag that sat in the corner and threw it over his shoulder. He turned to watch Alexa as she dressed quickly and sauntered over to him, her hand grabbing his crotch as she stopped in front of him.

'You know it is really rude to leave a girl hanging. You will pay for that later,' she said, giving him a little squeeze before tossing her hair and walking towards the door.

'I am sure I will,' Logan grinned, following her.

'By the way, I have a quick errand to run, but I will meet you in an hour or so at the warehouse,' she said turning to give him a quick kiss. 'And before you voice any objections about me heading out alone, Tommy and Dylan will escort me.'

'The thought of you not being able to look after yourself never crossed my mind, believe me. What errand are you running? I could come with you?'

Alexa shook her head. 'You will find out soon enough. I have a little surprise planned for you. Something that will help you get your brother back on side,' she replied, pulling open the door.

Tommy and Dylan waited out the front, standing alongside three dirt bikes. Alexa walked towards them and straddled the nearest bike, kick starting it with a roar.

'Do you want a lift?' she offered. Patting the back of her seat.

'Thanks, but not a chance in hell. I have an image to uphold, in case you hadn't noticed,' Logan replied.

'Your loss! Catch you later,' she laughed, the back wheels spinning as she took off in a cloud of dust with Tommy and Dylan hot on her heels.

Logan smiled and shook his head before adjusting the strap of his bag and beginning the hike to his hidden jeep.

Chapter 4

The trio of women walked slowly up the winding path to the falls, stepping around the strategically placed 'Do not Enter' sign that blocked the path. They eventually reached the rock face where the entrance lay buried beneath a layer of rocks and rubble.

'They have blasted it. I hope this spell works or we are never getting in there,' Evelyn said, pulling three candles out of her bag and lighting them.

The three women stood in a circle, each holding a candle as Giana began to recite the spell.

'*Pariter revertentur. Solve fasciculos spell.* May all be undone and returned to as once it was,' Giana chanted as the candles began to emit a brilliant red smoke.

'*Pariter revertentur,*' the women repeated in unison, blowing the smoke onto the rock debris.

The earth trembled beneath their feet and the rocks began to ascend, moulding back into the rock face with a loud cracking sound. The entranceway cleared, and the women quickly made their way inside. Shining their torches across the inscribed walls, they poured over every detail.

'There is nothing here,' Leila said, banging the wall in frustration after a futile, forty-minute search.

'Keep looking, Leila, I know it is here somewhere,' Evelyn replied, walking towards the far corner.

Giana suddenly stopped in the middle of the room; her hands pinned stiffly to her side. Her eyes rolled back in her head and she began to whisper softly. Evelyn shot Leila a puzzled look from across the cavern and made her way quickly to her friend.

'Giana, what is it?' she said, touching her shoulder.

'The eye,' she said quietly, 'we must find the eye.'

She began to walk through the passageways, guided by an unseen force as she navigated through the dark tunnels without the aid of a torch. Evelyn and Leila struggled to keep up with her, racing around each bend and calling her name. They came around a corner and nearly ran into the back of Giana as she came to an abrupt stop in the entranceway of a large chamber. Brilliant light shone through a hole in the ceiling, illuminating a patch of ground in the centre of the room. *The Cathedral Cavern!* thought Evelyn as she stared in awe at the inscriptions and diagrams that filled every space on the rocky wall.

Giana walked into the beam of light and suddenly dropped to the ground, digging at the dirt with her bare hands. Her hands began to bleed as the scraped against the small sharp rocks that littered the floor, but she continued unrelentingly. Evelyn and Leila knelt down to help her, and it wasn't long before the outline of a mosaic eye emerged from underneath the dirt.

The air around them swirled with whispers and Leila reached for Evelyn in alarm.

'What is going on?'

'I'm not sure yet, Leila,' she replied, listening intently to the hushed voices. 'They are talking about a crystal.'

'Ash said there was a large Selenite crystal in a chamber below this one. It was heavily inscripted, from what he said, but he didn't get the chance to decipher any of it.'

The ground beneath their feet suddenly began to rumble and the women took a step back as the black stones in the eye motif started to move. The women watched in fascination as a thick black liquid began to seep through the ground and pool in the centre of the motif. It bubbled like tar and a dark vapour quickly filled the air. Coughing and spluttering, Evelyn and Giana gasped in their desperate efforts to draw breath. Unaffected by the vapour, Leila tried to move towards her friends, but she could not move her legs. A voice sounded from across the room and everything went black as the three women slumped to the ground.

'Thank-you ladies, you have been most helpful,' the shrouded woman said as she stepped over the unconscious bodies and dipped a flask into the viscous liquid.

****

The naked man ran through the maze of corridors; his bare feet occasionally slipping in the red liquid that pooled on the cement floor. He reached another dead end and turned his head to the sound of a woman screaming. He called out to her and she continued to scream, her voice muffled as she begged him to find her. Rounding a corner, he found himself in a large warehouse. It was empty except for a white shipping container that sat in the middle of the space.

The man visibly shivered with the cold, wrapping his arms across his chest in an effort to warm his freezing skin. He cautiously inched towards the container, scanning the space around him for any sign of life. Finding none, he continued until he reached the sliding door and yanked it open.

A blast of cold air impacted with his already chilled skin and he audibly gasped. Ignoring his discomfit, he stepped into the container, pushing aside a bloodied, plastic sheet that hung from the ceiling. A pale body came into view and the man found himself staring at the torso of a blonde-haired woman. She was suspended on a pair of meat hooks that protruded through each nipple and a large hole gaped in her chest where her heart should have been.

'Rana?' said the man as he tentatively reached up to touch her cold skin. She flinched, and her eyes instantly shot open.

'Help me, Ash, please help me!' she whispered as blood began to pour from her mouth.

Ash frantically tried to free her from the hooks, but his hands were shaking so hard, he couldn't open them. Seeing a large knife mounted on the wall behind him, he reached for it and slashed the rope attached to the meat hooks.

Rana fell to the ground and he caught her, pulling her into his arms.

She reached out to touch his face, her hands shaking as they traced his jawline.

'Be careful, my love. He will find her too,' she said. Taking her last icy breath, her green eyes fixed on his and her hand dropped limply by her side.

Ash held her close to his chest and sobbed; gently rocking her in his arms.

Hearing laughter behind him, he spun around to see a group of men standing in the entranceway, each brandishing a knife or bone saw.

'You never learn, do you brother?' a tall man said, pointing to the back of the container. 'You can't keep them hidden from me. I will find everyone you love and kill them all.'

Ash turned to look in the direction the man was pointing. His eyes resting on the mutilated body of a red-haired woman that hung lifelessly from another hook. He stared in despair, feeling bile rise in his throat as he tried to cry out.

'Nooo!' he finally screamed, jumping to his feet and running towards the men.

The tall man laughed and shut the door in his face, entombing him in the container along with the bodies of the two women he loved.

****

Anya yawned loudly and flung her right arm out, reaching for Ash, but instead, found an empty space in the bed beside her. She pulled the sheet up around her in confusion and sat up, blearily scanning the dark room.

'Ash?' she said, clearing her throat and taking a swig from the bottle of water next to the bed.

She took a deep breath and hugged her knees to her chest. For the briefest of moments, she entertained the thought that perhaps she had dreamt the whole encounter with Ash, but the sight of his shirt hanging over a nearby chair, quickly dispelled that theory. She rose from the bed and walked over to the shirt, pressing her face into its soft folds and relishing its strong, masculine smell. Pulling the shirt on over her semi naked body, she pulled the heavy drapes aside and looked out the window, spotting Ash sitting by the pool. A wave of relief swept through her and she quickly made her way out the door.

Ash lay reclined on a plastic pool lounge, watching as the sun rose in the distance. He heard Anya's footsteps approaching and looked up to see her standing in front of him, silhouetted by the brilliant morning sun.

'Hey,' he said softly, motioning for her to sit with him.

'What are you doing out here? For a moment there, I thought you had done a runner,' she said.

She straddled his lap and he leant in to kiss her; his hands running through her long hair.

'Your hair looks even more beautiful in this light,' he mumbled, brushing against her slender neck.

'I bet that is what you tell all the girls,' she replied, sitting up straight. 'You didn't answer my question, Ash. Why are you sitting out here all alone? It looks like you have been here for a while.'

Ash shook his head and looked away, pretending to study the patterned arm of the plastic pool chair next to him. He took a deep breath and his shoulders visibly sagged.

'Now, you are really starting to worry me,' she said. 'First, I wake up in a cold, empty bed and now you can't even look at me. What is with you this morning?' she said, tears pricking at her eyes.

Ash finally looked back at her, his eyes full of sadness.

'Anya, hurting you is the last thing I wanted to do, but last night was a mistake. I should never have let things go as far as they did,' he said, reaching for her hand.

Anya pulled her hand away and stood up, glowering at him.

'A mistake? Are you fucking kidding me, Ash? There is no way that what we did together last night was a mistake. I know you felt the same way about me as I did for you. What has happened for you to have done a complete one-eighty since then,' she challenged.

'Anya, last night was incredible. You were incredible, and I want you more than you will ever know,' he said, standing up to face her. 'That is not going to change anytime soon.'

'Then what is your problem?' she demanded angrily. 'Why are you trying to push me away?'

'Because I can't keep you safe,' he shouted, running his hands through his hair in frustration. 'God, Anya! Can't you see? Being with you makes me vulnerable and weak. Logan will use my feelings for you to his advantage.' He turned his back to Anya and stood facing the main road. 'I had another nightmare last night,' he continued, 'and this one felt so real.'

'It was just a dream, Ash, nothing more.'

'No, it wasn't just a dream, Anya, it was a warning. Logan had killed you just to get at me and I know he would do it for real if he had the chance, because he did it with Rana,' he said. 'You are not safe with me Anya. I can see that now. If he found out about us, he would hunt you down. I can't lose someone I care about again,' he said, choking up. 'It would destroy me.'

'Ash, you are not going to lose me. Do you know how long I have wanted this? How much I have longed to have you look at me the way you did last night? I didn't just want you when I first saw you at the diner, I fell head over heels for you. You looked like you hadn't slept or shaved in a week, but I have never wanted a man more than at that very moment. Last night was the most amazing experience of my life and it is going to take a lot more than a stupid, fucking dream to keep me away,' she replied, grabbing the back of his head in an attempt to pull him closer.

Ash gently pulled away and held her at arm's length.

'No. It can't happen again, Anya, it is too dangerous for you to be around me. I am so sorry if I have hurt you, you have to believe that it was never my intention to lead you on,' he said softly.

Anya angrily shoved his hands away and slapped him hard across his face.

'Go fuck yourself,' she said, fighting off tears. 'I thought you were different, but you are like every other guy I have ever been with,' she raged. 'Was this all part of your master plan? To fuck me, and then ghost me at your first opportunity? You could have at least waited twenty-four hours before doing that!'

'No, Anya, it wasn't like that. I didn't plan any of this. I genuinely do have feelings for you, I always have. I just don't want to see you get hurt or worse because of me,' Ash replied.

'Well, it's a bit fucking late for that because you have hurt me more than anyone else ever has,' she said. 'I knew already how dangerous it was to be with you, but I was still willing to give it a shot because I cared about you and I thought you were worth fighting for. It's a real shame that you don't think the same of me,' she retorted, turning on her heels and heading back to the room.

****

Leila slowly sat up and scanned the dark space around her, groping the dirt floor for her torch. She heard soft groans next to her and after finally locating the torch, she shone it onto the prone form of Giana. Groggily getting to her feet, she made her way to the stricken woman and tried to help her sit up. Giana's head lolled heavily against Leila's chest, smearing a trickle of blood from her nose against her blouse.

'Giana! Wake up! I can't find Evelyn,' said Leila desperately trying to rouse her friend.

Giana opened her eyes with great effort and focused them on Leila's worried face.

'She's gone. A woman took her. She led us all into a trap,' she whispered weakly.

'What woman? What are you talking about?'

'There was a dark-haired woman here. She tricked us into finding this room and revealing the eye. The eye that has contained the Nequam for over a thousand years,' Giana explained.

Leila shone her torch across the dirty floor, illuminating the eye motif a mere two metres away from where they sat.

'There is black liquid seeping through it. Do you know what it is?' Leila asked as she helped Giana to her feet.

'Yes, I know what it is. It's the blood of the Nequam and whoever took it has sinister plans for its use. Anyone who drinks that blood will turn into a werewolf and be used at whim to do the Nequam's evil bidding,' she lamented. 'But that is not the worst of it, Leila. I have a bad feeling that the blood is part of a plot to control Ash. If they somehow manage to get Ash to drink it, they will have complete control over the Triune and he will be powerless to stop it!'

'Shit, Giana!' Leila swore. 'We need to find Evelyn and warn Ash!'

The two women staggered to their feet and made their way back to the entrance of the chamber only to find it blocked off by a pile of large rocks and debris.

'We are trapped!' said Leila frantically as she tried to move one of the rocks. 'Can you use one of your spells?'

Giana shook her head slowly, her face drawn in worry.

'I need another witch to cast the reversion spell, I can't do it on my own,' she said sadly.

'Shit, shit, SHIT!' yelled Leila, banging her hands on the rocks in frustration. 'You could not have picked a worse person to be trapped in a cave with, Giana!'

'It will be okay, Leila,' reassured Giana. 'At least now we have a great opportunity to examine the inscriptions in more detail. Who knows? Perhaps we will even find something to help us stop the Nequam,' she added.

'I wish I shared your optimism, Giana, you really do believe that every cloud has a silver lining, don't you. Alright, we might as well make the most of it. I'll take the far passage, you can keep looking in here,' she said, shining her torch along the walls as she walked away.

****

The warehouse roller door squealed as it slowly lifted up, alerting the group of men that patrolled the entrance inside. They jumped to their feet as a woman confidently strode into the space followed closely by two men carrying a shrouded body. She gave the sentries a seductive wink as she walked by and they instantly relaxed and resumed their positions. Nudging each other, they watched as the leather clad woman disappeared into a back room and out of sight.

Alexa entered the back room to find Logan standing over a large table, pointing at the blueprints that were spread out in front of him. A large group comprising of mostly men, surrounded the table and they each turned to look at Alexa as she stood by the doorway. Logan looked at her in surprise as Tommy carried a body into the room and removed the sheet from her head, revealing the pale face of Evelyn Giuliano.

'What have you done Alexa? Is she …' he began.

'No, she is not dead, Logan,' she interrupted. 'That was never part of the plan.'

'Everyone. Get out. We will go over these plans later,' Logan said dismissing the group around him. They reluctantly filed out the door, curiously eyeing the unconscious woman before they left. Logan shut the door behind them and removed the blueprints from the table before motioning for Tommy to lay Evelyn down. He waited until Tommy had also left the room before banging his hand down hard on the table.

'What the hell were you thinking, Alexa?' he said angrily. 'Once Ash finds out she is missing, he will come looking for her.'

Alexa calmly walked over to Logan and held his face in her hands.

'That is the plan, Logan. We need Ash to come looking for her.'

Logan pushed her away angrily.

'Do you have any idea what my brother is capable of? What were you planning on doing when he gets here?

Offering him a cup of tea and hoping he doesn't tear your head from your shoulders? God! Alexa, have you thought any of this through?' he said, seething in his frustration.

'I have thought this through, Logan. In fact, I have been thinking a great deal on how we can trap Ash and get him to switch sides. His mother is the bait we need to get him here and this,' she said holding out a gold flask, 'is how we will make him one of us.'

Logan reached out for the flask and unscrewed the top. Sniffing it, he looked at Alexa in shock.

'How did you find this?' he asked incredulously.

'I knew Evelyn and her friends were planning on reopening the cavern. Once they were inside, I used their own spells against them, and they summoned the eye. I was able to draw out the Nequam blood and steal Evelyn away,' she said. 'Do you know what will happen if we can make Ash drink this blood?'

'Yes, I do, but my question is, how the hell do you know?' he asked, walking towards her.

'I am not your average werewolf, Logan. I was never turned, I was born this way,' she explained, walking to a nearby stool and straddling it. 'My parents lived in Lockwood Valley, a town about three hours from here. When my mother was eight months pregnant with me, they were both attacked by a homeless guy outside a McDonald's restaurant and my dad was killed trying to protect her. My mother went into premature labour and was rushed to hospital with a large gash across her stomach. She died shortly after giving birth to me and from what I have been told, I was born with a cut on my face where the knife had penetrated her womb. If you look closely, you can still see the scar,' she said, pointing to a small line across her left cheek.

Logan touched her cheek, running his fingers along the light scar.

'It is so light, I wouldn't have noticed it, if you hadn't of shown me,' he commented.

'That wasn't a man that attacked my parents and it wasn't a knife that was used to stab my mother. He was a werewolf,' Alexa said, getting up from the chair. 'I was sent to live with my Aunty Sonia in Westmont, and she knew there was something remarkable about me, even as a young child. I was extraordinarily strong and resilient. The doctors thought I was just a sturdy baby, but the truth was, I had werewolf blood flowing through my veins. My entire childhood, I never got sick and I was ten times stronger than any person I knew. It wasn't until I hit puberty that I realised I had something else remarkable about me; the ability to read and manipulate other people's minds,' she said, stroking Evelyn's hair.

'So, you can read minds,' Logan said, nonplussed. 'Does that make you a witch of some sort as well?'

'No, I am not a witch, I am a "whisperer". I don't just read minds, Logan, I can enter people's heads while they are asleep or awake, it doesn't really matter, and plant thoughts. I don't even need to be in the same room,' she said, taking Logan's gun and emptying the cartridge before placing it back on the table. 'Watch this.'

Seconds later, Tommy walked in and strode towards Logan, snatching the gun from the table beside him. Logan watched in shock as Tommy pointed the gun to his own head and pulled the trigger. The empty gun clicked several times before he put it back down on the table and walked out of the room. Logan looked across at Alexa in disbelief.

'How the hell did you do that?' he said. 'Have you been controlling me this whole time too?'

Alexa shook her head and walked towards him, wrapping her arms around his neck.

'I couldn't control you, Logan, even if I wanted to. You are already being controlled by the Nequam. I can't manipulate your brother either, but your mother is a different story altogether,' she replied.

'Is that how you got her to reopen the cavern?' he asked, looking back towards Evelyn.

'Yes. I planted the idea and the others went along with it. Once they were inside, I made her witch friend lead them to the eye and unearth it. The rest, as they say, is history,' she said smugly.

Logan gently untangled Alexa's arms from his neck and walked over to his mother.

'This is the first time that I have been able to get a close look at her. She looks a lot like Ash, just not as tanned as him,' he said, studying her face.

'Have you ever spoken to her before?' Alexa asked, picking at her fingernail.

'No. I saw her at the cavern when I went to find Ash, but we didn't speak directly. I don't even know what I would say to her, she is like a complete stranger to me,' he replied. 'When do you think she will wake up?'

'Soon, I would imagine. Perhaps we should move her to the bunk next door where she will be more comfortable,' Alexa suggested.

Logan nodded, deep in thought. The door opened and without a word, Tommy walked over to Evelyn and carried her out.

'It is going to take me a while to get used to this mind control business,' he said.

'That's okay, I am not planning on going anywhere, anytime soon. We have all the time in the world to learn each other's special talents. Now, I don't know about you, but I am starving. Do you feel like going on a date tonight? I would kill for some Chinese food,' she said.

'Only if it is delivered. We cannot risk being seen just yet. Once we get rid of our enemies, we can walk the streets whenever we like,' he said, grabbing her hand and pulling her into him. 'Thanks for bringing me Evelyn, and I am sorry I shouted at you,' he said kissing her neck.

She smiled and moved her hand down the outside of his jeans, her touch making him stiffen beneath her fingers. He groaned in appreciation as she rubbed her palm against him and ran her tongue across his neck. His fingers found the waist of her leather pants and he deftly unzipped them, pulling them down her slender hips. She moaned as he moved his hand to cup and gently probe her depths.

'Apology accepted,' she said, ripping his shirt from his back.

****

Ash rode his bike into Rockdale passing a steady stream of traffic heading out of town. Each vehicle was fully laden, their roof racks crammed full of luggage and anything else that could be tied down in their effort to evacuate the once peaceful town. The mayor had attended a press conference the previous night and had given a voluntary evacuation order for all non-essential personnel within the town. Many residents, especially those with young families had decided to take the mayors advice and leave their homes to escape the escalating crime wave. Dozens of people were still missing, including the SWAT team and police had been unable to find any trace of them. At first, people on the outskirts of town were targeted by the murderous horde of werewolves that hunted every night, but it wasn't long before the inner suburbs also came under attack. The werewolves were becoming bolder and even day time attacks were becoming more prevalent. Residents had already begun to flee Rockdale, but the mayor's address added further urgency and it was the catalyst for a mass exodus.

Ash's mind wandered back to Anya; the way her body had felt in his hands and the sweet taste of her skin. She had been everything he had expected, and much more. He yearned to feel and taste her again, but his need to keep her safe overruled any carnal desires he felt for her. After their heated argument, he was certain she would want to put as much distance between them as possible and he was counting on her newfound hostility towards him to ensure this. He had offered to give her a ride back into town, but she had shot him a look of pure derision and stormed out the door, heading to the nearest bus stop. He had watched her safely board a bus before he left the motel himself and began to ride back to Rockdale.

As he now passed the vandalised town limit sign, he shook his head sadly. The sign sported a large pestilence symbol that covered its entire surface and obscured its welcoming words. *Welcome to Rockdale, the town that nobody ever wants to leave*, the sign affirmed, the irony of which was not lost on Ash as he eyed the congested northbound lane opposite him.

Riding through the mostly abandoned streets, Ash glanced at the missing posters that plastered the power poles, their torn edges flapping in the autumn breeze that collected the fallen leaves around them in something akin to a merry dance. He evoked suspicious stares from remaining residents, many of whom sat on their porches with an assortment of firearms, cleaning and loading them like soldiers preparing for battle.

Ash hastily picked up speed, not wishing to become the innocent victim of a trigger-happy resident hell bent on shooting anything that moved. He sped through the inner suburbs until he reached a gas station and pulled up behind a black pick-up truck. A middle-aged man was filling a jerry can while a teenaged girl watched from within the jeep. They both turned to stare at Ash as he began to fill his bike and he nodded courteously in their direction. The man rudely ignored his friendly gesture and whispered something to the girl in the truck before heading in to pay. Ash shrugged and finished fuelling his bike, aware of the girl's stare as she followed his every move. Putting the fuel cap back on, he finished up and began to walk towards the automated doors, instinctively stepping out of the way as the man exited and pushed past him.

'Hey pal, what is your problem,' Ash demanded angrily.

'Freaks like you. That's my problem,' the man sneered before turning his back and getting into his truck.

Ash watched as he sped off and shaking his head, entered the store.

****

Paige and Doug drove off in silence. Paige watched through the rear window as the man at the gas station disappeared into the store before turning back around in her seat and looking across at her uncle.

'What was he, Uncle Doug?' she asked.

'I don't know for sure, Paige. He was definitely a supernatural being, but I was getting a weird read from him. It was almost as though he was a mix breed,' Doug replied, turning the truck off the main street.

'Do you think he is dangerous?' she asked curiously.

'Probably. There are not too many that aren't, but I intend to find out for sure. I will let the others know about him and they can round him up. Did you take down his plates?' Doug asked as he pulled into his driveway.

'I did better than that,' Paige answered showing Doug her phone. 'I got a photo of him as well.'

****

Logan took a seat next to the sleeping form of Evelyn, studying her peaceful face as she softly groaned in her slumber. For his entire life until just recently, he had lived not even knowing of her existence. His mother, Melinda had never even told him that he was adopted, and he now felt conflicted as he watched the woman who had carried him in her womb, lying completely helpless in front of him. He tentatively reached out to touch her face but stopped when she suddenly twitched and moved her arm. She whispered something incoherently and her eyes fluttered open, staring around the room in shock.

'Where am I? Where are Leila and Giana?' she murmured, trying to sit up.

'You are safe, for now, Evelyn. I don't want to harm you and I won't need to if you cooperate,' Logan replied, fixing her with a firm gaze.

'Logan? Is that really you? Where are my friends?' she fretted, trying to push past him off the bed.

Logan grabbed her arm and forced her back, pinning her to the side of the bed.

'Look, calm down! Your friends are not here, Evelyn. You were the only one brought to me. They were left unharmed in the cavern,' he replied irritably.

She dropped her arms by her side and relaxed. Letting her go, Logan stepped back; unsure of what to say to her.

'Logan, why did you bring me here? Everyone will be looking for me. I need to get back before they begin to worry,' she said desperately.

'You will not be going anywhere, Evelyn, not until I have Ash,' Logan replied coolly.

'You had me kidnapped to trap your brother? That was your plan? He will destroy you and your friends if you keep provoking him, Logan. The Triune is subdued for now, but it could come back at any moment,' she warned.

'And so can the Nequam, Evelyn and it is ready for a war. Ash will come to rescue you, I am counting on that, but he will not walk out of this place the same man.'

Evelyn reached out to touch Logan's face as tears sprang to her eyes.

'How did it come to this, Logan? Both of you so consumed with hatred and anger towards each other and trying to fight a battle that I am not sure either of you can even survive. You both need to start fighting the beings inside of you and not each other; it is the only way you will be saved. You can fight it Logan if you really try,' she said softly.

Logan moved away from her, shaking his head in frustration.

'Will you just shut up!' he snapped, reeling on her. 'I can't fight it! Don't you think I have tried? Do you think I wanted to kill Ash's girlfriend or anyone else for that matter? I had to. I had no choice. The Nequam consumes me and I cannot control it. It wants me to kill Ash, but if I can get him on my side, he will be spared. Can't you see? I am trying to help him!'

'You cannot help him by turning him into a monster!' she seethed through clenched teeth.

'He is already a monster! He has equal parts werewolf and vampire blood running through his veins. You need to accept facts, Evelyn. You cannot save him anymore than you could save me!' he yelled, slamming the door hard behind him.

He stormed into the next room and punched the nearest wall sending plaster debris falling to the floor.

Alexa looked at him with a bemused smile and continued to file her nails.

'Mummy issues?' she said calmly.

'She is not my mother!' he said, shooting her a look of unbridled contempt before heading out the door.

Chapter 5

Leila jumped down into the dark hole, landing on her feet in the cramped passageway. She had been exploring the cathedral cavern with Giana for over an hour, their torches lighting the way as they felt around the walls for anything to help them. Giana had discovered the hole in the back corner of the cathedral cavern where the ground had previously given away and Leila had decided to investigate it, leaving Giana to continue exploring the far wall. Leila crawled through the passageway until she came across a large chamber dominated by an enormous Selenite crystal. As she approached the structure, a loud boom could be heard in the distance and the whole chamber shook, sending dirt and dust reigning down on her. *Bloody hell Giana! What are you doing up there?* she thought as she reached out to touch the crystal.

It hummed and vibrated beneath her touch and the room seemed to whisper around her as she stepped behind it, her fingers brushing its cool, hard surface. She gasped as a jagged section suddenly stabbed her side, instantly drawing blood. She stopped, examining the small painful wound that appeared, expecting it to heal immediately, but instead, the wound remained open and a light trickle of blood began to soak through into her shirt. *I need to feed,* she thought, turning her attention to the offending piece of crystal that jutted out from the rest of the structure.

It was a fragment measuring approximately fifteen centimetres long with the same thickness as a knife. Leila touched the piece and it snapped cleanly off the rest of the crystal, its milky white colour changing to auburn as it rested in the palm of her hand. Leila watched in awe as an inscription appeared across its length. *'Dedi malum,'* she read aloud, recognising one of the words as the Latin term for evil. She tucked the piece of crystal into her pocket and made her way back to the passageway, crawling quickly back towards the hole where Giana now waited for her.

'Leila, I have blasted a hole through, we are free!' she said excitedly.

'Holy shit, Giana, how did you manage that?' said Leila as she climbed back into the Cathedral Cavern.

'I found a box of explosives under that table over there in the corner.'

'It must have been left here by the professor that Ash worked with. How did you know how to use them?' Leila asked.

'I didn't, I just lit the fuse and ran for it,' Giana replied sheepishly.

'You could have been killed,' said Leila shaking her head in disbelief.

Giana just shrugged and smiled. 'Well at least we can get out now,' she said, her face suddenly blanching as she noticed Leila's side.

'Leila, you are bleeding! What happened?'

'Oh, I nearly forgot! I found this below,' she said calmly, pulling out the crystal fragment and handing it to Giana. 'I broke it off a huge crystal rock.'

'Wow, this could be something important. Do you know much Latin?'

'No, but I am guessing you do. What does it mean?'

'Dedi malum means surrender all evil. Leila, this crystal means something. The voices we heard when we first came in here spoke of a crystal. They wanted us to find it,' she said excitedly.

'What are we supposed to do with it?'

'I am not sure yet, but I will find out. Let's get out of here. I need to make a very important phone call,' Giana stated, grabbing Leila's hand as she left the room.

'It sounds good to me! Besides I need to feed,' replied Leila, her voice reverberating off the walls as they made their way out of the cavern.

****

Doug woke from his sleep with a start, frightening the cat that had decided to share his bed. He patted the ginger cat apologetically before swinging his legs over the side of his bed and quickly pulling on some pants. As he padded down the hall, his bare feet barely made a sound against the wooden floorboards in his effort to be quiet. A creaking sound startled him, and the face of his niece suddenly appeared in front of him, her eyes wide in fear.

'Paige, you nearly gave me a heart attack!' he whispered. 'What are you doing up?'

'I have that feeling again, Uncle Doug, the same one I had at my house.'

'I know. I have it too. Something is moving around outside the house,' he said. 'I need to get to the armoury. Stay right behind me,' he ordered, gently pushing in front of her.

They both walked through the hallway and into the living room, where Doug stopped in front of the coffee table and bent down. Pushing a button on the side, he waited as the top slowly slid apart, revealing a cache of weapons hidden within the cavity. Grabbing a handgun, he thrust it into Paige's trembling hands before selecting a shot gun for himself.

'You know how to use it, Paige, don't be afraid. Remember, you were born to do this,' he said, pressing her shoulders reassuringly.

Paige nodded feebly and took a deep breath before cocking the gun and moving behind the armchair. The sound of breaking glass followed by the wail of the security alarm announced their intruder and Doug straightened up with his gun trained on the empty doorway. Paige rested her arms on the top of the armchair, willing her hands to stop shaking as she waited for her uncle's instructions.

An explosion at the front of the house, shook the entire room and Doug and Paige were both knocked off their feet. Painful screams and groans sounded throughout the house as Doug helped Paige get back up and made his way cautiously back into the hallway. Doug's booby trap had been activated when the intruder had triggered the alarm and now his hallway was a splintered mess. The walls had been blown out and broken glass from the large mirror that had graced the left-hand side wall, now littered the floor. Paige gasped in horror as a naked bloodied man attempted to drag himself along the floorboards, leaving a trail of blood in his wake. The man spun around as he heard them approach, his amber eyes drilling into Doug's as he faced the barrel of his shot gun. Without a moment's hesitation, Doug pulled the trigger, shooting the man in the middle of his forehead and killing him instantly.

Paige didn't have time to register her shock as she felt the familiar sensations rippling through her body again. She spun around in time to see another werewolf appear from her bedroom and lunge at her. A shot rang out from behind her and the wolf fell to the ground, landing at her feet. More shots sounded as Doug put another few rounds into its skull. A sudden movement to their right caught them off guard and Doug went sprawling across the floor, hitting the side wall with a loud thud. Paige screamed and ran into the kitchen as the large wolf pursued her, its sharp claws scrabbling on the slippery kitchen tiles behind her. She slid across the marble benchtop and landed safely on the other side, spinning around as the wolf lunged at her from behind. Swiftly raising her gun, she fired as its body barrelled into her and knocked her to the floor.

****

Doug groaned as he tried to sit up, his head throbbing with pain from a large gash on his forehead. He peered frantically around him willing his bleary eyes to focus in the darkened hallway.

'Paige!' he yelled, scrambling to his feet and staggering down the hall, side stepping the inert forms of the two dead werewolves. 'Paige!' he yelled again, his voice choking up with worry. Hearing a groan from the kitchen, he raced in, scanning the room for any sign of his niece. Another groan sounded from behind the island bench and he rushed around it to find Paige lying on the tiles, pinned by the body of a man, her blonde hair turned red from the pool of blood beneath her.

'Oh God! Paige!' he choked, rushing to his niece's side. Pushing the dead man off her, he pulled her into his arms and frantically felt for a pulse. Her eyes fluttered open and she smiled wearily at her uncle.

'I got him, Uncle Doug. Right between the eyes just like you showed me.'

'Are you hurt? Did he bite you?' Doug asked, searching her body for any wounds.

'No, that's his blood, I shot him before he could bite me. I must have been knocked out when he landed on me,' she explained, groggily getting to her feet.

'Oh, Paige, I thought I had lost you!' said Doug, hugging her to his chest tightly.

'I am okay, Uncle Doug,' she laughed, feeling embarrassed by his affection.

'Have you got any idea of how bloody proud of you I am right now? You just single handedly killed a werewolf!' gushed Doug, ruffling her hair.

'Yeah, I kinda did, didn't I? Uncle Doug, what are we going to do about these bodies and this mess?' she said, gesturing to the hallway.

'Don't you worry about that. I will bring in the rest of the crew to clean up. We are going to need their help anyway now that the werewolf leader is obviously onto us. Logan Smythe needs to be put down and I intend to be the one to do the honours,' declared Doug, reaching for his phone.

'Not if I beat you to it.'

'Now, that is the Newman spirit,' Doug laughed. 'You had better go and have a shower. You look like something out of a Stephen King movie right now,' he said dismissing her as he dialled a number in his phone.

****

Ash pulled his bike to a halt in Leila's driveway and after killing the engine, swung his leg over. He undid his helmet and held it to his chest as he began to ascend the porch steps.

Leila burst out, of the front door, her face grim with worry as she addressed Ash.

'Thank God you are finally here!' she said, 'I was beginning to think you would never come home.'

'I did try calling and texting you both, but no one answered. Where have you been all day?'

Walking into the living room, he was surprised to see a blonde woman standing by the fireplace, her face instantly lighting up at the sight of him.

'Ash, this is your mother's best friend, Giana,' said Leila, stepping forward.

'Oh, Ash. It is so lovely to finally meet you. You are such a handsome man, just like your father,' she gushed, kissing him affectionately on each cheek.

'Hi,' said Ash, a little taken aback by her obvious affection for him. 'You knew my father?'

'Yes, very well. I would love to tell you all about him one day.'

'I would love that too. Mum hasn't spoken much about him. Speaking of Mum, where is she?' he said, peering over her shoulder.

'Ash, please don't freak out, but we don't know where she is. Someone took her this morning while we were in the caves,' Leila said softly.

'Took her? What the hell are you talking about, Leila?'

'We went to the caves looking for a spell to expel the Triune. Your mother was convinced we would find it there, but we were ambushed. Someone was there waiting for us, Ash. A young woman. She did something to us and we all blacked out. When we came to, your mother was gone.'

'Why would she want my mum?'

'We think it has something to do with Logan, but we can't be sure that Lillian is not involved as well. We received news today that she has escaped the hospital and perhaps the two are working together. It is a strong possibility,' Leila replied.

'For fuck's sake, Leila, why didn't you tell me any of this earlier? I should have been looking for her already,' Ash stormed.

'We couldn't tell you because we were trapped in the caves ourselves. We only got out because of a box of explosives that had been left behind. Ash, you cannot go after your mum without a plan or you could be walking straight into a trap,' Leila warned.

'I don't have time for a plan,' he snapped. 'Do you have any idea of where she might be?' he said, looking across at Giana.

'Yes, we do,' replied Giana, pulling out a map. 'I did a location spell and she is somewhere in this industrial area,' she said pointing to a small circle on the map.

'I know where that is. I think I will be able to pinpoint a building,' Ash replied, pulling his phone out of his pocket and clicking on Google Maps.

'There!' Ash said triumphantly, pointing to a large square on the map. 'She has to either be at the old Mill Warehouse on Lakeview Road or the fertilizer plant. Whichever it is, I will find her.'

Ash quickly pocketed his phone and began to make his way to the front door.

'Ash, wait! You can't go in without a plan. The woman who took Evelyn, also took something else from the caves, a flask of Nequam blood. It will turn anyone into a werewolf permanently, including you,' she warned.

'I'm already part werewolf. Besides, Leila, I do have a plan. I plan on tearing apart anyone who gets in my way, including my brother,' he replied, picking up his jacket.

****

Logan rolled the last heavy drum into the Mill, while one of his men secured it in place. He stopped to admire his handy work; the row of drums and pallets piled high on each side, capable of concealing his men and offering them temporary sanctuary in the event of an attack. Alexa, in her usual calm manner, observed the work from a metal platform high above the large concrete floor processor, blowing a kiss at Logan as he caught her eye.

'Are you going to stand up there all day distracting me or are you going to give us a hand,' Logan yelled up to her.

'I think I would rather stand up here and distract you. Besides, I just did my nails,' she quipped.

Logan smiled and shook his head, returning his focus to the group of men around him.

'We are almost ready. When Ash gets here, I am not expecting too much of a fight as his mother and her safety will be his number one priority. I will deal with him, the rest of you need to stay out of sight,' he instructed the group. 'Will, have the others come back yet?'

'No and I haven't heard from them either,' Will replied.

Logan looked towards Alexa who had moved down from her high position and was now making her way towards him. 'Can you do your mind control thing to find them?' he enquired.

'Logan, I have already tried, and I can't find any of them. Something must have gone wrong,' she replied.

'What could possibly have gone wrong? They only had to take out one man and his teenage niece! Can you get into his head and find out what the hell has happened?'

Alexa shook her head. 'I can't reach him or the girl. They are either dead or immune to my whispering. Perhaps they are not ordinary people like you first thought,' she suggested.

'And perhaps your range for whispering does not extend as far as you claim,' he sniped. 'We will find them later. Right now, I need to concentrate on my brother.' With one final look at the barricade his men had built, he walked out the door hoping he would not have to wait for long.

****

Tyson Johns threw the last of the lumpy garbage bags into the back of his pick-up truck before removing his bloodied gloves and disposing of them in them in a separate bag.

Looking across at Doug and Paige, he caught the pretty teenager staring at him and gave her a cheeky wink. Blushing profusely, she quickly turned her head and feigned interest in her uncle's conversation.

Tyson, or Jonno as his friends called him, was accustomed to female attention with his sun-bronzed skin, muscular build and dark wavy hair. On top of his physical attributes, he had an Australian accent that sent women weak at the knees.

He had moved to the States three years prior to pursue a career in football, but when that had fallen through, he decided to take up a job in security. After applying for a position that Doug Newman had advertised, Jonno had been offered a job assisting the Custodians with clean ups and protection. He was paid well and soon became good friends with the rest of the team.

Today was no different to any other day as Jonno was called in to clean up the remains of three slain werewolves and dispose of them. In total, he had disposed of seven dead werewolves, all killed at the hands of Doug or one of the other Custodians.

'Hey Dougie!' he yelled across the yard, 'How did the bastards find you?'

'Probably through scent,' Doug yelled back, placing his arm around his niece. 'Can you give Paige a lift back to her house? She needs to pick up the last of her things,' he added, as Paige quickly walked over to Jonno's waiting truck.

'Sure, no worries. I will incinerate these remains and then bring her back straight after.' Jonno opened the door for Doug's beaming niece and gestured for her to climb in.

'Now don't you get any ideas, young lady, I am a taken man,' he joked as Paige settled into the front seat.

'Having a crush on a celebrity does not mean you are taken,' Paige replied with a giggle.

'It does in my books,' grinned Jonno. 'I am just waiting until she realises that the douche bag she is with is not worthy of her. Then she will come looking for me.'

'Jessica Alba is not going to come looking for you, Jonno. Keep dreaming!'

'I sure will. Every night!'

Jonno started the truck and it lurched forward, its tyres chewing the gravel as they drove out of the property and back onto the main road. There were no other cars in sight as Jonno picked up speed. Most people had left now, and Rockdale resembled a ghost town.

Paige's family had also left town after their close call with a werewolf the previous week and Paige had made the decision to stay with her uncle, much to her parent's dismay. There was little they could do to stop her at her age and they reluctantly entrusted her safety to Doug, knowing that he would defend her with his life.

Paige sat alongside Jonno and stared out the window at the passing empty houses. It was all so surreal to know that everyone she knew from school had either fled or been killed. She hoped it wasn't the latter, but she couldn't know for sure, and she wondered if the houses would ever be filled with the laughter of families again. She wondered if anything would ever return to normal.

'Are you okay kid? That would have been some pretty scary shit to go through,' Jonno asked, noting her sudden pensiveness.

'Yeah, it was, but I'm not as freaked out as much as I probably should be. I mean, I just killed a man. One minute he was a living, breathing being, the next minute he was lying dead on top of me and I didn't even feel any remorse.'

'That is because he didn't deserve your remorse. He would have torn you and your uncle apart without a second's hesitation. You did really well today kid and I am super proud of you,' Jonno said ruffling her hair.

Paige pulled a face at him and fixed her hair in the mirror.

'I really wish you would stop doing that and please stop calling me kid,' she grimaced.

Jonno just grinned at her and continued to drive in silence. As they neared the driveway of her house, Paige looked across at him, her eyes full of mischief.

'There is something I just have to ask you,' she said, turning to face him. 'Did you really headbutt a werewolf once and knock him out?'

'Now, who has been telling you stories about me? Surely not your uncle?'

'No, Stu told me. He reckons you're crazy. Is he right? Are you crazy, Jonno?'

'Nah, I was just full of piss when that werewolf jumped me,' Jonno replied.

'Full of piss? What does that mean?' Paige looked at him quizzically.

'It means I was drunk. That bastard snuck up on me when I was walking home from the bar and I just instinctively headbutted him. I don't think it was the best decision I could have made, I had a lump on my forehead the size of a goose egg for three days afterwards and a pretty good shiner as well,' Jonno laughed. 'I don't know who looked worse, him or me?'

Paige laughed. 'I think Stu might be right, you are crazy!' she teased, winking as she opened the door and hopped out of the truck.

****

Ash pulled his bike up to the deserted lot and engaged the kick stand. The Old Mill loomed overhead, dwarfing him as he made his way down a laneway between it and several large shipping containers. The sun had descended behind the Mill and a series of automated lights surrounding the lot flickered, their soft light illuminating the buildings around him.

A scraping noise sounded to his right and he looked across to see several figures step out of the shadows, each of them brandishing a weapon of sorts. The nearest man rushed at him and swinging a metal pipe at his head. Ash jumped back feeling the pipe's momentum as it narrowly missed his face. Clearly agitated with his unsuccessful attempt, the man swung again, connecting with the underside of Ash's forearm as he brought it up to shield his face. Ash reached up and grabbed the pipe, throwing it and the man attached, against the nearest shipping container.

The two remaining men leapt into action and charged Ash, pinning him momentarily against the rendered wall behind him. A blue flash of light lit up the laneway and the men were sent flying through the air, landing in a heap a few metres away. Ash raised his hands and the three men began levitating above the ground in front of him, their faces drawn in terror as he spun them around to face him. '*Adflicto,*' he uttered, slowly bringing his hands together.

The men screamed in agony as every bone in their bodies slowly cracked and shattered, their limp forms contorting as they imploded from the inside out. Finally, Ash dropped them to the ground, their lifeless bodies impacting the hard path with a sickening thud. He stepped around them and made his way to a roller door, yanking it open effortlessly.

'What a surprise! It is good to see you, brother,' Logan said, stepping out of the warehouse in front of him.

'Where is Evelyn?' Ash demanded, his eyes flashing with anger.

'She is safe. You can see her soon, but first, you and I need to have a little chat,' Logan replied.

'Go fuck yourself, Logan. You and I have nothing to talk about.'

'I think you should hear me out, at least to see what I have to offer, Ash, and then I promise I will take you to Evelyn. Take a seat,' he said, motioning to a nearby wooden crate.

Ash shook his head and crossed his arms. 'I think I would rather stand.'

'Suit yourself. Firstly, I need you to understand something. I never meant to hurt Rana. That wasn't me,' he said studying his brother's face. 'I have no control over the Nequam once it surfaces.'

'I did not come here to listen to your excuses, Logan.'

'Hear me out, Ash. I have a proposition for you. The Nequam wants you dead, by any means necessary, but that is because of the threat you pose. The way I see it, you have two choices here. You can either join us or leave town and never return. We will overtake this town in the very near future and if you try standing in my way, I will be forced to kill you. If you decide to join us, you can share in our victory and the spoils of war that will ultimately come with it. We will all be together again, your brother and your best friends by your side and the world at your taking. The Nequam has promised us everything we could ever desire if we choose it as our leader,' Logan declared.

Ash began to laugh, shaking his head as he pushed his brother hard in the chest.

'You are fucking delusional if you think you can trust the Nequam. It has promised you everything, but it will give you nothing but pain and suffering, I can assure you. It is using you to wipe out this town and it will keep using you until it no longer has any use for you. Then you will be disposed of as easily as a snake sheds its skin. As long as I have life in my body, I will fight to protect this town and stop the Apocalypse from happening, even if it means killing you,' Ash warned.

'You are fighting a losing battle, Ash. You cannot stop the Nequam. There is only one of you, but I have an army behind me; one that grows with every passing day. Join us, Ash. Join us and take your place at my side where you belong,' Logan replied.

'I came here for one reason only and that was to find my mother and bring her back home. If you try and stop me, you will give me no choice but to kill you and the rest of your pack. You are already three men down,' Ash hissed, pointing to the laneway, 'Now, where is she?'

'I was hoping it wouldn't come to this, but if it is a fight you want, it is a fight you will get,' Logan replied, his eyes flashing red as he extended his claws and bared his teeth.

With a roar, Ash lunged at him and knocked him to the ground, the pair of them rolling into a wooden crate and smashing it. Logan slashed at Ash's chest, leaving deep gashes as he pushed him off and propelled him into the side of a shipping container. Ash sprung to his feet instantly, his chest wounds healing rapidly as he turned to face his brother. He positioned both hands in front of him and a blue ball of light travelled from his palms and hit Logan square in the chest, sending him sprawling across the warehouse floor. Ash pursued him, pulling him to his feet and delivering a well-aimed head butt to his nose that dropped him to his knees. Logan struggled to his feet and with a wave of his hand, sent Ash flying into the side of one of the oil drums, pinning him with an unseen force. He strode towards him and delivered an uppercut to his chin, followed by a sharp jab to his abdomen which doubled him over before letting him drop to the ground.

'Stop it! Both of you, stop it now!' came the shrill voice of Evelyn as she raced over to stand between them. 'You are brothers and I will not stand by and watch you hurting each other!'

Ash got to his feet and stared at Logan, his sides heaving in anger. 'Mum, you need to stay out of this,' he said sternly, his eyes never leaving Logan's.

Ash suddenly felt a sharp pain in his neck, and he stared down at his mother in shock as she withdrew a large syringe from his neck.

'Mum? What have you done?' he said, dropping to his knees.

'I... don't... know,' she stammered, looking at the syringe in confusion. She dropped it to the ground and knelt in front of Ash, catching him in her arms as he slumped forward in an unconscious state.

'Logan, what is happening?' she said, staring up at him, her eyes wide with shock.

Will and Matt bent down, and took Ash from Evelyn, propping him up between them as they dragged him away.

'Thank you, Evelyn. I now have what I need, and you are free to leave,' said Logan, turning away from her as two men escorted her outside.

Evelyn watched the roller door close in front of her, her throat constricting in shock as she pounded her fists against its surface frantically, screaming for Ash.

'Go home, Evelyn. There is nothing more you can do now,' said a husky voice from within the shadows. 'Go home and don't stop for anyone until you get there,' the voice insisted.

Evelyn stopped her fist pounding and turned around towards the road, walking past Ash's bike without any sense of recognition and disappearing into the night.

****

The squad car slowly patrolled the deserted streets. Officer Frank Hart shone a spotlight across the darkened porches and yards, looking for any sign of looters. The spotlight illuminated a long driveway where two teens were mounting their push bikes. 'Hey!' he shouted, and the boys quickly sped off, their laden backpacks jostling with each bump and corner. The squad car sped up, drawing parallel to the two boys as they pedalled madly down the sidewalk. One of the boys leered at Officer Hart and gave him the finger as they turned down a narrow laneway and disappeared into the night.

'Little shit!' swore Officer Hart as he picked up the radio to call for back up.

'Don't bother, Frank, they will be long gone before another car gets here,' his partner, Angus Frost said, turning the vehicle around and heading down a side street.

'That is the fifth one tonight, Gus, the little bastards just keep coming out of the woodwork,' Frank replied, shaking his head.

'We have bigger things to worry about than looters, Frank. Like what the hell has happened to that SWAT team. There has been no sign of any of them since their vehicles were discovered, not even that pretty detective has turned up. I think we are being lied to, Frank. There is no way that a small group of men, who, by the way, had squeaky clean records before now, are responsible for all the murders in this town,' he said bringing the car to a halt. 'We are dealing with an organized crime syndicate of which Logan Smythe is heavily involved and we need outside help if we are going to catch them and return this town to normal,' he added, taking a sip of his coffee.

'Yeah, maybe, but have you seen the bodies of the victims? I was chatting with Chris the other day and he reckons they have all been mutilated. The bodies were all missing hearts and sometimes other organs as well as presenting with animal bite and scratch marks. Some even had bones splintered as though they had been snapped with great force. He is convinced that whatever is killing all of these people is definitely not human,' Frank replied.

Gus shrugged. 'I wouldn't take too much notice of what Chris says. He likes to over exaggerate things, particularly when he has a receptive audience. No one is disputing that animals have interfered with the bodies once they were dumped, but we have witnesses that place Smythe at the scene of several of the murders. Not to mention, the human footprints that have been found at most of the crime scenes. The animal attack theory has long been put to rest, but I still think we are dealing with much larger numbers of suspects than we originally thought. Whoever it is, we will catch up with them eventually,' he said.

'I hope so. You can't even get a decent coffee now that Dolly has closed up Jo's. This stuff from the servo tastes like toilet water,' he said winding his window down and tipping the cups contents onto the ground outside. Hearing a noise, he looked ahead, peering into a stand of trees. 'Hey, look over there. Can you see something moving?' Frank asked, turning the spotlight onto a figure in the distance.

'That's a woman. What the hell is she doing out here alone at this time of night?' Gus replied, giving the siren a short burst. The dark-haired woman suddenly stopped and spun around like a startled deer in the headlights. She began mumbling incoherently and turned to run, stumbling in her attempt to escape. Frank got out of the car and took off after her, quickly catching the fleeing woman and attempting to restrain her.

'Jesus!' said Gus as he raced over to Frank as he struggled against her flailing arms.

'Calm down, lady, we are not trying to hurt you!' Gus yelled as she managed to slip from Frank's grip and deliver a well-aimed kick to his groin.

Frank dropped like a stone and rolled on the ground, groaning in pain.

'Jesus fucking Christ, we are only trying to help you,' he grimaced as Gus tried unsuccessfully to grab her.

She picked up a large rock and threw it at the officers, narrowly missing Gus's head.

'I have to go home. I have to go straight home!' she screamed at them both, turning to run.

Gus pulled out his taser and fired it at her back, sending her sprawling to the ground. As she lay twitching, he pressed his knee into her back and unceremoniously cuffed her before pulling her to her feet.

'You have just scored yourself a one-way ticket to the police station, lady. You will not be going home tonight. You are under arrest for the assault of a police officer,' Gus said sternly as he escorted her back to the waiting squad car.

As he read her rights, she stared at him open mouthed, her eyes wide with fear. Gus sat her in the back seat, and she looked up at him.

'What am I doing here, Officer? My son has been taken, he needs your help,' she pleaded.

'Look. lady, we are taking you to the station,' Gus said closing the door.

Frank turned around in his seat and looked at the woman through the barrier. Her long dark hair was plastered to her pale face and she visibly trembled.

'Please Officer, I didn't mean to hurt you, I don't know what came over me. My son needs your help! He was taken by his brother and I am worried he might hurt him,' the woman insisted as Gus started the car and began to drive off.

'Save it for the judge lady, my balls are still hurting because of you and needless to say, I am not feeling very accommodating right now,' Frank said, turning to Gus. 'Let's just get the hell out of here, we are supposed to knock off soon and now we will have to write an extra report, thanks to her.'

'Out of curiosity, lady, what are your son's names?' Gus called into the back.

'Ashton Wakehurst and Logan Smythe,' she replied quietly as the two men looked at each other in disbelief.

Chapter 6

Lillian woke with a loud gasp and anxiously peered around the strange room she found herself in. She tried to move her limbs, but even the slightest movement caused her pain and she cried out in her agony. Shaking, she held her hand out in front of her face, shocked at the condition of her skin. The flesh on her hand was almost translucent in comparison to the veins that snaked and bulged beneath the surface of her skin. Dropping her hand to her side, she turned her head to examine the musty space around her. Several candles flickered on a table alongside the bed she now rested in and the room was small and unkempt, the peeling wallpaper covered in a dark substance that, she assumed, could only have been mould.

Pushing the blankets off her chest, she slowly tried to sit up, flinching as pain and nausea swept through her body. The door to the room suddenly swung open and Bernard entered with a steaming cup of soup in his hands. He placed the cup on the table next to the bed and helped Lillian sit upright, supporting her back with a pillow.

'What is this place, Bernard, it smells awful!' she said, screwing her face up in disgust.

'It is one of the old prison guard cottages that were built in the fifties. It hasn't been used for years and it was the best

I could do considering everyone is out looking for us both,' he explained. 'Here, I made you some soup.'

'How long have I been here?' Lillian asked, taking a shaky sip of the soup.

'Only two days. You were in a coma in hospital for three weeks before you woke up. Whatever your grandson did to you, it almost killed you, Lillian, I thought I had lost you.'

'That wasn't my grandson, Bernard. He Awakened the Triune Spirit and it would have killed me only for Evelyn. It will try and kill me again if it gets the chance,' she replied solemnly.

'I won't let that happen. Besides, he has his hands full with his brother now anyway,' Bernard explained. 'Logan Smythe has blooded an army of werewolves and is taking over the town.'

'Then the prophecy has come to bear. There will soon be a battle and only one of my grandsons will be victorious. We must wait until that happens before we strike. I will have my revenge, Bernard,' she said menacingly.

'And I will be right by your side when you do, my love. Let's just get you back to good health for now, our plan can wait until later. How are you feeling?' he said, placing his hand on her knee.

'A bit weak, but this soup will pick me up,' she said, smiling weakly. 'I need some painkillers. Do you have any?'

'I did manage to find some at the twenty-four-hour drug store, but as it is the only one still open in town, it is going to be harder to find them in future,' he warned.

'It is just for a little longer Bernard, once the full moon arrives, I will be able to make an offering to Cerridwen. She will restore most of my power with the right choice of sacrifice,' Lillian replied, downing her painkillers.

'Who did you have in mind this time? Surely not your grandson again?'

'No, I aimed too high when I went after him and I won't be making that mistake again. No, I need someone young, preferably a virgin,' she replied.

'I am sure I can find the perfect person, but I may have to travel to Westmont. Rockdale is being evacuated.'

'We had better start making preparations then. I don't want to stay in this hovel any longer than absolutely necessary,' Lillian said taking another sip of her soup.

****

Anya stormed into the station ignoring the look of surprise on Officer Norman Radcliffe's face as he buzzed her in.

'Anya, where the hell have you been? Everyone has been out looking for you for the past three days,' he said, dropping his half-eaten brownie onto his lap in surprise.

'Not now, Norman, I need to see Harry,' she said dismissively, heading down the corridor.

She found the chief of police sitting at his desk with a phone cradled to his ear, deep in conversation. He looked up when she entered the room and nearly dropped the phone in shock.

'I'll have to call you back, Ruth, something has just come up,' he said placing the phone back in its receiver.

He stood up and made his way around to the front of his desk, embracing Anya like a long-lost daughter.

'You have no idea how happy I am to see you, Detective. I thought you were dead!'

Anya suddenly broke down in a torrent of tears, crying into the comfort of his shoulder. Harry held her until her sobbing subsided and then presented her with a tissue box from his desk. Anya gratefully took a tissue and dabbed at her eyes, furious at herself for breaking down in front of her boss.

'What the hell happened to you and the SWAT team? Where is John and the commissioner?' Harry probed as he sat across from Anya.

'They are all dead. Logan Smythe and his men set an ambush for them and killed them all.'

Harry shook his head in disbelief. 'How could this have happened? They were all highly trained men and women!'

'They never stood a chance, Harry. Logan is not an ordinary man, he is a werewolf.'

'What? Come on Anya, you know they don't exist,' Harry scoffed, 'You must have received a good knock to the head if you honestly believe in werewolves.'

'It is the truth, Harry. I saw them with my own eyes and John was also one of them. He set us all up and walked us right into Logan's trap,' Anya maintained.

'John? Are you suggesting he was working with Smythe?'

'No, I am not suggesting anything. I am telling you he was working with Smythe. He watched while the entire team was viciously slaughtered and then he abducted me. If it wasn't for Ash Wakehurst, I would be dead or worse right now,' she said coolly.

'Was Wakehurst involved in all this as well? John always said he couldn't be trusted.'

'Ash is not one of the bad guys here. He came looking for me and rescued me from John's basement. He dealt with John and helped me escape,' she said defiantly.

'And by dealt with, you mean killed, don't you?' Harry probed.

'Yes, he killed John, but in self-defence. That man was a psycho and he was trying to rape me. If it wasn't for Ash, he would have succeeded. Ash is not the one we need to be going after, Harry. We have to stop Logan before he hurts anyone else,' she said, getting to her feet.

Harry watched her pensively before picking up his phone.

'Frank, before you knock off, can you come in here? I need to ask you something,' he said, jotting something down in his diary.

Moments later the door opened, and Officer Hart poked his head around the corner.

'You wanted me for something, boss?' Frank said, reeling when he spotted Anya, 'Jesus, where have you been?'

Ignoring his obvious surprise to see Anya, Harry gestured for him to come in.

'Frank, the woman that you brought in earlier. Did you say she has a connection to both Smythe and Wakehurst?' Harry questioned, leaning back on his chair.

'Yeah, she is a real head case, that one. She claims that she is the mother of both of them. Twins apparently, and that Smythe has Wakehurst locked up somewhere,' he scoffed.

'Is her name Evelyn by any chance?' Anya asked, walking towards him.

'Yeah, how did you know?'

'Because, she is their mother, you fucking moron and if Logan has Ash, he is in great danger!' Anya raged, pushing past the bewildered officer and storming out the door.

'What the fuck is her problem?' asked Frank, shaking his head. 'Look, Harry, I have had my fair share of psycho women tonight and if you don't need me anymore, I'd like to head home now,' he added.

Harry nodded. 'Yeah Frank, I should get going too. We both need to be here nice and early tomorrow. See you in the morning,' he said grabbing his jacket.

****

Anya walked to the holding cell and scanned the inert forms for Evelyn. Calling out for her, she managed to waken the tired woman and beckon her to the cell bars.

'Mrs Giuliano, do you remember me? I'm Detective Chemarov and I have been helping your son, Ash,' she whispered.

'Yes, of course I do,' she said. 'Please help him, Detective. He is in great danger now that Logan has him,' she pleaded.

'Where is he?'

'At the Old Mill on Lakeview Road. You have to be careful, Detective, there is something you should know about my sons,' she warned.

'It's okay, Mrs Giuliano. Ash has told me everything. I know what they both are, and I will be very careful,' she said reassuringly.

'There's something else. A flask of Nequam blood. You need to find Ash and stop him from drinking it. If you don't, he will be turned into a monster and he will be lost to us both forever,' Evelyn warned.

'I will find him, I promise,' said Anya holding Evelyn's hand through the bars. 'Your son means a lot to me in case you hadn't already worked that out.'

Evelyn smiled sweetly. 'It is written all over your face, Detective. Trust me, he feels the same way about you. Please find my son and bring him back to me,' she said, tears pricking her eyes.

Anya nodded and moved away from the bars, turning on her heel and exiting through the automated doors.

****

Alexa walked slowly around the unconscious man, adjusting the chains that held his hands in place as he leant forward, suspended from the ceiling. She stopped in front of him and lifted his slumped head to study his face, instantly noting the features he shared with his brother. He had the same bone structure with an angular jawline that lay concealed beneath a growth of stubble. She touched the side of his face and felt him flinch beneath her fingers. Groaning, he moved his head and his eyes fluttered open, locking onto Alexa as she instinctively took a few steps backwards. She stared into his deep brown eyes, momentarily mesmerized by his intense gaze and unable to look away.

'Free me,' he whispered huskily, pulling against his binds.

Alexa took a step forward and reached for the gold chain that hung around his neck but stopped suddenly when she felt someone grab her arm.

'Don't do it, Alexa,' a stern voice ordered, and she turned her head to see Logan firmly gripping her arm.

'I… don't know what happened. He was looking at me and then, all of a sudden, I felt the urge to rip the chain from his neck,' she replied sheepishly.

'He was compelling you. It is a good thing I was nearby, or you would have done untold damage. You saw what he did to my men and that was without the Triune's help. That chain is all that keeps the Triune subdued,' Logan replied coolly, letting go of her arm. Turning his attention to his brother, he faced him and sneered.

'Nice try, brother,' he said, pulling a syringe out and plunging it deep into Ash's bicep.

Ash groaned, and his head lolled forward as he struggled to keep his feet, the copal sap all but paralysing him as it coursed through his veins. Alexa, now fully composed, shot Ash an angry look and grabbed his chin, forcing his head up level to her eyes.

'Try anything like that again and I will kill you myself,' she said, her eyes flashing with anger.

'Many before you have tried and failed. What makes you so special,' Ash challenged, holding her stare defiantly.

'Quit it Alexa, we don't have time for this,' interrupted Logan as he stood between them. 'Where is the flask?'

Alexa fished into the waistband of her leather pants and pulled out the flask, angrily thrusting it into his outstretched hand.

'I hope I like him better once he drinks that,' she said crossing her arms.

Logan twisted the lid on the flask and held it up to Ash's lips.

'Drink,' he ordered, grabbing the back of his head and trying to force the liquid down his throat. Ash struggled against him and refused to open his mouth, turning his head away from him, like a toddler refusing food.

'We can do this the easy way or the hard way, Ash. Open your fucking mouth and drink or I will force it down your throat,' Logan said angrily, reaching to grab his head a second time.

In that instant, Ash swung his head back and delivered a head butt straight to the bridge of Logan's nose, sending a spray of blood across his chest.

Logan reeled and fell to one knee holding his nose as a torrent of blood poured through his fingers.

'You motherfucker!' Logan yelled as he cracked his broken nose back into place and stood up to face his brother, 'I guess you would rather do this the hard way.'

He took a swing at Ash and his fist connected hard with his jaw, whipping his head back violently. He followed this with a couple of quick jabs to his mid-section that doubled him over and left him coughing up blood. Groaning and gritting his teeth through the pain, Ash, glared at his brother and pulled against the chains.

'Is that the best you can do?' he said, spitting out blood at his feet.

Enraged, Logan lunged forward and grabbed Ash by his throat, his eyes turning an iridescent red as he slowly squeezed harder.

'Don't fuck with me or I will tear out your fucking throat!' he threatened as Ash's face drained of colour and he began to choke. The voice that came from his mouth was not his own, but rather a deep raspy voice that emanated from deep inside.

As Ash struggled to breathe, Alexa came up alongside Logan and touched his arm, causing him to momentarily lose his focus on Ash.

'Logan,' she said softly. 'Don't let the Nequam take over or you may do something you will regret.'

Logan's eyes flashed, resuming their normal colour and he immediately let go of Ash's throat, watching as he gasped for air and began to cough.

'Stop fighting me, Ash! You can't win. Just drink from the flask and it will all be over. You and I will fight side by side and we will never be enemies again,' he said holding up the flask.

The roller door suddenly creaked open and Logan and Alexa both spun around as a blindfolded woman was dragged into the room, kicking and screaming.

'Logan, we found her snooping around outside,' said one of the men holding her firmly.

Logan recognized her immediately and walked over to greet her.

'This is a surprise. It is nice to see you again, Detective Chemarov. Did you tire of our dear friend John?' he asked, placing his hand on her shoulder.

Shrugging him off, she turned in his direction. 'He's dead. Ash killed him, and he is coming after you next,' she retorted angrily.

'Is he now? Are you two working together these days?' he asked curiously.

'Something like that, not that it is any of your fucking business!' she replied.

Anya kicked out at him and Logan laughed out loud, gesturing for Alexa to join him.

'I swear you two could be sisters. You both have bigger balls than any man I have ever met,' he said. Alexa rolled her eyes at him in irritation as she walked over to him.

Switching his focus back to Anya, he gripped her shoulders and spun her around to face him.

'What are you doing here, Detective? Did you miss my wit and charm, or do you just have a death wish?' he enquired, ripping off her blindfold.

'Well, if you think I came here looking for you, don't flatter yourself, you are not my type,' she said defiantly.

'Ahh, but Ash is, isn't he? That's why you are here. You came looking for him, didn't you?' he said, spinning her around to face the back wall. 'Well, you have found him.'

Anya looked towards the wall and spotting Ash, broke into a run towards him. Her two captors made a move to grab her, but Logan stopped them both.

'Let her go to him, she can't escape us,' he said and they both nodded, before turning back towards the door. 'Alexa, make sure she doesn't rip that chain from his neck,' he ordered as he began to follow her.

Anya quickly reached Ash and cradled his face, searching his body for signs of injury.

'Are you okay? Has he hurt you?' she asked urgently.

'I'm okay, Anya. You shouldn't have come here,' he said sadly, bringing his head up to meet her eyes.

'I had to. Your mother was brought into the station frantic with worry. She told me you were in trouble and I knew I had to come. I couldn't bear the thought of losing you again,' she despaired, softly kissing his lips.

'Anya, promise me you will get Leila and my mother and leave town immediately. Logan let Mum go, but she won't be safe for much longer. Things are going to get a lot worse around here, now that I can't help any of you anymore,' he lamented.

'Ash, what are you talking about? Break the chains! Fight Logan and stop this once and for all,' she demanded.

'Anya, with you here now, Logan has the leverage he needs to control me. He knows I won't fight him with your life in his hands. I have to do what he wants, or he will kill you.'

'I can look after myself, Ash, I am hardly the damsel in distress type,' she replied haughtily.

'That is exactly what Rana thought and look what happened to her,' he replied, 'I am not going to lose you too!'

'How touching,' scoffed Logan and as walked up behind Anya and grabbed her by the throat. 'I hate to break up this little reunion, but I think Ash and I now have an understanding. Don't we, brother?' he asked menacingly.

Alexa approached Ash and held the flask up to his lips.

'Don't drink it, Ash!' Anya pleaded, 'Evelyn told me it contains Nequam blood. If you drink it, the Nequam will control you!'

'Logan, can you promise me that both Anya and Mum will be spared?' Ash enquired.

'You have my word, Ash. No one will touch either of them and you can visit Anya whenever you feel the urge,' Logan assured him, 'Now drink from the flask.'

'No! Ash, don't listen to him. You will kill innocent people and become a monster just like him,' Anya cried desperately. 'If you drink that blood, you and I can never be together again. I will not be your werewolf booty call!'

'I would rather you never spoke to me again than see you killed in front of me. I'm sorry, Anya, this is the only way,' he said as he allowed Alexa to pour the contents of the flask into his mouth.

Ash swallowed the thick liquid, gagging as it slid down the back of his throat. It burned all the way down and his whole body began to tremble. As the liquid took hold, it felt like molten lead as it raced through every artery and capillary in his body. Flashes of bloodied limbs and agonized screams filled his mind and his eyes rolled back in his head. Crying out, he arched his back in agony and strained against the chains that held him.

'Help me, Logan! It's tearing me apart,' he pleaded.

'Don't fight it, Ash. Give in and the pain will subside,' Logan replied, quickly reaching up and snapping the chains; allowing for Ash to fall to the floor where he continued to writhe in pain.

Anya screamed and tried to reach him, but Alexa held her back and whispered something in her ear, her body instantly relaxing. Ash pulled himself up to his knees, tearing off his clothes as his limbs began to change and his spine shifted alignment with an audible crack. His smooth skin contorted and stretched over his growing limbs and fur began to sprout across his body. In an instant, his remaining clothes tore at the seams and fell to the ground along with the gold chain that had snapped around his burgeoning neck.

Logan smiled at Alexa as a large white wolf now stood where Ash had lain, its brilliant red eyes fixed on Logan as it padded towards him. Logan patted its soft fur and turned to Anya; his obvious delight evident as he beamed at her.

'He is one of us now as he should have been all along,' Logan said. 'Go home, Anya, there is nothing you can do for him now.'

Anya stood transfixed, tears running down her cheeks as she watched the wolf follow Logan across the room. She bent down to pick up Ash's gold chain, letting it run through her fingers before dropping it into her pocket. Alexa approached her and, putting her arm around her shoulder, guided her towards the door.

'You will be safe from harm. Logan will keep his promise to Ash. Go home and wait. Ash will come to you when he is ready,' she said as the roller door creaked open.

'I won't be there waiting for him,' she said, shrugging Alexa's arm away. 'There is nothing in this town for me anymore.' With that, she walked off and headed back towards her patrol car.

****

Kyle Wagner trudged up the mountain path straining underneath the weight of his heavy backpack. A black Belgian Shepherd ran ahead of him, stopping frequently to sniff at the base of the occasional tree and rock, his tail wagging furiously. Kyle shifted his backpack and shrugged it off his shoulder, letting it drop gently on the ground next to a large rock. Taking a seat, he reached into the pack and pulled out his tripod stand, positioning it on the flat section of ground overlooking the valley below. He turned back to his pack, brushing up against the dog as it buried its nose deep into its contents and removed a brown paper bag.

'Luka! Get out of there. That's not your lunch,' he admonished, pulling the bag out of his mouth and taking out a chicken sandwich. Luka whined and turned his head to one side, his eyes never leaving the sandwich as Kyle tore it in half and threw the rest to him. Kyle patted Luka's furry head as he wolfed it down greedily and began to sniff around for more. Quickly eating the rest of the sandwich, Kyle rummaged through his pack for his camera and set it up on the waiting tripod. He repositioned himself on the rock and snapped a few shots of the magnificent vista that spread out before him, across the valley below.

Luka barked and nudged his arm, picking up a stick and dropping it at his feet.

'Not now, Luka,' he said, repositioning the camera.

Luka placed his paws on Kyle's knee and began to lick his face.

'Stop it Luka,' he said, pushing him away and picking up the stick. 'Go and chase your stick and leave me alone,' he added, throwing the stick into the bushes below. Luka happily bounded down the slope and disappeared from view, his excited barks reverberating back through the thick undergrowth.

Kyle smiled and shook his head, adjusting the filter on his camera and snapping several more pictures. Placing the lens cap back on his camera, he removed it from the stand and hung it around his neck. Standing up, he placed two fingers in his mouth, and whistled loudly for his dog, before packing the tripod back into his pack and shouldering it. Whistling again, he peered down the slope, listening for Luka and expecting him to come lumbering into view at any moment. When Luka did not appear, he shook his head in frustration. *Bloody dog!*

he thought as he began his descent down between the scraggly shrubs that dotted the side of the mountain.

'LUKA!' he called as he came to a flatter section of ground and caught his breath. He heard a whimpering sound and turned to see Luka emerge from beneath the thick undergrowth to his left. The dog nervously licked his face as Kyle leant down to pat him.

'What's wrong, boy?' Kyle asked the trembling dog.

Kyle looked over to the bushes and made his way towards them, pushing his way through their prickly branches and finding himself in a small clearing. He covered his nose as a foul smell of decay accosted his nostrils and he walked towards a section that suddenly dropped off over a steep embankment. Peering over the side, he fought his natural urge to retch and instead, pulled his t-shirt up over his mouth in an attempt to mask the smell. Pulling his camera up to his face, he removed the lens cap and began to snap pictures of the scene below him. A scene of abject horror and gore that he had never before encountered. In a mangled heap below him, lay the missing SWAT team, their bloated bodies now baking in the sun as a flock of ravens picked through their rotting corpses.

****

The crowd in the warehouse parted like Moses through the Red Sea as Logan made his way through, flanked by Ash and Alexa. He came to a stop in front and turned to silence them with a single wave of his hand. Looking over the assembled group in front of him, Logan felt the mix of excitement and nervousness that his followers exuded like an intoxication that slowly crept through his own veins. His eyes scanned the faces of the sixty-strong crowd as they waited patiently for him to speak and he smiled as an overwhelming sense of pride and paternalism swept through him.

'This is the day that we have all been waiting for. By noon today, we will have this town on its knees begging for mercy, but none will be shown except for the few that you have chosen to keep in your lives,' he shouted.

A huge clap of thunder sounded outside the warehouse as though proclaiming the approval of the Gods and rain began to patter on the tin roof overhead. Nonplussed by the brewing storm outside, Logan continued his speech.

'Dave, I want you to take a dozen men to Westmont and take out their police department. Leave no survivors. The rest of you will attack the council chambers and the hospital here in Rockdale. Ash and I will take care of the Rockdale Police Department,' he declared, his eyes flashing red in anticipation.

'And where do you want me?' Alexa flirted, touching Logan's chest as she passed them by.

'I need you by mine and Ash's side,' Logan replied.

'Oh, I always wanted to be the meat in a twin sandwich,' she said, playfully slapping Ash on the ass.

'Now is not a time for jokes, Alexa. You know what needs to be done,' he admonished.

'Who said I was joking?' she said, tossing her hair.

Ignoring her, Logan turned his attention to Ash.

'Are you ready, brother?' he said, taking off his shirt and letting it drop to the ground.

Ash nodded and stepped out of his jeans, quickly transforming into a wolf.

Addressing the men and women around him, he shouted, 'Well, what are you all waiting for? Get your gear off everyone, we are ready to go.'

The group quickly stripped and transformed to their quadruped forms. Impatiently, they paced the length of the warehouse, their snarls and growls reverberating off the corrugated iron walls.

Moving to the front of the pack, Ash took his place alongside Logan and Alexa and meeting their pace, raced out the door.

****

Officer Halle Montgomery scanned her ID card and waited for the lock to beep before walking through the automated gate to the holding cell. Her boots tapped noisily on the concrete floor, alerting the new inmates of her arrival and stirring them into action. Their taunts and protestations fell on deaf ears as she ignored them and singled out Evelyn, motioning for her to approach the cell door.

'It's your lucky day, Mrs Giuliano, bail was just posted for you. You are free to go,' she said warmly.

Evelyn stood up and stiffly made her way to the cell door, avoiding the glares of derision from her cell mates as she made her exit.

'Posh bitch! Think ya better than us, don't ya. Ain't none of us here got no sugar daddy to bail us out,' sneered a toothless woman, spitting at her feet.

'Quit it, Bianca!' officer Montgomery warned, 'and for God's sake, clean yourself up. You smell like a goddamn sewer.'

Bianca extended her middle finger and resumed her seat on the bench, muttering to herself.

Officer Montgomery guided Evelyn through the door and sealed it shut behind her with a loud clang.

'Don't mind her, Mrs Giuliano, she is mostly harmless. Her bark is a lot worse than her bite at least,' she laughed, clearly delighted with her joke.

Evelyn gave her a blank look and Officer Montgomery stopped laughing and rolled her eyes.

'Doesn't anyone have a sense of humour anymore? I was referring to the fact she has no teeth, therefore she can't bite…oh forget it…it was a dumb joke anyway,' she reasoned.

They came to the automated gate and Officer Montgomery swiped her card.

'Oh, I have been meaning to ask you. How did it feel to kick Officer Hart in the balls? I have wanted to do that for ages!' she asked, ushering her through the gate.

'What time is it, Officer?' Evelyn finally spoke.

Looking at her watch, Officer Montgomery replied. 'It is a little after nine am. Time for a coffee, I think. Sign out at the desk and you can leave with your friends.'

With that, she patted Evelyn warmly on the arm and walked off towards the tearoom.

Evelyn watched her leave and then made her way over to the front desk where a portly gentleman instructed her to sign a form. Handing her a brown paper bag, he dismissed her, returning to his crossword puzzle.

'Evelyn!' a voice sounded, and she spun around to find Leila and Giana standing behind her. They both embraced her warmly and kissed her cheek.

'What happened to you? We have been so worried,' Leila said as they began to walk outside.

'Logan had me kidnapped so that Ash would come looking for me. He has him now, thanks to me,' she lamented.

'Evelyn, it wasn't your fault. There is no way you could have stopped him from coming for you,' Leila said, hugging her. 'Believe me, I tried to stop him myself, but you know how determined he gets at times.'

Evelyn shook her head sadly. 'You don't understand, Leila. I am the reason Logan was able to overpower him. They were both fighting and when I tried to stop them, something happened to me. I can't explain why, but I injected Ash with something, and he collapsed. It was like I was being controlled by someone else,' Evelyn explained.

Giana and Leila looked at each other. 'The woman from the caves,' they said in unison.

'She made me dig up the eye. I knew what I was doing, but couldn't stop myself,' said Giana.

'She could be very dangerous with a power like that. We will need to cloak ourselves in future,' said Leila. 'What did they do with Ash?'

Evelyn shook her head. 'I don't know. They took him inside and the woman told me to go straight home. When the police found me, I was still under her spell and that is why I attacked them,' she replied sheepishly.

'It's okay, you are out now. Nothing else has happened in the two days you have been incarcerated so no news is good news, right? Ash will be okay, at least we know Logan won't try and kill him,' she reasoned as she unlocked her car.

Evelyn climbed into the front seat and Leila shut the door behind her.

'Why didn't you tell her the truth?' Giana said, whispering in her ear.

'How could I? From what Anya has said, he is now a werewolf hell bent on destroying everyone in this town. It is better that she doesn't know yet. We will tell her when she is feeling better,' she said dismissively, opening the driver's side door and climbing in.

Starting the engine, she began to reverse the car out of the parking space, but something in the distance caught her eye and she stopped, staring open-mouthed at the scene that unfolded in the street behind them.

Chapter 7

The cane rocking chair creaked beneath the weight of Clive Porter's portly frame as he slowly rocked it back and forth on his porch. Listening to the rain as it fell steadily outside, he flipped over another page of his newspaper and began to read the obituaries. Shaking his head, he called out to his wife through the open window beside his head.

'Marg, have you read the obituaries? There must be thirty odd death notices since last week and they are not old folks either!' not waiting for a response, he continued to read on, intermittently sipping on his hot coffee. He, along with his wife Marg, had decided to stay in Rockdale as he was reluctant to leave his aviary and prize-winning vegetable garden behind. He wasn't convinced by the mayor's long speech regarding the town's irretrievable decline and preferred to wait out the bad times with his trusty double barrel shotgun by his side.

Pippa, his miniature poodle suddenly looked up from her bed at his feet and began to growl. Getting to her feet, she yipped shrilly and ran to the front gate, seemingly oblivious to the heavy rain.

Clive slapped his newspaper down and slipped his feet back into his slippers before standing up.

'Pippa! Get back here girl and stop that racket!' he yelled from the top step.

The dog ignoring him, continued to bark, sticking her head through the wrought iron gate.

Struggling to see through the torrential rain, he peered across the street to see dark shapes dashing past.

'Marg, have you given me the wrong medication again? I could swear I am seeing wolves out the front of the house,' he shouted back towards the open window.

Marg stuck her head out and gave Clive a stern look.

'What are you prattling on about, Clive? I am trying to do the dishes,' she said irritably.

'Look for yourself, Marg. There would have to be at least thirty wolves in the street, big ones they are too,' he said, pointing towards the road.

Marg and Clive watched in disbelief as the wolves raced past the house en masse. Pippa's barking escalated and one of the wolves stopped and double backed, glaring at her through the gate. The dog moved forward and in an instant the wolf attacked, biting the little dogs head clean off its shoulders, its body twitching as it dropped to the ground.

Marg screamed, and Clive stumbled back in alarm, quickly grabbing his gun and running back to the safety of the house. The wolf sniffed at the dead dog's head and picked it up in its mouth before swallowing it whole and racing to catch up with the rest of the pack.

****

Norman filled in the last of his crossword puzzle and checked his watch. *Nearly morning tea time,* he thought, and his stomach grumbled at the promise of a slice of his wife's banana cake. He glanced around the waiting room, contemplating whether an early escape to the tearoom would go unnoticed. A woman sat on the chair closest to the door, speaking loudly on her mobile phone while another woman stared into space as she leant against the wall. *Nothing more I can do for those two,* he reasoned, knowing that they had both already given statements and were waiting on a formal interview.

He stood up from his desk and pushed the chair back, reaching into the drawer for his swipe card.

The sound of the automated doors opening caught his attention and he looked up towards the doorway. His mouth dropped open as a beautiful young woman stepped into the waiting room with two huge wolves; one jet black in colour and the other as white as snow. She was completely naked, her long wet hair hanging lankly across her breasts and shoulders as she stood stroking the fur of the two wolves. Norman openly stared as she made her way towards him and stopped at his desk, placing her elbows on the counter and leaning in through the service window.

'Excuse me, Ma'am,' he stuttered nervously, 'you can't bring dogs in here.'

'Dogs? I don't see any dogs, Officer. These two beautiful creatures are wolves,' she said, smiling at him seductively.

'Ma'am, I must insist. Please take the dogs, I mean, wolves outside,' Norman said handing her his jacket, 'and please cover yourself up, this is a public place.'

'Why? Don't you like my body? You know we are all naked underneath our clothes,' she teased.

Yes, but not everyone looks like you! he thought, willing himself to keep his eyes on her face.

'Perhaps you would like for me to put something on. A fur coat maybe?' she replied, tossing her drenched hair.

'Yes, that would be more acceptable,' Norman replied in earnest.

The woman suddenly sneered at him and her eyes flashed red.

'Be careful what you wish for,' she said menacingly as she reached in through the service window and grabbed Norman's hand. 'Open the door,' she said, looking into his eyes.

Norman robotically pushed a button underneath his desk and the security door buzzed open.

'Why, thank you sir, you have been most helpful!' she said as the two wolves swung into action and lunged at the startled man, his screams becoming gurgles as they tore him apart.

****

Leila watched in amazement as a naked woman walked through the street surrounded by dozens of wolves of various shades of white and grey. Some of the wolves peeled off from the rest, continuing down the road towards the main precinct, but two remained behind and followed the woman into the police station.

'Are you seeing what I am seeing?' said Leila, craning her head in the direction of the woman.

Giana and Evelyn both turned to see the woman and Giana immediately gasped. 'That is the woman from the caves!'

'And those wolves must be my sons,' announced Evelyn, opening the car door.

'What are you doing?' demanded Leila as she tried in vain to grab Evelyn's arm.

'I have to stop them. I can't let Ash be a part of their murderous plans, it will destroy him!'

Leila got out of the car and raced after her, restraining her before she could enter the building. Evelyn struggled to free herself and swore at Leila when she realized her efforts were futile.

'Let me go, Leila! I have to save my son!'

'No, I will not let you put yourself in danger. They will tear you apart!' Leila replied.

Screams suddenly broke out from within the building and a woman came running out, her eyes wide with fright. She barely made it within a foot of the building when a white wolf lunged through the doors and knocked her to the ground. A sickening crunch sound replaced the woman's screams as the wolf bit into her skull, killing her instantly. The wolf turned to face Leila and Evelyn as they stood cowering on the footpath and began to walk towards them. Within seconds the wolf transformed, and Ash now stood in front of them, his naked body streaked with rivulets of blood. His red eyes bored through Evelyn's and she began to openly sob, reaching out to touch his face. He flinched at her touch and quickly resumed his quadruped form, loping back into the station without a backward glance.

Evelyn collapsed to the footpath, sobbing hysterically in Leila's arms.

'It is too late, I can't save him,' she cried as shots broke out from inside the building.

The sound of gunfire spurred Evelyn into action and she stood up, breaking away from Leila and racing towards the car. Rummaging for her phone, she began to dial for help.

'Who are you going to call, Evelyn? There is no one to help us now. Can't you hear the screams? They are being slaughtered in there,' Leila said.

'I can't stand here and do nothing,' she despaired, dialling Anya's number.

After several minutes, silence finally descended over the scene and the automated doors opened. Three wolves walked out and picked up their pace as they made their way back down the street, the black wolf's howls chilling the shocked women to their very core.

****

The sound of tapping reverberated through the valley below as Austin Mackay, hammered away at the rock face in front of him. Austin and his fellow Geologist, Steve Pratt, had arrived at Mount Westmont, a few hours prior, to investigate the recent seismic activity from the area. Using thermal imagery, they had discovered an unusual heat signature on their equipment some forty metres down the eastern side. Eager to find its source, Austin had abseiled down the steep cliff to obtain samples, updating Steve through his hand-held walkie-talkie.

The wind picked up and he felt himself being swung to the side like a pendulum as he tried to regain control. Bending his knees, he sat back into his harness, shifting his centre of gravity to minimise the sway as he dangled over the steep precipice.

Quickly regaining control, he continued digging into the russet-coloured sandstone. After a few moments, he stopped; surprised to find a sticky tar-like substance oozing through the porous rock. After placing some of the substance into a specimen jar, he tentatively reached out and touched it with his gloved finger, bringing it up to his nose. It had no obvious odour, so he placed a small amount on his tongue, hoping to identify the substance through taste. Instantly he gagged and began to shake, his limp body banging into the side of the cliff with every convulsion. Red froth began to form at the side of his mouth and pour from his nose as he eventually lost consciousness and slumped back into his harness.

Steve sat topside, drinking a can of Pepsi and impatiently looking at his watch.

'Austin, what is going on down there?' he said, clicking on his walkie-talkie and moving to the side of the cliff. 'Austin, come in, we need to finish up soon,' he added.

Hearing no response, he peered over the edge, swearing when he spotted Austin's limp body hanging precariously down the rock face.

'Holy shit,' he swore, activating the winch on his Range Rover and quickly retracting Austin's climbing rope. He managed to winch him up within minutes and pulled him to safety, frantically examining his body for obvious signs of injury.

Austin opened his eyes and Steve involuntarily took a step back. His friend's eyes were bloodshot and jet black in colour as they stared at him in desperation. Steve fumbled for his phone and called for help as he watched Austin attempt to crawl towards him, his bones snapping and cracking with every feeble movement. Screaming in agony, Austin writhed uncontrollably before retching blood and bile onto Steve's boots and collapsing at his feet.

****

Doug Newman walked into the Psychiatric wing at the hospital and was quickly waved through into the visitor's room where Paige was meeting with a patient. Upon entry, he smiled at his niece who sat opposite Natasha Reid, a pretty, dark-haired woman. They were deeply engrossed in conversation and Natasha laughed out loud at something Paige had whispered prior to Doug's arrival.

'Well you two certainly look cosy,' he said, sitting in the chair alongside Paige and beaming at Natasha.

'We have so much in common and it's not just a shared hatred for werewolves,' replied Paige, reaching for Natasha's hand. 'Tash wants to be a part of our program and I think she would be perfect.'

Doug nodded, recalling the night Natasha's dorm mates were slaughtered. As the sole survivor, if anyone had the right to hate werewolves, it was definitely her.

He studied the pale girl in front of him with a mixture of pride and trepidation. He was immensely proud of her for overcoming her debilitating fear and agoraphobia brought on by her close shave with death, but at the same time, he knew she was risking her life to fight with them. The Custodians had handpicked dozens of young people as part of the "Purge Program", as it had been aptly named and Natasha was one of the newest recruits. The rest of the hospital was due to be evacuated that afternoon and she was being released into Doug's care based on the remarkable improvement she had shown since Paige's daily visits. She would now be trained in hand-to-hand combat and weapon use as part of the program intent on decimating the werewolf population in Rockdale.

'Let's get you out of here, Tash. Your training begins today,' he said warmly, gripping her shoulder.

Natasha nodded and collected her bag eagerly, following Doug out the door.

As the trio made their way down the corridor into the main hospital ward, they stopped, stepping out of the way as a gurney was quickly pushed past. Paige caught her uncle's eye and glanced at the man on the gurney as it disappeared from view.

Doug quickly grabbed the girl's arms and escorted them into the waiting room.

'That was a werewolf in transition. I have to go back there and kill it before it transforms. Paige, take Tash to the truck and wait for me there,' he ordered.

'I want to help,' Natasha said, her eyes bright with excitement.

'Not yet, Tash, you are not ready to see one of these things up close, let alone kill it. Go with Paige, I won't be long,' he said turning away from the girls and heading back towards the doors the gurney had entered.

Suddenly, the hospital's loudspeaker hailed, *'Code red, Code red. We have an emergency situation. Everyone please remain calm and make their way to the roof in an orderly fashion. I repeat, please make your way to the roof of this building. This is not a drill.'*

The sound of smashing glass heralded the breach of the hospital doors and the waiting room became a scene of mass panic. Doug frantically pushed the girls into the nearest storage cupboard and grabbing a broom, snapped it in half to use as a weapon.

'Stay here and don't make a sound,' he whispered, locking the door behind him.

Racing into the waiting room, he was unprepared for the carnage that now presented itself. Werewolves had torn through the room, killing everyone in sight. Their bloodied bodies were strewn across the floor like mutilated rag dolls. The wolves had moved on and their howls could be heard mingling with the terrified screams of patients and staff further along the corridor. Desperate to get to his truck, but not wanting to leave the girls, he double backed and yanked open the storage cupboard door, coming face to face with the other splintered half of the broom stick wielded by his niece. Narrowly ducking out of the way, he knocked it from her hands and pulled both her and Natasha into the corridor.

'We have to get out of here now,' he screamed at them both and they sprinted into the waiting room. Sidestepping several mutilated bodies, they made it to the front desk and rounded the corner. Losing her footing, Natasha suddenly slipped on a pool of blood and slid across the floor, banging into the body of a woman. Pulling herself up, she spotted movement as something squirmed in her arms.

'Oh, my God!' said Natasha as she spotted a swaddled baby that was concealed in its dead mother's arms. She picked up the unharmed baby and cradled him protectively in her arms as she hastily followed Paige and Doug out the door. They ran across the carpark and reached the safety of the truck, diving inside and shutting the doors behind them. Doug grabbed his two-way radio and quickly called for help before exiting the truck and arming himself.

'Paige, you take Tash and the baby back to the compound. I am going back in. Those people in there are completely defenceless,' he said, throwing her the keys.

'You can't fight them on your own, Uncle, not even with your weapons. Let me stay and help you,' Paige pleaded.

'The others will get here soon. I need to know you girls are safe, I can't go in there fighting if you are still in danger. Now go! I will be fine, I promise,' he shouted, shutting the truck door abruptly.

Paige stifled her sobs and started the truck before noisily crunching the gears and taking off.

****

Anya walked into the police station with her gun drawn at the ready and her heart in her throat as she took in the eerie silence.

Moments earlier, she had received a garbled message from Evelyn Giuliano describing an attack on the station by Logan and Ash. When she had found Logan and his werewolf posse at the Old Mill, they had been planning something big, but she never suspected they would do something like this, especially in broad daylight.

She scanned the waiting room, puzzled by the lack of signs of struggle. The security door was opened, but still intact, suggesting that it hadn't been forced open, but rather, opened voluntarily. A woman sat on a chair against the window with her head slumped forward as though she was deep in slumber. Blood slowly trickled down from her fingertips, pooling on the floor beneath her. Anya gently lifted her head and it flopped back revealing a gaping hole in her throat that morbidly reminded Anya of a giant Pez candy dispenser.

Inching past her inert body, Anya cautiously made her way through the security door to find the body of an officer lying on the floor.

Kneeling down beside him, she tried to steady her trembling hands as she turned him over. Reeling in shock, she fell backwards at the sight of her colleague's disfigured face and body. Struggling to contain her sobs, she covered his face with the jacket that was hanging over the back of his chair. *Poor, harmless Norm,* she thought, sniffing as she pulled herself up. She continued through into the tearoom to find more of her colleague's dead, some still with their hands on their holsters indicating that they were struck very quickly without having the chance to fire off a shot. The corridor told a completely different story as it was riddled with bullets and the two armed officers slumped against the wall had obviously fought for their lives. Officer Hart and Frost were ironically partners in life and in death as they sat side by side on the cold hard floor.

The holding cells were a horrific sight. It was hard to imagine that the mutilated bodies had once been living and breathing human beings as not a single person was left intact. It was scene reminiscent of a fox attack in a hen house and at the sight of such carnage, Anya's normally strong stomach failed her, and she retched onto the floor, her stomach contents mixing with the blood and gore all around her.

Heading back towards the main offices, she steeled herself, refusing to look at the dead faces of the people she had once worked with, her mind focused on Harry's office and the movement she could see through his frosted glass door. Breaking into a run, she pushed open the door and stood frozen at the sight of her boss hanging from the ceiling fan as it slowly oscillated. He had been stripped naked and skinned from the chest down, a crude pestilence symbol cut deep into his bloodied chest. Dropping to her knees in despair, Anya could no longer suppress the tide of emotions as she finally broke down, screaming for the horror she had witnessed and for the knowledge that Ash, along with Logan, had been responsible for the brutal deaths of so many innocent people.

****

As heavy clouds rumbled overhead, ready to let loose on the hospital carpark, Doug stormed into the reception area with his rifle at the ready. Rounding a corner, he looked up the corridor to see a terrified man and woman hurtling towards him, carrying a small child. Doug screamed at them to get down before aiming his gun at a werewolf in pursuit and dropping him with a well-aimed shot to the head. As the wolf struggled to get back on its feet, Doug put another round into its head, killing it instantly. The horrified family ahead of him scrambled to their feet and quickly exited the hospital doors to safety.

Doug checked each room on the first floor, finding the bodies of nurses and orderlies that had been unable to escape. Most of the hospital patients had already been evacuated earlier that morning, but those who remained were on the top two floors and in the psyche ward. Doug hoped he wasn't too late to help them.

Hearing a rush of footsteps behind him, he turned to see five armed men enter the corridor. Waving his hand and gesturing to the ceiling above, two men peeled off and double backed whilst the remaining three silently followed Doug as he climbed the stairs. As they neared the top of the stairs, Doug came across the slumped body of a nurse. Quickly checking her pulse, he realized she was still alive and crouched down beside her.

'Are you okay?' he asked as she struggled to hold her head upright. Shaking her head, she moved her hand away from her stomach to reveal a huge gash from which her intestines protruded.

'Good God!' cursed one of the men behind him, doubling over.

'It's okay. Everything will be okay, nurse. We will come back for you once we kill them. Do you know how many there were?' Doug probed gently.

'There were four,' she replied weakly, 'you have to stop them. We haven't evacuated the Children's Ward yet. There are a dozen kids up there,' she said desperately.

'Don't worry, we will stop them,' Doug said turning to the nearest man.

'Nate, take Joe with you and go to the far end of level three. Mitch and I will cover this end and meet you in the middle. Hopefully, the others will have no trouble covering level two,' he ordered.

'Nurse, we will come back for you, I promise,' he said before heading up the steps to the top floor.

When he reached the top, he pushed open the swinging door that led into the Children's Ward and stepped into the brightly coloured corridor. It was eerily quiet except for a television that had been left on in the empty waiting room. Carefully, Mitch and Doug checked each of the rooms and the nurse's station but found them all empty. Doug looked over at Mitch and shrugged.

'They must have already gone to the roof,' he suggested, and they began to make their way back to the stairwell. Hearing gunfire on the floor below them, they both stopped in their tracks and headed back downstairs to the second floor. Bursting through the doors, Doug and Mitch opened fire on the two werewolves that were trying to escape the other Custodians. One of the wolves dropped to the floor as it finally succumbed to its gunshot wounds, but the other one smashed through the outside window and made its escape.

'Jonno, there is still one more wolf unaccounted for, plus they were wheeling in a man who was transitioning before the wolves attacked. He could have turned by now,' Doug said, addressing the nearest man.

'We only encountered these two, but not before they killed everyone on this floor. The poor bastards didn't stand a chance,' Jonno replied.

'We need to get to the roof and find the kids before it's too late,' Doug declared, glancing at the body of a dead nurse as she lay spread-eagled on the floor. Blood was pouring from a huge hole in her chest where her left breast had once been, and her mouth was frozen open in shock.

Shaking his head, Doug quickly raced back to the stairs with the other Custodians close on his heels.

****

Lillian woke from a fit full sleep and rolled over to find Bernard sitting on the edge of the bed with his head down.

'My love, are you okay?' she whispered, slowly pulling herself up to rest on the pillows.

He turned to look at her, his dark eyes intermittently flashing red.

'The Nequam is calling me. I can feel it under my skin trying to control me. Something big is happening out there, Lillian,' he said, reaching out to touch her hand.

'Oh dear, Bernard, you are shaking like a leaf!' Lillian replied, clutching his trembling hands.

'It is taking everything I have not to transform. Even with your amulet, I am worried I won't be able to resist for much longer,' he despaired.

Lillian reached for the small leather amulet that hung around his neck. It contained crushed Agate stone, Amaranth leaves and a powerful herb known as Mullein; all working together to combat the Nequam's control. She had made it for him before she had been hospitalised, and it was in dire need of respelling.

'*Da fortitudinem*,' she whispered, blowing onto the amulet.

'That should keep you safe for a bit longer,' she said, watching as Bernard visibly relaxed. 'As the Nequam becomes stronger, the amulet will slowly lose its power. Don't worry my love, as soon as I am renewed, I will do a stronger spell. Speaking of which, did you find me a suitable sacrifice?'

'Yes, I did. A young woman from Westmont. She is being prepped by the girls and we will be ready to proceed tonight, as planned,' he replied.

'And what of Morgan? Did you manage to find her?'

Bernard shook his head. 'She was at the manor, but as soon as she found out you had escaped the hospital, she disappeared. She had a werewolf staying with her, so I imagine they are hiding out somewhere together,' he replied.

'I will find her eventually, but right now I need to go home,' she insisted.

'It's too risky, Lillian, the police have been watching the house since you escaped.'

Lillian smiled and touched his face gently. 'I had a vision, Bernard, while you were out. I know why the Nequam has suddenly gained more power and it is something that will benefit us both greatly, despite your earlier issue. Logan and his merry band of werewolves have wiped out both the Rockdale and Westmont Police Departments. There is no one looking for us now. We can return freely to our home and once again look forward to the coming of Cerridwen for she will come, believe me,' Lillian replied, kissing him softly on the lips. 'Oh, and one more little snippet of information that you might find reassuring is that Ashton is now under the control of the Nequam. He won't be looking for us either and we no longer need to fear the Triune. We are free to do what we desire, my love and no one can stop us,' she added gleefully.

****

The heavy fire escape door creaked in protest as Doug swung it open and stepped out onto the roof. Heavy rain stung his face as he ran for cover under an overhanging air conditioner vent. After scanning the roof, he motioned to the others to follow and they joined him with their guns drawn. The sound of a baby crying broke through the incessant patter of the rain and Doug looked over at Jonno.

'That came from the other side of the roof. You and I will go and check it out. "Mitch",' he said, addressing his friend. 'You can stay here and make sure nothing gets through those doors. Stu, we will need you to cover us,' Doug instructed before moving off and running to the other side of the roof.

Soaking wet, they both made it to a large greenhouse that was situated on the eastern side of the roof. Doug slowly opened the door and a woman screamed, launching a pot plant at his head. Ducking out of the way, the pot smashed against the wall behind him, narrowly missing Jonno.

'It's okay,' Doug whispered. 'We are here to help you!' he reassured the panic-stricken woman in front of him.

Huddled in the corner of the greenhouse, Doug could see a group of children being consoled by five nurses, one with a small, squalling baby in her arms.

'Is anyone hurt,' Jonno asked, walking towards the nearest nurse.

'No, we all made it out safely, but not before we heard the screams from the floor below us. What the hell happened down there?' the nurse sobbed. Jonno put his arm around her protectively and looked towards Doug.

'Trust me, you don't want to know.'

The door to the greenhouse swung open and Stu raced in, his long hair slick to his face.

'Guys, we have trouble,' he announced, looking back over his shoulder.

Doug swung into action, instructing the nurses to keep the children quiet before heading back outside with Jonno.

'What is it Stu?' Doug enquired.

'Something big is banging into the fire escape door and I don't think it will hold for much longer,' Stu replied looking back across the roof anxiously.

'Well, whatever it is, we cannot let it out. Jonno, stay here and protect the kids, Stu and I will help Mitch,' he replied, racing off into the rain.

As they ran past the helipad, gunshots sounded from the other side of the air conditioner vent and Doug and Stu both instinctively ducked for cover. A loud clang reverberated across the roof and Mitch was suddenly propelled through the air, hitting the far brick wall with a sickening thud. From out of the rain mist, a single werewolf stepped, fixing its hungry eyes on Doug and Stu.

'Fuck!' both Doug and Stu swore in unison as they raised their shotguns and fired.

With a snarl, the wolf suddenly veered to its left and raced along the far wall, stealthily avoiding the volley of bullets as it zigzagged across the roof towards the greenhouse. Fifty metres behind them, the greenhouse door swung open and Jonno calmly strode out with his assault rifle at the ready. Dropping to one knee, he carefully raised the gun and waited until the wolf was almost upon him before opening fire. The wolf stopped in mid-air and fell to the ground, sliding to a halt mere centimetre's short of Jonno's boots. It immediately changed back into its human form and Jonno kicked out at the now dead man as he lay at his feet.

Running back to join him, Doug and Stu slapped his back appreciatively before examining the body.

'You, crazy bastard! Doesn't anything scare you?' Stu laughed, shaking his head.

'Yeah, women. They scare me a lot more than werewolves,' Jonno joked and the other men laughed out loud.

'Well if Aussie women are half as crazy as you, I can see why you would be afraid of them,' Doug remarked, dragging a nearby tarpaulin across and over the dead man. 'We need to check on Mitch and get these people out of here,' he added, turning back towards his injured friend.

While Stu and Jonno herded the survivors safely across the roof, Jonno rushed to Mitch's side.

'Are you okay, Mitch?' he asked as he helped him to his feet.

'Yeah, I think my arm is broken though. I wasn't expecting him to come through the air vent, he caught me by surprise,' he said, cradling his arm.

'He nearly caught us all by surprise, but thanks to Jonno, he is now well and truly dead. We will get these people to safety and then find out what happened to Joe and Nate,' Doug said as they began to slowly make their way down the stairwell.

On their way down, the group found Nate in the stairwell as he carried the body of the badly injured nurse they had encountered earlier.

'Boy am I glad to see you lot. We could hear the gun shots but didn't know if any of you had made it out. Joe's alright too, he has just gone back into the psyche ward. Something had killed everyone there, but I don't think it was a werewolf, it was something different altogether. Joe killed it and he has gone to retrieve its body. I tell you Doug, it was the scariest looking thing I have ever seen,' Nate said earnestly.

'I will have a look at it when we get it to the lab. It may be a mutation of a werewolf as I saw a patient earlier who was giving me a weird read like he was transitioning. Paige sensed it too, but I didn't have time to investigate before we came under attack. We managed to save most of the patients and staff on the top level as they made it to the roof, but a lot of people have died here today. Is she going to be okay?' Doug said, gesturing to the unconscious nurse in Nates arms.

'I don't know. She has been hurt pretty bad, but she still has a pulse,' Nate replied as the group of survivors filed past him. 'I will take her back to the compound and do what I can for her. We can't send her to another hospital as she may yet transition.'

'Yes, of course. Stitch her up and keep an eye on her. We don't need another werewolf in our midst,' replied Doug.

Nate's CB radio crackled, and Joe's voice sounded over the airwaves. Carefully placing the nurse in Jonno's waiting arms, Nate retrieved the CB from his belt.

'Nate here. Did you find the body?' Nate answered.

'No, it has gone. I must have only wounded it. What about Doug and the others? Did they all make it?' Joe enquired.

'Yeah, Doug is here with me now. They killed the last werewolf on the roof and are now walking the survivors out through reception,' Nate replied.

'Holy shit!' interrupted Joe, 'Have you guys looked outside? The fucking Calvary has finally arrived!'

Nate and Doug quickly made their way down the last of the steps and pushed open the fire escape door onto the ground floor. The corridor was swarming with soldiers and Doug and Nate raised their hands cautiously as the men quickly trained their guns on them. Grinning from ear to ear, Doug stepped forward and hugged a highly decorated officer that had stopped in front of him.

The officer embraced him back with unabashed affection and held him at arm's length as he examined his old friend.

'I can't believe it is you, Dougie. I haven't seen you in twenty-five years! Fuck, you haven't changed a bit!' the officer exclaimed, patting him on the shoulder.

'I can't say the same for you, Lawrence, you have gained a few more pounds and a few more stripes since we parted company,' Doug joked. 'I see you finally made captain.'

'Yes, you are presently looking at the new captain of the United States Army, Captain James Lawrence. It has a nice ring to it, don't you think?' the captain said proudly.

'It sure does. Who would have ever thought that Lanky Lawrence would become a captain? Old Crusty would be turning in his grave,' Doug remarked, grinning at his old friend.

Doug and James had first met as new recruits at the Fort Benning Army Base in Georgia where they had undertaken training as soldiers. They had initially bonded over their shared hatred for Sergeant Crustmore whom James had aptly nicknamed "Old Crusty", much to the other soldier's delight. Unfortunately, Sergeant Crustmore did not share the same pleasure in the learning of his new moniker and he made James's life as uncomfortable as possible during his training. Doug was also targeted as one of James's friends and the pair often found themselves partaking in 3 am hikes in torrential rain and cleaning lavatories, among other unsavoury activities. This unfair treatment only cemented their bond and they were inseparable for the five years they lived, trained and fought together.

Doug had slowly risen through the ranks and was a respected corporal when he was severely injured by a roadside bomb in Iraq. Three other soldiers traveling with him, including James were also badly injured with one later dying from his wounds. Whilst Doug's physical injuries eventually healed, the shock of what he had witnessed on that fateful day could not be cured and he was later diagnosed with Post Traumatic Shock Disorder and given a medical discharge from the army. James made a full recovery and later returned to the Gulf War, but Doug was so ashamed of what he deemed as a weakness, that he severed all ties with his army mates and moved to Nebraska.

Now looking at his old friend, he wished they had been reunited under different circumstances. The arrival of the army in Rockdale now heralded the start of martial law and an uncertain future for those still living in Rockdale if they chose to remain.

'Captain, we have a lot to talk about and you are definitely going to need to sit down for what I am about to tell you,' he said earnestly.

'I am all ears, my old friend. My chariot awaits,' he said, motioning to the jeep parked outside.

Chapter 8

The small group of caped girls pushed a bound woman ahead of them as they made their way up the path that snaked towards the waterfall entrance. Bernard followed closely behind them, his dark brow slick with perspiration as he carried Lillian. They finally reached the entrance and the women stopped short, turning to Lillian in surprise.

'The water has turned red!' one of the girls remarked, pointing to the reddish-brown water that spilled over the top of the waterfall and thundered down on the rocks below.

"When the waters doth turn crimson and the earth haemorrhages its precious life blood, mankind will tremble in the light of a new dawn of death and destruction of which they have never before witnessed. The Goddess will walk the earth with her brothers and sisters and the faithful will bask in her glory and in her mercy," Lillian quoted. 'Do not fear my loyal subjects, the red water is a sign from Cerridwen that she will be reborn soon. You, as the faithful will be rewarded when she comes. We will all be rewarded,' she added.

The girls whispered to each other before bowing to Lillian and stepping into the mouth of the cave.

Rounding the corner to the Cathedral Cavern, Lillian stared at the room before unleashing her hostility on the nearest girl.

'Someone has been here. This cavern was meant to be secured so nobody could get in,' she snapped.

'We did secure it! Someone has used a spell to open it up again,' the trembling girl replied.

'That bitch!' Lillian swore, realizing that Evelyn was the only one who could have reopened it. Motioning for Bernard to set her down, she scanned the chamber.

'What was she looking for in here? It had to have been something important,' she muttered, lighting the candles against the wall.

'I think I might know,' Bernard replied pointing to the exposed eye motif a few feet away from them.

Lillian limped over to the motif and knelt on the ground, cautiously poking at the sticky substance that bubbled and oozed around the eye.

'It's Nequam blood!' she said in amazement, turning to face Bernard. 'Why would Evelyn want Nequam blood? It is toxic to humans. It doesn't make any sense,' she ranted.

'It may not have been for her use, Lillian. Perhaps that was how Logan managed to turn Ashton?' Bernard suggested.

Lillian walked to the closest wall and placed her hand on the cold stone.

'Memento omnium,' she chanted, her eyes suddenly turning white. Her body jolted violently, and Bernard raced to her side, catching her in his arms. As her eyes returned to normal, she looked up at Bernard and smiled.

'We have another player with their cards on the table. The Whisperer. You must find her Bernard and bring her to me,' she ordered.

'A Whisperer? Where would I find her?' Bernard questioned.

'Go to Logan. Answer the Nequam's call and she will be found,' she replied. 'I haven't laid eyes on her in over twenty years and back then, I wasn't sure which path she would take. I know now though, she has made it perfectly clear with her latest actions,' she added.

Bernard nodded and looked across at the terrified woman that cowered between two of Lillian's followers.

'I will go as soon as the sacrifice is complete,' he said, striding towards the woman and wrenching her up from the ground.

****

Ash, Logan and Alexa exited the back room to the sound of adulation as a loud cheer rose up from the gathering throng of werewolves in the warehouse. Beaming with delight, Logan moved steadily through the crowd, graciously accepting each congratulatory back slap before reaching a large white shipping container that stood in the centre of the room. Turning to face the crowd, Logan silenced them all with a single hand gesture.

'It has been done and with minimal loss to our numbers. Rockdale has been purged. The next wave will bring the army to our door, but we will be ready and waiting,' Logan declared, pausing as the crowd cheered. 'This town is ours and many more will follow, but for now we celebrate. Drink and feast to your hearts content, my fellow wolves, for tomorrow is a new day for us!' he shouted jubilantly, yanking open the container door and stepping out of the way as Matt and Will dragged a group of frightened men and women outside and passed them onto to the waiting mob. Taking a beer from a carton inside, he held it up before taking a long swig. Cheering, the crowd clamoured for the cartons of beer and groups paired off, dragging their struggling captives with them.

Logan looked across at Ash as he turned away from the rest of the group and began to head towards the back entrance.

'Ash! Where are you going? Come and celebrate with us, you deserve it after what we have achieved today,' Logan said as he reached his side.

'And what exactly did we achieve today, Logan? You made me kill innocent people. People who have never harmed me and didn't deserve to die,' Ash seethed. 'Excuse me if I don't feel that murder is an action worthy of celebration,' he added before turning away.

Fuming, Logan grabbed him by his shirt and pulled him back, forcing his head up to look at the screaming women behind them. Ash tried to avert his gaze as one of the men pinned down a young woman and forced her legs apart, but Logan gripped his jaw firmly.

'Look at her! That is all humans are good for,' he spat, spinning them both around to watch the woman struggling to push the man off her. 'You cannot tell me this doesn't excite you. I can see it in your eyes!'

'No, I can't watch this. Please don't make me watch this,' Ash begged.

'You listen to me, brother. Humans do not deserve your sympathy. If they knew what you were, they would hunt you down and destroy you. You know I am right. For us to exist, humans must die or be under our control,' Logan reproached.

Shaking his head, Ash freed himself from Logan's grip. 'Anya knew what I was, and she loved me anyway. If you choose to live peacefully with humans, they don't have any reason to fear us,' he added.

'Don't be so naïve, Ash. Do you honestly think that humankind would accept us? Anya only did because she wanted to fuck you. Trust me, she would betray you in a heartbeat if you ever pissed her off enough. *"People fear what they don't understand and hate what they can't conquer"*, remember Andrew Smith's words. What do you think they would make of you as a hybrid wolf?' Logan replied, pushing him hard in the chest.

'I don't know and now I won't ever have the opportunity to find out. Enjoy your celebrating without me, Logan. You might be able to make me kill for you, but I will never take any pleasure in it,' Ash retorted, leaving the warehouse.

'What's up his ass?' Alexa said as she pressed her body up against Logan's back.

'Just his moral compass,' he replied, leaning back into her and closing his eyes as she ran her hands up his shirt.

'Enough about Ash, how about you and I do some one-on-one celebrating while everyone is distracted with their free alcohol and acts of debauchery,' he suggested, spinning around and lifting her up onto his hips.

'I wouldn't mind experiencing some debauchery for myself,' she said seductively, kissing him as he carried her into the back room.

Once outside, Ash punched the side of the warehouse wall in frustration and headed towards his bike. Angrily ripping the tarpaulin cover off, he straddled the seat and revved its motor noisily, before taking off in a cloud of squealing rubber.

****

The large wolf raced through the streets and parks relishing the power that surged through his body as it effortlessly leapt over fences and walls. The moon shone full and bright in the night sky, illuminating the empty streets and guiding the wolf to his destination. As the old Mill loomed into view, the wolf suddenly stopped and began its instant transformation to its bipedal form. The naked man stood up and strode towards the group of men who stood around a makeshift fire pit outside the building.

'Who the fuck are you?' shouted one of the men as he approached.

'My name is Bernard. I have come to see the Whisperer,' the naked man announced.

'Alexa? You think you can just walk in here and see her? It is not going to be that simple, old man. I don't know you and definitely don't trust you and neither will she,' he sneered, pushing him back. 'Now do me a favour and fuck off back to where you crawled in from.'

'I am one of you!' Bernard insisted.

'If you are one of us, where have you been and how have you not heeded the Nequam's call. No full-blooded werewolf can resist the call, not unless you are a half breed like Logan's brother,' the man challenged.

'I am a full blood and I need to speak with Alexa,' Bernard said, stepping forward.

'Over my dead body,' spat the man.

'That can be arranged,' replied Bernard, standing firm.

'Boys, boys, boys!' a female voice chided from nearby and Alexa stepped out from the shadows. 'You know I would normally like it when two men are fighting over me, but you two are definitely not my type,' she said haughtily.

'Alexa, I have a message for you, and I am not leaving until you hear me out,' Bernard retorted.

'Oh, do you now? And what makes you think I want to hear this message of yours?'

'Because it comes from someone who knew your mother,' Bernard answered.

Bristling, Alexa turned on him and grabbed his jaw firmly.

'How do you know about my mother?' she said suspiciously, her eyes flashing as they bored into his mind.

Bernard cried out in pain as she kept her vice-like grip on his face and scanned his mind. Finally letting him go, she turned to the stunned men behind her.

'Tell Logan that I will be back tomorrow. There is someone I need to meet,' she said as she stripped off her clothes and handed them to the nearest man. Quickly transforming, she glanced up at Bernard expectantly, her piercing red eyes prompting him into action. Shooting the men a look of pure derision, he also transformed, and the pair of wolves raced off into the cold night.

****

Anya wearily picked up the scattered clothing that littered her bedroom floor and stuffed it into her waiting suitcase along with a worn photo album and framed picture. Zipping it shut, she hauled the heavy suitcase into the living room, sidestepping the broken glass and upturned furniture that dotted the floor.

'Fucking bastards,' she cursed, kicking the remnants of her once favourite vase across the floor.

In her absence, looters had smashed their way into her apartment and taken anything of value and trashed the rest. Her neighbour's apartments had fared much the same and not a single pane of glass had been left intact in any of the buildings. She had gathered what little she had left and had planned on returning to the motel out of town as soon as she was packed.

Her left foot came into contact with a small object, sending it hurtling across the room and into the sofa. With tears in her eyes, she retrieved the object, an antique Babushka doll that her mother had given her as a child. It had been her favourite toy once, and she had spent hours playing with the little doll family that resided within the shell of the larger doll. Wiping the dust from it, she carefully opened the outer shell and pulled out the smaller dolls that were nestled inside. There painted faces smiled up at her, bringing cherished memories of her mother to the surface. *I wish you were here, Mamochka, I could really use one of your hugs right now*, she thought as she broke down and cried, clutching the wooden dolls to her chest.

The sound of an approaching motorbike outside in the street brought her back to reality and she carefully placed the dolls down on the stand behind her before moving towards the window.

A strong gust of wind eddied through the room and Anya spun around to find Ash standing behind her.

She stared at him in disbelief as he slowly walked towards her. Holding her hands out, she shook her head furiously, tears springing to her eyes.

'No! Don't you dare come any closer,' she warned.

Ignoring her, Ash gently grabbed her arms and pulled her towards him. Anya lashed out, scratching at his chest and face, but her nails only found air as he pulled her into a strong embrace. Heaving with sobs, Anya finally let herself collapse into his arms, burying her face into his chest. He held her tight, running his hands through her hair and down her back until her sobbing eventually subsided.

Looking up at his face, she lightly traced her fingers along his jawline as his simmering dark eyes stared back at her with a tenderness that left her weak at the knees.

'You have no idea how much I needed to see you look at me like that,' she whispered as he wiped away her tears. 'I never thought I would see that look again.'

'I'm still the same man, Anya, and my feelings for you have never faltered. I have a connection with you that nothing will ever break, not even the Nequam,' Ash replied, brushing a stray strand of hair from her face.

'What are you doing here, Ash? Did Logan free you?' she asked.

Ash shook his head sadly. 'I am not free of the Nequam, but it is dormant for now. At least until the next time I am needed.'

'Ash, you have to fight it. What you did today, what the Nequam made you do, that wasn't you. This will destroy any humanity you have left if you continue to kill on his behalf. I know you are a good man. You have to find a way to beat this,' Anya replied.

'I can't fight it, Anya! The Nequam blood burns through my veins like molten steel. It takes over my mind and has complete control of me. Now I understand why Logan hasn't been able to resist it. It is not possible,' he lamented. 'Anya, I am so sorry for what happened at the police station. I know it would have hurt you to find your colleagues like that,' he added, reaching out to touch her face.

Anya's eyes flashed with anger and she turned away from him. 'They weren't just my colleagues, Ash, they were my friends, and Harry was like a father to me,' she sniffed, walking from the room.

Following her, Ash grabbed her arm and spun her around to face him.

'Please don't do that, Anya. Please don't look at me like that,' he said.

'Like what, Ash?' she replied, rolling her eyes.

'Like I'm some kind of monster.'

'How else am I meant to look at the man who peeled the skin off my boss like he was a banana?' she reeled. 'Would you have done that to me too, if the Nequam commanded it?'

'No. I could never hurt you, Anya. I would rather die than see anything bad happen to you,' he said, pulling her close. 'If it is any consolation, I didn't kill your boss, that was Logan's handiwork.'

'It is not much of a consolation, Ash. You still killed dozens of innocent people,' she said coolly.

Ash lowered his head and nodded.

'I'm sorry, Anya. I never wanted any of this to happen,' he said sadly. 'All I want is to be with you.'

He began to kiss her neck; running his hands up the back of her head. She threw her head back, relishing the feel of his firm lips on her skin as they brushed against her slender neck and the hollow of her collar bone. Effortlessly picking her up, he carried her to the bedroom and laid her down on the rumpled bed, his hands wandering up her blouse and setting her skin on fire as he hungrily kissed her parted lips.

'Ash, I love you so much,' she whispered, pulling his shirt up over his head and throwing it on the floor.

'I love you too, Anya,' he replied, cradling her head and kissing her fervently as she began to remove her clothes.

****

As the son rose up behind the mountain, the captain walked around the makeshift camp, proudly pointing out the weaponry and vehicles at his disposal. Doug, suitably impressed, whistled as he stopped in front of an eight-wheeled, armoured vehicle.

'The major must have been expecting some serious action to send you a Stryker. She's a beauty!' he said, running his hand along its hull.

'Yeah, she sure is and now that you have filled me in on what we are dealing with here, I am glad we brought her with us. She will tear through any werewolf pack like a knife through butter,' Captain Lawrence boasted.

Doug smiled and slapped his old friend across his shoulders, admiring the .50 calibre M2 machine gun, mounted on its roof. He had told the captain everything he knew about the werewolf attacks on Rockdale and had been surprised when he had believed him without any hesitation. The captain had then ordered the immediate evacuation of all remaining residents within a fifty-mile radius of the town and sent out units to search every residence and building. Doug knew there would be some opposition to the mandatory evacuation, but it was paramount that civilians would not be caught in the crossfire when the wolves launched their next wave of attacks. Martial Law had officially been declared and Captain Lawrence was now in charge of Rockdale's defence under the authority of General Parsons.

They walked on from the armoured vehicles and made their way into the captain's quarters where he gestured for Doug to sit.

'Tell me what you know about the werewolves. Didn't you say you captured one of them recently?' the captain probed.

'We did have one in captivity. I had all but dissected him. I took blood work, skin and hair samples, but we still don't know enough about their physiology. One thing we have learnt though, is that they appear to be linked. When the wolves attacked the station and hospital, our cameras recorded the captive werewolf transforming and throwing himself against the cage in an effort to escape. He was a bloodied mess by the time we returned and later died. My guess is that the ringleader, Logan Smythe, has some form of psychic control over the others. We have been looking for him for a few weeks now, but so far he has alluded capture,' Doug replied.

Pausing to reach into his pocket, Doug pulled out his phone and scrolled through the photo gallery. Thrusting the phone into the captain's palm, he continued.

'This is another man we are interested in catching. He is not like the rest of the wolves and I want him brought in alive,' he said pointing to the photo that his niece had snapped of the mystery dark-haired man at the gas station. 'I believe he will be instrumental in stopping this scourge.'

'Send this pic to me and I will make sure that all my men have a copy of it. We will find him, it is only a matter of time,' he promised, handing the phone back to Doug.

'Time is not something on our side at the moment, so I hope you are right my old friend,' Doug replied solemnly.

****

The humming of the water pumps in the Westmont Municipal Water Treatment Plant were drowned out as Bruce Simmons and his fellow work colleague, Max Clune pulled up outside the large reservoir. 'Bad Moon Rising' blared from the stereo as Max opened the door of the council truck and made his way around to the rear of the vehicle. Yanking the tailgate down, he pulled a heavy metal box towards him and undid the clasp, revealing a myriad of test tubes and labelled vials inside. The music suddenly ceased, and Bruce walked up alongside him, pulling on his rubber gloves before reaching into the box for a glass beaker.

'I'll get a sample from the reservoir first and then we will check in on Davy in filtration,' he said as he walked over to the concrete wall of the large treatment reservoir.

Max nodded and lined up the vials before pulling on his own gloves and fishing his reading glasses out of his pocket.

'Holy shit!' Bruce swore, motioning for Max to come over. 'The water is fucking red!'

Max rushed to the reservoir wall and leant over the edge, adjusting his glasses in the process.

'Davy's head is going to roll for this, what the fuck has he put in the water,' Bruce cursed, dipping a beaker into the russet-coloured waters.

'If that is rust, the plant manager is not going to be very happy. You know how hard it is to get extra funds out of the council and with every pipe possibly having to be pulled up and examined, it is going to cost a fortune!' Max declared.

'I don't think it is rust, it has a different smell,' Bruce surmised, screwing up his nose as he sniffed the contents of the beaker. 'If I didn't know any better, I would say it was blood!'

'Well, whatever it is, it won't be safe to drink. We had better call it in,' Max replied, pulling off his gloves and walking back towards the truck.

Sliding across the vinyl seat, he reached over and picked up the CB radio.

'Come in Davy, this is Max,' he said. After waiting a few seconds, he tried again. 'Davy, what the fuck are you doing down there? Pick up your goddamned CB,' he persisted.

Having packed up the equipment, Bruce slid onto the driver's seat alongside him and closed the cabin door.

'No luck?' he said, fishing for the keys.

'No, he is not answering the CB or his phone. We will have to drive down there and see what is going on. I'll call it in with the boss first and get him to turn off the pumps. We do not want this water getting into the town supply,' he stated as Bruce started the engine and began to drive in the direction of the filtration plant.

The trucks tyres crunched on the loose gravel as they pulled up outside the plant and parked alongside Davy's car.

'Well, he's definitely still here. The fat fuck has probably fallen asleep in the control room again,' Bruce said, opening the truck door. 'I'll get the samples while you go and find him,' he added, disappearing around the side of the truck.

Shaking his head in frustration, Max exited the vehicle and made his way towards the plant door. Swinging it open, he called out to Davy and began to climb the metal grate stairs to the top level overlooking the treatment tanks. Finding the viewing platform and control room empty, he cursed and made his way back down the steps and headed to the kitchenette. He stood in the small doorway, shaking his head at the mess that confronted him. The fridge door was wide open, and packets of food and drink bottles littered the small space. Max walked over to the sink cupboard and picked up a smashed coffee cup from the floor, the words, "World's Best Dad" staring up at him.

'Fucking hell, Davy, you useless prick,' he said aloud, 'That was my favourite mug!'

Hearing approaching footsteps, he swung around to find Bruce standing behind him, his face like thunder as he scanned the messy room. Storming past Max, he strode to the fridge and opened the freezer compartment.

'I am going to fucking kill that prick. He ate my pies!' Bruce bemoaned, angrily kicking an empty milk carton into the wall.

'Something is not right here, Bruce. This is too much mess even for Davy. We need to find him,' Max said backing out the door.

'I'll look in the toilet. If he's not there, he might be in the test room,' Bruce said, heading in the opposite direction.

Max quickly made his way along the side of the filtration tanks and into the back room. Various samples of water sat on one of the sampling tables along with Davy's laptop and a microscope. Max walked around to the other side of the table, his boots crunching on the remnants of a shattered beaker that now lay in pieces on the concrete floor. Bending down, he picked up a piece of the glass and examined the sticky substance that had congealed to its side. Placing it on the table top, he turned his attention to the five vials that sat nestled in their stand. Reading each label, he used a pipette to drop a small amount onto a glass slide and position it under the microscope's lens. Lighting it up, he magnified the sample and jotted down notes on the notepad he kept in his pocket. Repeating the process with the other samples that had been left on the table, he finally pushed his chair back and put his hands on his head.

'That's strange,' he said aloud, switching on the laptop and logging on.

Bruce entered the room, his ashen face immediately causing concern.

'Max, something weird is going on. The toilet has been completely trashed and there are large scratch marks up the wall like a bear was in there trying to get out,' he said quietly.

'That's not the only strange thing. I just examined the samples of groundwater that Davy must have been looking at. They all have traces of blood in them. These samples came from an underground spring near Mt Westmont. There is no scientific explanation for contamination of this kind. The whole plant is going to have to be shut down immediately,' he declared.

The laptop screen reverted to its last action and Max jumped back in horror as screams rang out from its speaker.

'What the fuck!' Max swore, and Bruce raced to his side. The laptop audio continued as a large creature suddenly emerged in the frame before running off.

'Rewind it back!' Bruce demanded, and Max replayed the footage again. They watched transfixed as Davy worriedly spoke about the samples he had been sent. He meticulously labelled each one before safely sealing and storing them on the stand. Holding up a beaker full of a reddish-brown substance, he dipped his finger in and gave it a stir. Immediately, his hands clutched at his throat and his eyes bulged in their sockets. His face contorted as he fell back wards off the chair and disappeared from view. Guttural screams filled the small room and moments later, the mystery creature came back into frame. Quickly hitting the pause button on the video, the two bewildered men stared at the creature on the screen. Its red eyes and snarling mouth sent shivers down their spines and they both instinctively began to head for the door.

'What the fuck happened to Davy?'

'I don't know, Bruce, but we need to get out of here and fast. If that thing is still around, I don't want to run into it,' he said as they raced back towards the exit door.

Max reached the door first and pushed on it only to find it had been jammed shut. Bruce soon joined him and they both charged into the door in an attempt to open it. Failing with both attempts, Bruce picked up a length of steel piping and swung it into the door desperately, refusing to give in.

'It's not going to budge, Bruce, something is blocking it. Let's try the back door instead,' he said fearfully and they quickly made their way through the plant.

Upon reaching the back door, the two men were relieved to find it ajar.

'Hey, this door was definitely shut when I walked past it earlier,' Bruce said nervously.

'Well, it's open now and we need to get the fuck out of here!' Max retorted, running through the door.

After a few moments, Bruce reluctantly followed him out into the delivery bay, frantically scanning the empty area for any sign of Max.

'Max, where are you? You better not have taken the truck without me,' he warned, racing around the side of the building to find the truck parked up against the plant entrance, blocking the door.

'What the fuck!' he shouted, running towards the idling truck.

Hearing a strange whimpering sound, Bruce looked around the side of the truck to see Max slumped up against the back wheel. His face was very pale and his eyes wide with shock as he looked down in the direction of where his legs should have been.

'Oh my God!' Bruce said, panic and terror rendering him incapable of movement as his heart thumped within his chest. Feeling hot breath on the back of his neck, he turned around slowly, coming face to face with the hideous creature that had appeared on Davy's laptop. Its deformed body and head were covered in patches of grey fur and its piercing red eyes oozed with a foul yellow liquid that slowly trickled down the sides of its misshapen jaw. It opened its mouth revealing a row of sharp incisors that dripped with a mixture of saliva and blood. Bruce screamed as the bipedal creature picked him up and snapped him in half like a brittle twig, throwing his lower limbs to the ground. As his bowel and intestines slowly unravelled and plopped onto the ground, Bruce's last agonizing moments were that of the creature tearing the flesh from his face.

****

Doug put his phone down and grinned across at Jonno and Stu as they sat across from him in his living room. The men had been discussing a united attack on the Old Mill with the army, but he had been hesitant as he needed to ensure that the mystery dark-haired man was not caught up in the crossfire. He was too valuable to their research. The captain had just confirmed what he had hoped for; that the man had slipped off on his own. They would never have a better chance than now to bring him in unharmed.

'They found him,' he said cheerfully. 'The captain has just confirmed a sighting of his motorbike out the front of an apartment in Crampton Street. We also have his name, Ashton Wakehurst,' Doug said, opening up his armoury.

'What's the plan? You know he won't go down without a fight,' Jonno said, scratching his chin.

'The captain's men will draw him out and engage him first. We will be waiting until he is distracted and shoot him full of sedatives. I trust you will be the perfect man for the job, Jonno?' Doug replied, tossing a rifle across to him.

'You betcha. I won't let you down,' Jonno promised. 'Do you have everything in the lab ready to contain him? He is going to be pretty pissed off when he comes to.'

'It has all been taken care of. We just need to bring him in alive. He will be too drugged up on Wolf's Nettle to cause us any grief once he is contained,' Doug replied. 'As soon as he is delivered safely to us, we can attack the Old Mill.'

'What are we going to do about the creepers?' Stu asked, stretching back in the chair.

The captain's men had discovered another concerning issue as they systematically searched and evacuated every residence; creatures that appeared to have morphed between humans and werewolves. They were surprisingly fast and strong despite their awkward appearance and extremely aggressive. They moved around on two legs, but their long gangly arms dragged by their sides like that of a primate. The Army had shot and killed dozens of the mutated creatures, now known as "creepers", including one in the hospital and it was now believed that one of them was responsible for the deaths of two Westmont water plant workers whose bodies had been discovered the previous day. Both men had literally been torn apart before being partly consumed, their faces were barely recognizable when they had been found a few hours later.

Following the discovery of a recording on a laptop found within the facility, the captain was convinced that both Westmont and Rockdale's water supply had been compromised by an unknown toxin that was causing the mutations. He ordered for the immediate cut to both town's water supply and the evacuation of Westmont as a precaution. He directed his men to only drink bottled water and to wash with the water that had been being trucked in from interstate. In the meantime, the Army had prioritised the hunting of the creepers or "ugly bastards", as Jonno referred to them and a mass grave had been dug for the disposal of their grotesque bodies.

'I don't know about you, but I plan on steering clear of the creepers. Let's just let the Army sort them out and we will concentrate on the greater threat, the werewolves. We move out in one hour,' he stated, loading his rifle.

Chapter 9

Loud rapping on the front door startled the three women as they poured through Gwynn Wakehurst's extensive collection of witchcraft and occult books. Having retrieved the books from Ash's house, Evelyn, Leila and Giana had been engrossed in the old books when the knocking on the door had disturbed their study. Reluctantly getting to her feet, Leila walked to the door and opened it cautiously, staring in surprise at the five heavily armed soldiers that now stood on her porch.

'Can I help you?' she said, defensively crossing her arms.

'Ma'am, we are here to evacuate you and any other residents by order of Major Crawford of the United States Army. Please pack your belongings and secure the premises. The transport truck will be here within the hour to escort you out of here,' the soldier said.

'We are not going anywhere,' Leila said haughtily, proceeding to shut the door in the soldier's face.

He quickly placed his boot between the door jamb and the door before it closed and swung it open again.

'I must insist, ma'am. Our orders are to leave no one behind. The town water is now contaminated with a deadly toxin and the entire town is being evacuated as we speak. You must pack your things now or we will remove you by force,' he said resolutely.

Leila stepped out of the house and fronted the group of soldiers. Placing her hand on their arms, she whispered to each of them and they nodded before turning back to their vehicles and driving away.

Walking back into the house, Evelyn gave her a bemused look and returned her focus back to the book in her hands.

'What did you tell them?' Giana asked, as Leila resumed her seat next to her.

'I told them to declare this house as empty and continue on to the next one,' Leila said with a wry smile. 'They won't be bothering us again,' she added.

'I wish I could compel people,' Giana bemoaned.

'What did the soldier say about contaminated water?' Evelyn asked, closing the book and reaching for another one.

'The town water has been contaminated with a toxin. There was a news report about it last night. Apparently, the town water supply has turned red. We don't need to be concerned though as this place isn't hooked up to town water, only rainwater tanks,' Leila replied.

Evelyn's face suddenly blanched and she stood up, glancing at each of the women in turn.

'Oh no,' she said softly. 'My mother used to quote something about the waters turning red. She told me it would herald the end of humankind and was a sign that demons would once again walk the earth.'

'Evelyn, it could be anything, algae blooms, rust in the pipes or even bacterial growth. Your mother was barking mad! I wouldn't believe anything she ever said,' Leila replied.

'I hate to be the bearer of bad news, but I think for once, Lillian may have been onto something,' Giana said, turning the book on her lap towards them. 'Look at the illustration,' she instructed.

The women peered at the manuscript that depicted a lake of blood with dozens of demons and creatures emerging from the red water. Dead bodies littered the shoreline as ravens pecked at the eyes of the dead. A red moon hovered in the sky, giving the cliff face below an eerie red glow.

'Is that Lake Rockdale?' Evelyn asked, taking a closer look. 'Oh my God, Giana did you read the inscription below?'

"The final millennium will pass, and the earth will tremble with the dawn of the Nequam and his minions. With the deaths of a thousand souls, the undead shall crawl from the earth and be reborn from its blood. The hordes will feed on the flesh of humans and wolves alike and they will once again walk the earth."

'A thousand souls? How many people have already died here in Rockdale alone?' Giana replied.

'At least half that number,' Evelyn suggested. 'There have also been numerous attacks in Westmont. We are running out of time. If the Nequam reaches its quota, we will have hell on earth right here, with Rockdale at its epicentre,' she warned.

'How many soldiers have come to Rockdale?' Leila replied. 'Even though most of Rockdale's residents have been evacuated there are still hundreds of soldiers camping out at the showgrounds. If the wolves attack, the Nequam could reach the quota within days. We have got to warn the army!' Leila added, reaching for her phone.

'Whose number are you calling?' Giana asked curiously.

'Just an old flame who will pass our warning on,' Leila responded. Noticing Evelyn's curious stare, she added, 'Yes, even I had a love life once.'

'Giana, we also need to warn Logan and Ash. If this prophecy comes true,' Evelyn said, pointing to the illustration, 'they will be in danger too!' she warned. 'The Nequam will dispose of them all to feed the demons that come through.'

'We need to find out more about the crystal first. If it is indeed a weapon, we must find a way to use it. It could change everything,' Giana said, closing the book on her lap. 'There are only three more books to go through and I pray the answer is within one of these pages,' she said, picking up a heavy leather-bound book. As she opened the first page, she noticed the edge of a yellowed piece of paper poking out from the book's spine. Flexing the book, she reached under the leather dust jacket and pulled the paper out. Carefully unfolding it, she gasped and looked across at Evelyn.

'Evelyn, are we still fully cloaked from the whisperer woman and Lillian?' she asked as Leila re-entered the room.

'Yes, neither of them can access or manipulate our thoughts. What did you find Giana? Anything useful?' Evelyn probed.

Giana nodded and grinned at her two friends.

'Just the answer to all our problems,' she said triumphantly, passing the handwritten note to Evelyn.

'Oh, my goodness! This changes everything!' Evelyn gushed, warmly hugging Giana.

'Just one question. How did Gwynn Wakehurst know that one day we would need this?' Giana replied.

'She was an extraordinary woman; something I sensed from the minute I met her. It always puzzled me how she appeared to have been expecting me the day we met. She even had the kettle boiled and two cups of tea sitting on the kitchen bench when I staggered in with Ash in my arms. She knew I was coming and that I would trust Ash into her care. Gwynn was a psychic vampire and everything that has happened to date, she knew would come to pass. She couldn't interfere with the prophecy, even when she foresaw her own death, but she has ensured by this message, that we now have the means to help Ash and Logan. Now we just have to find them both before it is too late,' Evelyn explained, picking up the crystal shard and turning it over in her hands.

****

The sounds of agonised and terrified screams cut through the air as the crowds of people fled along the narrow ditch. The earth around them was muddy with blood as demonic hands reached for them relentlessly, picking them off one by one and sucking them into the ground. Ash stood at the top of the ditch, watching as the demons devoured the humans, their screams drowned out by the unearthly shrieks of the eyeless demons as they sated their hunger.

Two women remained, clutching each other and crying as a snarling demon crawled out of the mud and began to slither towards them. Using its arms to pull its giant snakelike body through the soft mud, it brought itself up to full height in front of the women and stood over them menacingly. The entire length of its body pulsated from within as its previous victims struggled in their last moments of life to escape their horrific fate.

Ash stiffened as he recognised the women's faces and tried to move to save them. His body refused to budge, and he looked down at his bare feet to find them slowly sinking into the putrid mud. Struggling to break free, he tried to scream out to the women, but no sound would leave his lips. One of the women looked up at him and a single tear slid down her face as the demon opened its mouth full of needle teeth and consumed her whole, her body sliding down its throat and becoming dislodged in its body like a Tapir inside an Anaconda. He watched in horror as the next woman met the same fate and the demon burrowed back into the ground, disappearing with a flick of its tail.

The sky suddenly darkened, and Ash felt a pair of hands moving up the inside of his thigh. He looked down to see a long-haired demon looking up at him as she slowly made her way up his body. Her yellow eyes demanding his focus as she ran her scaly hands over his chest and along his jawline.

'In aeternum meus es tu, you are mine forever,' she whispered, as her serpentine tongue flicked in and out of his ear.

Bringing her lips to his, she kissed him feverishly and began to pull him down into the mud.

Waking with a start, Ash sat up and kicked off the bed covers, before jumping out of bed.

'Ash! It's okay. It isn't real,' Anya soothed, reaching for him. 'It's just another nightmare.'

Ash, breathing hard, sat back on the bed with his back to her as he held his head in his hands and tried to calm himself down. He flinched as he felt Anya's warm hand run up the side of his back and stroke his hair, but he didn't move.

'Baby, are you alright? You are shaking all over,' enquired Anya as she sat beside him.

He nodded his head slowly and turned to look at her, giving her bare knee a gentle squeeze.

'I will be okay. I just need a minute or two. Did I hurt you?' he asked.

'No, but you scared the shit out of me. You were groaning and talking in your sleep again, so I rolled over to spoon you, but as soon as my hand touched your stomach, you jumped up like you had just been electrocuted. What the hell were you dreaming about Ash?' she replied.

'Trust me, you don't want to know,' he said sadly.

'You kept saying the word "Cerridwen" over and over. Does that mean anything to you?' she probed.

Ash nodded. 'She is a demon that keeps reappearing in my dreams and telling me I am hers. It's fucking creepy as hell especially as it feels so real,' he said. 'You were also in my dream.'

'Did you watch me die again?'

'Yes. You and Mum both and I couldn't do a damn thing to save either of you,' he said, shaking his head.

'It was just a dream. Your mum and I are both fine,' Anya soothed, leaning over to kiss him.

Pulling her onto his lap, he ran his hands up her naked back and rested his head on her chest, relishing the softness of her skin.

'I feel so useless, Anya. I want to stay with you, but I am being drawn back to Logan even now as I speak. I made a huge mistake denying the Triune. If I hadn't have switched it off, maybe things would be a lot different right now. I have let everyone down, especially you and it kills me to have to leave you again,' he despaired.

'Hey!' Anya replied, stroking his face. 'None of this is your fault. You did what you thought was right, you always have. The future is not yet written, not while we still have time to fight back. Just don't ever give in, promise me that. I don't ever want you to become one of the Nequam's brain-dead puppets. Promise me that you will fight with every ounce of your strength,' she replied.

'You know I will, Anya. I want us to have a future together and I haven't given up on that dream yet,' he replied determinedly.

'I love you, Ashton Wakehurst, don't you ever forget that,' Anya replied, kissing him deeply, before hopping off his lap. 'Now, I had better get ready, Leila is coming to get me in an hour and as there appears to be no water here, I will have to forego a shower until I get to her house.'

'I am so glad you decided to stay with her and Mum, rather than the motel. You will be a lot safer with them,' Ash replied.

'It just made more sense and besides, I want to be close by, so I can keep an eye on you,' she said, winking as she pulled on her satin robe.

'Clingy much?' Ash joked, pulling on his jeans and t-shirt.

Hearing a rumbling sound in the distance, he walked to the window and peered out.

'I should get going too, it looks as though the army are moving everyone on,' he said giving her a quick kiss on her forehead and heading out the door.

****

Doug and a group of his men watched the apartment from the relative safety of an abandoned house across the street. Thermal imaging had confirmed that Ashton was still inside the opposite apartment and the army were preparing to engage him as soon as he left the premises. They had contemplated raiding the apartment while he was distracted with his human companion, but Doug was reluctant to risk the safety of the innocent woman and they certainly couldn't risk her getting caught up in the crossfire.

The sight of the front door finally opening nearly caught them off guard and they each scrambled into position. Jonno, with his gun trained on Ashton, watched calmly through his gun scope as he strode to his motorbike and pushed it out into the street. Straddling it, he looked back towards the apartment as a stunning red-headed woman appeared in the doorway dressed in a satin robe. Jonno's breath caught in his throat as the woman quickly opened her robe and flashed her naked body at Ashton before closing it up again and leaning against the doorframe with a grin.

'Lucky bastard!' muttered Jonno, returning his focus back to Ashton only to discover he had gone.

'What the...?' Jonno said as the window in front of him suddenly smashed and he found himself being propelled through the air. Landing in a heap on the front lawn, he groaned as he tried to get to his feet. Ashton loomed into view and stood over him, his eyes flashing red in his obvious fury.

Shouts rang out from the street ahead and Jonno ducked as bullets whizzed past him, pummelling into Ashton's chest and knocking him backwards. Ashton jumped to his feet and walked calmly onto the street, temporarily ignoring Jonno as he scrambled back towards the house.

'Holy fuck!' said Stu, passing Jonno's gun through the window. 'Are you okay?'

'Just a little winded,' he said dismissively, grabbing the gun and repositioning himself on the front steps of the house.

'Focus everyone,' Doug's voice boomed. 'No more fuck ups, we can't afford to lose this guy!'

Shots continued to be fired at Ashton, but he now deflected each bullet with an unseen forcefield that surrounded his entire body. Doug and the others watched in amazement as he lifted his hands and shot balls of blue light at the convoy of army vehicles that assailed him. Soldiers jumped for cover as the jeeps and trucks exploded upon impact, catapulting into the air.

'Holy shit!' Stu swore. 'He is more powerful than we first thought. How the fuck are we going to stop him?'

'Every man has a weakness,' Doug quipped calmly. 'And I have a feeling that that beautiful creature across the road, is his. Nate, I want you to double back and grab that woman,' he ordered.

'Me? You want me to piss him off even more? This is a fucking suicide mission!' he protested.

'I'll do it,' Jonno offered. 'I was the one who stuffed up in the first place getting distracted with his missus. Stu can shoot him up with the serum, he is just as good a shot as I am,' he said throwing his gun to Stu and disappearing up the street.

The gunfire continued and a loud whoosh sounded followed by a blinding flash that shook the foundations of the house and knocked Doug and the others off their feet. Doug reached for his walkie and screamed into it as he got to his feet.

'An RPG? What the fuck are you doing, Lawrence? We need him alive!'

'I'm sorry, Dougie, we need to neutralize him as a matter of national security. I have received orders from the general to take him out,' came the captain's reply through the walkie.

'And when were you going to tell me? Jonno is out there and there is also a civilian woman in the apartment across from us!' he fumed.

'Collateral damage, I am afraid. Wakehurst is our number one priority. He must be stopped now,' the captain responded.

'Let me take him out. Give me ten more minutes and if we can't capture him alive, then you can put him down however you feel necessary,' Doug implored.

'Dougie, I can't take the risk, you know that,' the captain replied.

'Please, trust me on this, Lawrence. I need this guy alive. He is crucial to our plans and he might be our only chance of stopping Smythe. Please, for old time's sake, you have to let me bring him in alive!' Doug pleaded.

The walkie was silent for a few moments and then cackled back to life.

'Okay Dougie, for old time's sake, I will call my men off. You have ten minutes,' he said before the walkie went dead.

'Thank God for that,' said Doug, rubbing his temple. 'Don't you fucking miss, Stu,' he said, slapping him on the shoulder. 'If you do, Jonno is as good as dead.'

'No pressure then. This will be like a walk in the park,' Stu said sarcastically.

****

Anya pulled herself into a sitting position, her ears ringing as she pushed a length of twisted guttering off her legs. She wasn't badly hurt, with only a few cuts and bruises, but she couldn't say the same for the neighbourhood. The street had erupted around her and the burning ruins of her neighbour's houses filled the air with acrid smoke. She finally managed to get to her feet and staggered down her front steps, wincing as her bare foot stepped on a fragment of broken glass. The whole street was filled with smoke and eerily silent except for the crackling of fire as it quickly engulfed the abandoned houses around her. Glancing back at her apartment, she was relieved to find it had only suffered minor damage at the front and was not yet on fire, but as her neighbour's house had taken the full brunt of what she assumed was a missile blast, she knew it wouldn't be long before her apartment caught fire as well.

She made her way to her security gate and cried with relief when she spotted Ash crouching unscathed in the middle of a shallow crater. His hands were held up in front of him, but his attention was clearly focused on the house opposite hers. She was about to call out to him when a hand grabbed her firmly around her mouth and pulled her back, knocking her off balance. She struggled against her unknown captor and dug her fingernails into his arm, but he wrenched her to her feet and held a sharp blade to her throat.

Hearing her muffled screams, Ash turned around and began to move towards her.

'Don't take another step or I will hurt her!' warned the man in his thick Australian accent.

'If you harm her, I will hurt you in ways you wouldn't have thought possible! Get your fucking hands off her!' stormed Ash.

'Easy now mate, back up,' Jonno said, inching out the gate. 'Don't make any sudden moves or I might accidentally cut up her pretty face. We wouldn't want that, now would we?'

A shot rang out from across the street and Ash reached for the side of his neck, pulling out a dart and throwing it to the ground. Another volley of shots followed and several more darts struck his bicep and shoulder. Ash roared in anger and lunged for Jonno, knocking him away from Anya and disarming him. Grabbing him by the throat he began to lift him off the ground, ignoring the stings as several more darts found their target. Anya grabbed Ash's other arm, forcing him to look at her.

'Don't do it, baby, let him go,' she said softly.

Ash began to sway on his feet and his head lolled forward as the dart's sedatives finally began to take effect. Dropping to his knees, he let go of Jonno and fell forwards into Anya's arms, slipping into unconsciousness.

Holding him, Anya reeled on Jonno.

'You have gone after the wrong man! Ash isn't evil, he is being controlled by his brother!' she raged.

Ignoring her, Jonno pulled her away from Ash's prone form and held her back as Doug and the others raced across the street.

'Well done, Jonno and Stu! Every dart hit home,' he said pulling the darts from Ash's back and arm. 'Let's get him back to the lab before the captain has a change of heart.'

Anya continued to struggle in Jonno's grip and delivered an elbow to his groin, dropping him to the ground.

'You, fucking asshole,' she said kicking him in the face.

'Get her back inside and help her pack before her house goes up in flames,' he ordered two soldiers and they nodded, dragging her up the stairs.

Doug knelt down next to Jonno and put his hand on his shoulder.

'Are you okay?' he asked with genuine concern as Jonno groaned and struggled to stand.

'I told you, it's women you have to be afraid of, not werewolves,' he rasped and the men around him snickered with laughter.

'She is a wildcat, that one. It looks like you may have met your match in her,' Doug replied as he helped Jonno to his feet.

'I have always liked a challenge,' Jonno joked as he limped towards a nearby army truck.

Doug laughed and shook his head, following Jonno to the truck.

Hearing a vehicle pull up, Doug spun around to see Captain Lawrence alighting from a jeep and giving orders to the drivers of the truck.

Storming towards him, Doug fronted him angrily.

'What are you doing? I thought you and I were supposed to be on the same side! You just ass-fucked me and my entire team back there and now you plan on taking him after we brought him down?' Doug fumed. 'What about our deal? Did you ever intend to stick to it or were you just playing me this whole time?'

'Dougie, I have no choice, I am under orders myself, I have been since we arrived,' the captain replied.

'And what were your specific orders, Lawrence?' Doug probed.

The captain hesitated for a moment before responding. 'My orders were to evacuate everyone, including you and your men and set up a perimeter around the town before blowing it up. The general believes this is the best option to wipe out the remaining creepers and werewolves before they head to Westmont,' he replied.

'Fuck your orders! The general has no idea what is going on here! He is probably balls deep in a hooker somewhere giving orders between thrusts. He doesn't give a shit about this town. He just wants his little problem sorted out as quickly and cheaply as possible, so he can take all the credit at the next press conference. Fuck him and fuck you!' Doug seethed, pushing him in the chest.

A soldier suddenly grabbed Doug's arm and Doug instantly reacted, bringing his elbow up to the soldier's face and breaking his nose.

Several more soldiers joined the fray and Jonno raced in, smashing his fist into the nearest soldier's face and knocking him out cold. He took out two more soldiers before being hit across the back of his head with the butt of a rifle and falling to the ground. Doug rushed to Jonno's side and pulled out his gun, aiming it the captain.

'Call them off, Lawrence, and let us leave with the truck as planned,' he ordered as the remaining soldiers drew their weapons on him. 'We shouldn't be fighting each other. The enemy is out there, and it is mobilizing for its next attack, most likely, on your base! That man in the back of that truck is the key to stopping it all. His power can be used to our advantage, I know it. I just need you to trust me!'

'Enough!' yelled the captain. 'Enough! Everyone, put your guns down now. You are right, Doug,' he said walking towards him and lowering his gun. 'I need to trust you and we need to join forces.'

Turning back towards his men, he addressed them. 'Change of plans. Doug and his men are taking Wakehurst to a secure location. We need to prepare for an attack on the Old Mill.'

'What about the general's orders?' the First Lieutenant asked.

'Fuck the orders. I am now taking complete charge of this mission and to hell with the consequences,' the captain affirmed. 'I am sorry, Doug, I should have been upfront with you from the start,' he said gripping Doug's shoulder.

'That's okay, Lawrence, I appreciate your trust in me now,' Doug said, pulling his old friend into a strong embrace. 'You know what you are risking by defying the general's orders, don't you?'

'Yes, I am very aware, but I can't focus on that now. If we don't stop this maniac, the general is going to have more to worry about then an insubordinate captain,' he replied.

'Is the Stryker within range?' Doug enquired.

'She will be very soon. We will strike within the next hour at 1100 hours. I will be in touch, old friend,' he said, returning to his jeep.

Doug smiled and looked over to where Stu and Nate were half dragging a very groggy looking Jonno to the truck.

'Where the fuck were you two when I needed you,' Doug chided, positioning his shoulder under Jonno's arm pit and helping him walk.

'We were in the jeep in front and didn't know what was happening, it all happened so quick. Thank God Jonno was there to back you up!' replied Stu.

'Yeah, even with throbbing balls, he still wasn't going to miss out on a good fight, the crazy bastard. We better get him back to the house and patch him up,' Doug said as they helped him into the truck.

****

Will and Matt pulled up outside the Old Mill in Logan's jeep and made their way into the warehouse along with several other men. Logan had ordered the immediate return of all wolves within the vicinity for what he was calling, "The Final Wave" and the last of them had finally arrived.

As he walked, Will fidgeted with a thin herringbone chain that hung around his neck; a present from Morgan when they had still been together. Rubbing his thumb over the small Celtic cross that hung from the chain, he looked across at Matt to find him watching him pensively.

'When was the last time you saw Morgan,' Matt said as they walked through the laneway and entered the warehouse through a side door.

'It has been over a week now,' Will replied. 'I thought she might come around, but she doesn't want anything to do with me. I can't really blame her though.'

Matt nodded. 'Women just complicate everything, anyway. Trust me, you are better off single,' Matt said.

'You are probably right, but I can't help but miss her. Anyway,' he said, promptly changing the subject, 'I wonder if Ash has arrived back yet, I didn't see his bike out the front.'

'He probably can't tear himself away from the detective,' Matt remarked. 'I don't blame him, she is smoking hot!'

'As long as he has managed to avoid the army patrols and hasn't gone looking for trouble.'

'This is Ash we are talking about. He does not go looking for trouble,' Matt remarked.

'No, but trouble certainly has a way of finding him and you heard those explosions. Let's just hope he is nowhere near that part of town. Logan is going to be pissed if he doesn't turn up soon.'

'Logan is already pissed. Alexa didn't return yesterday after she took off with that old black dude. He sent Stiles and Charlie after her, but they came back empty handed. They reckoned they couldn't even find her scent, it was like she had just vanished into thin air,' Matt said, approaching the back room.

As they entered the room, they found Logan deep in conversation with several of his men. Upon seeing them arrive, Logan quickly dismissed the men and turned his attention to Will and Matt.

'It's about time that you two got here. Did you hear the explosions downtown?'

'Yeah, we heard them. There are rumours that whole streets are now on fire and with no fire brigade or water supply, the fire is quickly spreading. Do you think the army might have something to do with it?' Will replied.

'My guess is that they are trying to smoke out any werewolves as they have already evacuated the town,' Matt chimed in. 'I just hope Ash wasn't caught up in it.'

'So, you haven't heard from him either? He should have returned by now. His girlfriend lives in that part of the town and he would be with her, unless he went to stay with his mother. Wherever he is, he shouldn't have been able to resist my call for this long. Something is wrong,' Logan replied.

'Maybe we should go and look for him?' Will enquired.

'Not on your own. I can't risk you getting caught by the custodians. They would shoot you on sight and we know that they have bullets that can kill us now,' Logan replied. 'We need to strike the army camp first as planned and then we will go looking for Ash. Let's just hope that the custodians don't get to him before us.'

The door suddenly burst open and the men looked up as Tommy walked in and stood in front of them. His eyes were rolled back in his head and only the whites of his eyes were visible as he opened his mouth to speak.

'You need to leave now!' a garbled voice spoke from within Tommy. 'The army know you are here, and they are on their way.'

'Alexa?' Logan enquired, moving towards Tommy. 'Alexa, is that you? Are you okay?'

'I am safe. Warn the others before it is too late,' the voice warned.

'Matt and Will, get them all out of here, we will retreat to the forest,' he said, turning back to Tommy.

'Alexa, do you know where Ash is?'

'The custodians have him, but he is alive, for now. Please hurry, you don't have much time,' the voice persisted.

'We are leaving right now. Bring Tommy back,' he said as he grabbed him by the arm.

With a shake of his head, Tommy returned to his normal self and began to run from the warehouse.

Logan and Tommy made it outside just as the first missile whistled through the air and hit the warehouse; the force hurtling them both into the side of a shipping container. Another missile struck, and Logan and Tommy were both covered with debris as the building collapsed on top of them.

****

Alexa slowly opened her eyes and looked back across the valley, watching as a thick cloud of black smoke arose from the horizon line. Sensing Lillian's approach, she pulled her eyes away from the distant explosion and looked across at the older woman.

Alexa had dreamt of Lillian ever since she had been a small child. At first, she had been confused by the ever-present visions she had of the strange dark-haired woman with piercing blue eyes, especially as her Aunty Sonia had been unable to explain who she was. She had eventually pushed her out of her mind, but she had always resurfaced whenever she felt distressed or alone. Lillian was like a ghost mother for her entire life and was a great source of comfort for her. She had always felt that one day they would be reunited and had not hesitated to meet with her when Bernard had arrived at the Mill seeking an audience with her.

Lillian stood beside her now, pulling her shawl across her chest as she surveyed the scene ahead of them. Her face remained expressionless as though she had been expecting the current events to take place. With her long dark hair tied up in a tight bun, she looked formidable, but Alexa felt a strong maternal connection with her and a sense of comfort in her presence.

'I don't know if he got out in time,' Alexa said softly. 'I can't whisper to Tommy or any of the others. No one is responding.'

Lillian had warned her that the army were mobilising. Her view from the top floor of the mansion took in the sprawling valley below and the showgrounds that hosted the temporary army camp. Bernard had been watching the army for days now and in the past few hours, he had reported them positioning their heavy artillery and missile launcher. Several explosions in the centre of town had also been heard and the town's skyline was now shrouded in a haze of smoke.

Alexa returned her gaze to the town below, listening as the muffled sound of distant gunfire echoed up through the valley. Near panic, she gripped the handrail in front of her and began to tremble as she struggled to hold back the wave of emotions that threatened to engulf her. Lillian, sensing her distress, placed her arm across Alexa's shoulder and squeezed her tight.

'He made it out, I can still feel him. You reached him in time,' she said reassuringly.

Alexa nodded as a single tear slid down her face and she bit her trembling lip.

'How did you know this would all happen, Lillian? Did you have a vision?'

'I have had prophetic visions ever since I survived a traumatic event as a child. My visions rarely fail me, and they are becoming stronger as the Apocalypse draws near. Trust me, my dear, the end times are very close,' she replied. 'You know what you have to do now. The Nequam must have a thousand souls for the prophecy to come true and you now need to do what you were born for.'

Alexa nodded and sat down cross-legged on a papa-sun chair behind her. Closing her eyes, she concentrated on reaching the minds of the men who threatened to ruin all their plans.

Chapter 10

Coughing and spluttering, Logan opened his eyes and rubbed them; peering through the dust and smoke around him. His head was filled with a persistent ringing noise, making the screams and moans in the vicinity appear muffled and distant. Removing the lighter debris that covered his body, he tried to move his legs but discovered they were pinned down under a large block of concrete. Grunting with exertion, he slowly began to push the heavy block off his leg. With a final shove, it rolled away and he was able to get to his feet. With his ears still ringing, he glanced around at the aftermath of the missile strike.

The Old Mill was gone and, in its place remained a blackened, smoky crater filled with twisted iron rafters, corrugated sheeting and burning rubble. The debris from the decimated Mill scattered as far as his eye could see and was mingled with the remains of those who had not been quick enough to escape the blast. Hearing his name, he turned around and ran towards a large, blackened cinder block, quickly pulling it away.

Momentarily shocked, he looked down on the charred and mangled body of his friend, Will, as he moaned in pain.

'Jesus Christ!' he swore quietly before crouching down and trying to comfort him.

'It is going to be alright, buddy. I need to get you out of here, so you can heal,' he soothed, trying to pull him to an upright position.

Will cried out but didn't resist as Logan put his head under his left arm and hoisted him over his shoulder. Carrying him to the parking lot, he found one of the few vehicles that had not been destroyed and gently laid him down on the back seat.

'I have to see if anyone else has survived and then I will be right back. Was Matt with you?' he asked.

'No, he was on the other side of the building with Alex,' Will replied weakly.

The sound of gunfire suddenly broke out in the direction of the Mill ruins and Logan spurred into action, quickly returning to the blast sight.

****

First Lieutenant, Kurt Sommers surveyed the scene using his thermal imaging binoculars to see through the thick smoke. Raising his right hand in the air, he hesitated briefly before giving the signal to move forward. His men were waiting behind him, armed with mercury bullets that would kill any werewolf instantly if shot in the head and within minutes if a body shot was made.

'It is time to go in men. Kill anything that moves. That is an order!' he shouted and with a flick of his hand, the soldiers ran headlong into the thick smoke.

Following close behind them, he scaled a partly demolished brick wall and scanned the rubble, picking up a heat signature under a pile of debris.

'Over there!' he shouted to his men and they raced over and pulled up the iron sheeting that concealed a wounded werewolf. He lashed out at them, but the soldiers quickly fired several rounds into his head, killing him instantly. As fire crackled around them, the soldiers moved on, flushing out several more surviving werewolves from beneath the rubble and putting them down.

First Lieutenant Sommers gradually veered away from the rest of his men and accompanied by two other soldiers, he began to search what remained of a laneway. As he rounded the twisted remnants of a shipping container, he stopped, alerted by a soft thud from behind him. Spinning around, he moved his boot out of the path of an object that rolled awkwardly towards him, recoiling in horror as he recognised the pale face of one of his soldiers staring up at him. Quickly aiming his machine gun, he fired into the dense smoke ahead of him before stepping into the haze. He took a few steps before almost tripping over the bodies of his two men and falling against a shipping container. With his heart thumping in his chest, he steadied his nerves and scanned the area for any sign of life. As he stepped away from the container, he heard a growl and looked up to see a pair of red eyes staring at him from the top. Firing his weapon blindly at the creature, he fell backwards over the dead soldiers. Scrambling to get to his feet, he shouted for assistance and several more soldiers soon joined him.

'There is something up there!' he yelled. 'It killed Ronnins and Crickshank!'

One of the soldiers, stepped forward with a grenade and lobbed it over the top, while the rest ducked for cover. The subsequent blast rocked the shipping container and sent a shower of debris over the crouching men.

'Did we hit anything?' Lieutenant Sommers asked, coughing and brushing off his uniform.

'No, you didn't!' sounded a gravelly voice from within the haze and a flash of blue light burst from behind them and knocked the men to the ground. First Lieutenant Sommers, momentarily stunned, reached up to push a soldier off his chest, but recoiled as his hand came into contact with a spongy slickness on the side of the soldiers back. Shoving the soldier aside, he gasped in shock at the sight of the man's back. The skin on his entire back was gone, as was most of the muscle tissue, leaving his spine and the back of his rib cage exposed. Frantically examining the rest of the soldiers around him, he discovered they had all met the same fate. Only he and one other soldier remained intact.

A tall man suddenly emerged from the smoke haze, his piercing red eyes never leaving the lieutenant's. He raised his left hand and the stunned soldier beside him began to scream, clawing at his clothes. Lieutenant Sommers watched in shock as the soldier's exposed skin erupted in blisters and his eyeballs burst from their sockets with an audible popping sound. The soldier finally fell to his knees at the lieutenant's feet.

'Good God!' the lieutenant said, scrambling for his gun.

Without a word, the red-eyed man raised his hands in front of him, sending a shockwave that picked up the lieutenant and sent him hurtling into the side of the shipping container where he remained pinned. The shockwave thrummed and intensified as the lieutenant's shirt and cargo pants tore and disintegrated in a heap on the ground. Naked and completely paralysed, the lieutenant screamed as he felt the top layer of his skin slowly begin to peel back and come away in large pieces. His agonised screams pierced the air as, one by one, each limb was flayed, and he was skinned alive. As he finally succumbed to his horrific injuries, his screams ceased, and Logan let his body drop to the ground with a sickening thud.

****

Will opened his eyes and instantly, his body was wracked with unbearable pain. Crying out, he tried to reposition himself, but both of his legs were broken and his pelvis sat at an unnatural angle. He never thought it would be possible to ever experience such intense agony and he suddenly wished that Logan had left him to die. Hearing the car door slam, he looked up to see Logan seated behind the wheel.

'Did you find Matt?' he croaked; his voice barely a whisper.

Logan put his head down and nodded before turning to look at Will.

'He was gone. You were the only one I found alive,' he said, before hot wiring the car and putting it into gear. 'I need to find you somewhere safe to heal. I will deal with the army later,' he said as the back wheels spun, and the car lurched forward.

****

The kettle whistled on the bench top, shrilly announcing its readiness as the two girls prepared the lab for Ash's arrival.

'Do you really think that Ash is evil? I mean, he seemed like such a nice guy,' Tash said, picking up the kettle and pouring the boiling water into a bucket of disinfectant. 'Rana and I went to see his band a few times and he was just a regular guy, albeit an extremely hot one, but there was nothing unusual about him. Rana was obsessed with him though. I think she must have followed him around for a year or so before she finally got the courage to approach him.'

'I think your friend Rana may have been something supernatural as well, according to Uncle Doug. He believes that she was the one that turned Ash after he got attacked by a werewolf,' Paige replied.

'Are you for real?' said Tash. 'No, she was just a regular girl like us. I would know, surely, if she wasn't human?'

'Don't be so sure about that, Tash. Supernatural's can blend in very easily if they don't draw attention to themselves by killing people. Rana would have been very discreet and fooled everyone into thinking she was an ordinary woman,' Paige replied.

'She sure did,' said Tash. 'She did everything that a normal twenty-one-year-old woman would do, and I never suspected a thing.'

'Not many people would notice anything unusual. Custodians are the exception, and Doug and I can sense any supernatural being the minute we come into contact with them. That was how we first discovered Ash, although he did seem different to the others. I think that is why he is so important to Uncle Doug's research,' Page replied, opening the cell door and pulling a face. 'This is so gross! How did we get stuck with cleaning up this mess?' she despaired.

'I asked the same question but was pretty much shot down by your Uncle Doug. Apparently, it is all part of our training as custodians,' Tash replied, scrubbing the cell bars.

'Well it sucks! Next, he will have us scrubbing toilets,' Paige complained.

'Whatever you do, don't plant that idea in his head. He will have some logical explanation of how it would benefit us in the future. I can hear him now, *Paige and Tash, you need to learn all the ins and outs of the custodians in order to become one,*' Tash replied, mimicking Doug's voice.

'Learning the "outs" anyway,' Paige quipped, and the girls burst into laughter.

The girls spent the next hour cleaning the containment cell and wiping down the examination table and equipment. Paige had only just removed her gloves when the door buzzed, and Nate and Stu entered, carrying the unconscious form of Ashton Wakehurst. Strapping him down on the examination table, the two men double checked the restraints before walking to the counter and setting up the equipment.

Doug and Jonno entered next and Paige audibly gasped at the sight of Jonno's battered face. His left eye was swollen shut and caked blood covered his scorched shirt from a nose bleed.

'What the hell happened to you?' Paige asked, grabbing a clean towel and wetting it.

'You should see the other bloke,' Jonno joked, unbuttoning his ruined shirt and throwing it in a nearby bin.

'You look like you have been in a fight with the devil himself,' Paige declared, wiping the soot and blood from his face.

'No, just the army and a six-foot werewolf hybrid. All in a day's work,' he grinned.

Paige looked across at the prone form of Ashton Wakehurst. Her uncle had removed his bullet riddled shirt and was placing electrodes on his bare chest and forehead. She walked towards the table and positioned herself between her uncle and Tash.

'He doesn't look like a killer,' she said, reaching out to touch the silver wrist restraint that firmly held his arm in place by his side.

'No, but I can assure you he is capable of killing everyone in this room in a matter of seconds,' Doug replied. 'You should have seen him, Paige, he is even more powerful than we first thought. He took a direct hit from a missile strike that should have blown him apart, but it didn't even leave so much as a scratch on his body. If we can work out what he is exactly, maybe we can control him. And use him to our advantage.'

'Whoa!' Nate exclaimed from the foot of the table. 'His heat signature if crazy. Check it out,' he said throwing the thermal image camera across to Doug.

Doug hovered the camera over Ash's body, displaying a standard red heat signature. After a few seconds, the red disappeared and was replaced by a blue flush that pulsed momentarily before resuming its red colour.

'What the hell?' Doug said in confusion, banging the camera with his hand. 'It must be a malfunction.'

'No, there is nothing wrong with that camera. He has something inside him giving off another reading. Something is controlling him,' Nate replied.

'Why hadn't we noticed this at the apartment?'

'Maybe we just couldn't see that far away or maybe he wasn't being controlled at that point,' Nate proffered.

'And maybe, it has something to do with the link between him and the head werewolf,' Doug replied excitedly. 'Get some blood work from him. Let's find out what makes him tick.'

****

Anya threw her suitcase on the ground outside reception and fished out her phone, angrily scrolling for Leila Merrin's number. She had been forcibly removed from her apartment after the army had allowed her a mere ten minutes to finish packing her things and then driven to the Mountain Retreat Motel, where she had previously stayed with Ash. The two burly soldiers that had escorted her, then drove off ignoring her numerous insults and threats to their manhood. Now fuming and frantic with worry for Ash's safety, she dialled Leila's number and prayed she would pick up.

After four rings, Leila's voice finally answered.

'Anya, what is going on downtown? Are you okay?' Leila asked.

'I am safe, but Ash has been taken. The army blew up my neighbourhood trying to catch him and I don't know where they have taken him or what they plan on doing with him,' Anya fretted.

'Where are you now, I will come and get you,' Leila replied.

Giving her quick directions, she resumed her conversation.

'Leila, please tell me you and Evelyn have a plan. We have to save Ash,' she said.

'If we can find him, we do have something that can help him,' Leila reassured her. 'Did the army take him?'

'No, it was a group of men. Civilians. One of them was called Jonno and I think their leader was someone named Doug,' Anya replied.

'Was Doug tall, middle aged with a tattoo on his neck,' Leila probed.

'Yeah, he had a weird symbol on the side of his neck and so did the other men, now that I think about it,' Anya replied.

'I know who Doug is and more importantly, where he is. Wait out front for me Anya, I will be there in twenty minutes,' she said, hanging up.

****

Evelyn jumped to her feet when she heard the front door open and rushed to embrace Anya.

'Is he alright, Anya?' she probed before pulling away.

'The custodians have him,' Leila said bluntly, making her way to the hall stand and opening the top drawer.

'The custodians? Why would they want him? He is not evil!' Evelyn declared.

'Excuse my ignorance, but who are the custodians?' Anya interrupted.

'It's a long story, but they are essentially hunters of anything that threatens human lives. I have a bit of a history with their leader,' she announced, pulling a map out of the drawer. 'Hopefully, he still lives in the same house,' she said unfolding the map.

'Is he the old flame you rang the other day,' Giana enquired, walking towards the women and kissing Anya on both cheeks. 'Hi detective, I'm Giana. I am an old friend of Evelyn,' she said warmly.

'Yes, Giana, Doug and I had a thing a few years back, but it didn't work out,' Leila explained.

'Did he know you were a vampire?'

'Yes, he did. He actually saved my life after I was captured by another group of custodians. If it wasn't for him, I wouldn't be here today telling you this story,' said Leila.

'Well, no wonder you have a thing for him,' Giana replied.

'Had a thing for him, Giana, that ship has long since sailed,' Leila said.

'Well, maybe that ship has since returned to port,' Giana replied.

Ignoring her, Leila shook her head and returned her focus to the map in front of her. Circling a section on the map, she looked up at Evelyn and Anya.

'This is where Doug used to live. Let's hope he is still there, for Ash's sake,' she announced, stuffing the map into her handbag.

Alerted by footsteps on the landing above their heads, Anya looked up to see a pretty, dark-haired woman descend the stairs whilst drying her hair with a towel.

'Gees, I needed that! Thank God you still have water, Leila,' the woman said.

'Anya,' said Evelyn looking up at the woman, 'This is my little sister, Morgan. She is staying with us for a while.'

'Ash has told me about you,' Anya replied, extending her hand to Morgan. 'He said that you helped save his life in the caverns when his grandmother tried to kill him.'

'Yes, I did. I had to save him. Afterall, it was partly my fault that he had been captured in the first place,' Morgan said. 'I hope he has forgiven me for my part in what happened. My mother, his grandmother, manipulated me into thinking I was doing a good thing, but I know now she is a psychopath.'

'He does not blame you for what happened to him,' Anya replied. 'Everyone makes mistakes and you made up for yours when you helped him.'

Morgan smiled and placed her hand on Anya's shoulder. 'Are you and Ash together?' she said with a shy smile.

'Something like that.' Anya replied. 'It's complicated.'

'I know all about complications! I used to date a werewolf too and I tried everything to keep him away from Logan Smythe, but he was under his complete control,' Morgan replied.

'Yes, I know what that feels like all too well.'

'Ladies, we need to move. God only knows what they are doing to Ash right now,' Leila interrupted.

They all nodded and quickly gathered their coats; making their way to the door. Hearing a car pull up outside, Evelyn peered out the window and put her hand to her mouth.

'It's Logan and he has someone with him,' Evelyn exclaimed.

Pulling a gun from her waist band, Anya pushed her way to the door and threw it open, coming face to face with Logan and Will.

'Anya, wait!' Evelyn shouted, grabbing her arm. 'Let him talk.'

'I am not here to cause any trouble,' Logan declared, struggling to hold Will up. 'I know Morgan is here and Will needs her help.'

'Oh my God, Will!' screamed Morgan, rushing forward and helping Logan bring him into the house.

Laying him on the sofa, Morgan quickly grabbed a towel and began to dab cold water onto his wounds.

'He will heal in a few hours, but I need to know he will be safe. The army is looking for us,' Logan said looking back at Anya. 'Where is Ash?'

'I wouldn't tell you even if I knew,' Anya seethed.

'Logan, Will is safe here, but you need to leave. We do not want the army aiming their missiles in our direction,' Leila stated, opening the door.

Logan nodded and walked towards the door, turning to look at the women.

'You should all think about leaving Rockdale. Some serious shit is about to go down and you do not want to be caught up in it, believe me. I will be back for Will once he has healed,' he said heading out the door.

Anya shook her head in disbelief. 'The balls on that man coming in here, he must be crazy thinking we would help him,' she raged.

'Not crazy, Anya, desperate,' Evelyn replied, patting her on the shoulder and bending down to examine Will. 'Morgan, let's help him upstairs to the bathroom where we can clean him up.'

After Morgan and Will had disappeared into the bathroom, Leila pulled out the crystal shard and held it up to Evelyn.

'We have been given an opportunity that we cannot ignore,' she said turning the crystal over in her hand. 'We now have someone that we can test the crystal on.'

'Well, if you are going to use it, you better wait for him to heal first or he will die from those injuries,' Evelyn warned.

'Let's give him half an hour and then I will stab him with it. I would much rather fail on him than on Ash,' Leila replied.

'I don't think Morgan will see it that way, but I have to agree. We need to delay our rescue of Ash to ensure that what we have will cure him, not kill him,' Evelyn stated.

****

Morgan sat on the edge of the tub and watched Will as he soaped up his hair and rinsed it off, turning the bath water into a dull grey colour. His burns and facial cuts had already begun to heal, and he sighed audibly as his broken leg and pelvis finally aligned back into place with a loud crack. Morgan stood up and walked over to the towel rack, selecting a dark blue towel and holding it out to Will.

'You shouldn't have gone back there, Will. I begged you not to go,' she said bluntly.

'I had no choice, Morgan, you know that,' Will said softly, emerging from the tub and wrapping the towel around his body.

'I can't do this anymore, Will,' Morgan said, fixing him with a firm gaze. 'You need to choose me or Logan. I won't sit back and watch you risk your life for him anymore.'

'Morgan, he saved my life. I can't turn my back on him now.'

'He is the reason you were nearly killed in the first place! Can't you see that?' Morgan fumed. 'God, Will! He is making you kill for him. Is that really who you are now?'

'I will do whatever it takes to survive, Morgan and right now, being by his side seems like the smartest move,' he replied, drying himself off and pulling on a pair of Ash's clean jeans.

'He is going to get you killed!' Morgan yelled, throwing a shirt at his feet in frustration. 'I am not going to stand in your way, but if you go with him, I never want to see you again.'

A knock sounded at the door and Evelyn poked her head around the corner, taking in her sister's tear-streaked face.

'Is everything okay in here?' she asked with concern.

'I'm fine. Will was just leaving,' Morgan snapped, walking out the door.

'He should stay a little longer,' Evelyn said, linking Will's arm. 'I am sure you would like a hot meal before you go.'

Ignoring Morgan's hostile stare Will nodded thankfully and followed Evelyn down the stairs to the kitchen.

Once seated at the table, Leila served him with a bowl of hot soup and Will hungrily spooned up the broth, stopping only to sporadically dip a bread roll in the bowl.

'This tastes amazing!' he gushed. 'What kind of soup is this?'

'It is an old family recipe,' Leila replied, walking towards the table. 'It is called Mulligatawny Surprise,' she said with a smile.

He suddenly slowed down and stopped, a look of realization crossing his face as he glared across the table at Leila.

'Wolf's Nettle?' he had time to blurt out before slumping forward on the table; his head connecting with the bowl and spilling its steaming contents across the table.

'Surprise!' said Leila as she pulled the crystal from her pocket.

Morgan screamed and rushed to his side, pulling his limp head back towards her.

'What have you done?' she screamed at Leila.

'Morgan, we have to do this. If it works, the Nequam's toxin will leave his body and he will be human once again,' Evelyn soothed, trying to put her arm around Morgan.

'And what if it doesn't work?' Morgan fumed, pushing her away. 'What then?'

'We hope it doesn't come to that, Morgan. If this works, we will have found a weapon to free all werewolves, not just Will. It will mean that we can rid both Ash and Logan of the spirits that possess them. We can be a family again,' she replied calmly.

'You want us to be a family?' Morgan seethed. 'You have betrayed me. How can I ever trust you? If anything happens to Will, I will NEVER speak to you again.'

'We are doing this, Morgan, whether you like it or not,' Leila replied, pulling Will onto the floor.

Giana and Evelyn held Morgan back as Leila pushed Will's shirt aside and held the crystal shard above his bare chest.

The three women, reciting the words that they had memorized from Gwynn's letter, chanted together before Leila brought the shard down into Will's chest.

'*Liberatio ab intra,*' she shouted as the room around them began to hum.

****

The mud beneath his bare feet rippled and pulsated as though it had a life of its own. He tried to move, but his feet were firmly planted in the sticky red sludge and his attempts proved futile. A lone, black tendril snaked its way up his leg and wrapped around his thighs, heating his skin upon contact. As panic set in, he could feel his heart rate accelerate and he cried out for help, peering through the smoke haze that stung his eyes. He could see his brother approach, his naked body caked with mud and blood as he walked towards him, agonizingly slow in his movements. 'Help me!' Ash screamed to his brother as he felt more tendrils coil around his lower limbs and he began to sink into the squelching mud.

His brother reached out and grabbed his arms, trying to free him from his certain doom and for the briefest of moments, Ash was able to move. A shrieking sound pierced through the air and Ash and his brother both covered their ears with their hands, cowering to the ground to escape the ear-piercing onslaught.

Logan's body suddenly jolted, and he looked up at his brother in shock, his eyes wide with fear. He began to make a choking noise and grabbed at his throat as a large tendril emerged through his open mouth. Ash looked behind him to see a long-haired demon staring back at him, her serpentine tongue flitting in and out of her fang lined mouth as she watched him with interest. Opening her mouth impossibly wide, she sank her teeth into the side of Logan's neck and tore a chunk of flesh away, gulping it down in seconds. As Ash looked on in horror, unable to move, she was joined by several other demons and they each tore into Logan's flesh, consuming him while he writhed in pain and struggled to free himself. In his remaining seconds of life, he was torn apart and different pieces of him were either carried away or sucked into the mud.

The demon wiped her mouth and reached out for Ash, cradling his trembling jaw as she stepped in closer and pressed her naked body to his chest.

'It is nearly time, my love. Soon my brothers and sisters will be reborn, and they will feast on the human's and beasts that walk this earth. You will be spared if you submit to me. You were destined to be mine, the minute you were born, and I will have you,' she whispered, running her hands down his stomach and reaching into his jeans. 'You will give me many children and rule by my side as you were destined to do. Give yourself to me and you will become my equal for all eternity,' she said, pulling him down on top of her and spreading her legs wide.

The heart monitor machine beeped erratically, and Nate walked over to investigate, pulling the electrodes from Ash's chest and repositioning them. Ash had been unconscious for several hours now, which had been somewhat of a relief for Nate, given that he was given the responsibility of running tests on Ash. He had completed all the tests but was still trying to analyse some of his bloodwork as some anomaly's had been discovered. It would take days to work through each genetic sequence, but so far Nate has ascertained that Ash was indeed a hybrid and that they would need to take extra precautions around him. He had hoped for more time before Ash awoke, but, judging by the spikes in activity on both the ECG and heart machine they had taken from the abandoned hospital, he was about to wake up and soon.

Ash murmured softly, his hands lightly twitching and his breathing increasing as he tossed his head from side to side.

'Dougie! You had better get down here, he is waking up,' Nate said, speaking into the intercom.

'I am on my way down now, give him a shot if he wakes before I get there,' Doug's voice replied, and the intercom went quiet.

Ash suddenly cried out and began thrashing against his confines, his eyes wide with panic as he quickly surveyed the room.

Reaching for a syringe, Nate tried to inject the copal serum into Ash's bicep, but it was knocked from his hand and sent rolling across the concrete floor.

At that moment Doug burst into the lab with Jonno, Paige and Tash following close behind him.

'Doug, he is completely freaking out! I can't keep him still long enough to sedate him,' Nate declared, retrieving the runaway syringe.

'Jonno, get on the other side of him and help me hold him down,' Doug ordered, and the two men put their body weight onto Ash's chest.

Finally managing to inject the serum, Nate wiped his brow and leant back against the counter, watching as Ash's heart rate began to decrease on the monitor.

'His heart rate was off the charts, I have never seen anything like it before, not from someone who lived afterwards, anyway,' Nate marvelled. 'He was in a deep sleep and then started muttering the name "Cerridwen" over and over again and something about eating werewolves. Whatever, he was on about, it was something that he was afraid of.'

'Paige, can you see if you can find anything about the word "Cerridwen" on the net? It might give us something to go from,' Doug requested, turning his focus back to Ash.

'Where am I?' Ash rasped feebly. 'What have you done with Anya?'

'Anya is safe. The army dropped her back at her motel room a few hours ago,' Doug replied. 'Ashton, who or what is Cerridwen?'

'You have to let me go!' Ash demanded, and the heart monitor began to beep erratically once more.

'Whoa big fella, take it easy, you will only hurt yourself if you try to escape,' Doug warned. 'Your restraints are made from a silver and mercury amalgamate and they cannot be broken. As an extra safeguard, I also have a gun trained on you and if you do anything stupid, my good friend Jonno here, will not hesitate to put you down.'

'You don't know what you have done!' Ash shouted, staring at Doug. 'You are fighting a battle you cannot win, and you are all doomed to die no matter what you decide to do to me. Logan will come for me when I don't return, and he will tear you all apart!'

'No, he won't,' said Doug. 'The army have destroyed your hideout and even with the slim chance that Logan has survived, his pack has been wiped out.'

Ash shook his head and began to laugh, his whole body shaking as he looked across at Doug.

'You think you have it all worked out, don't you? You and your men have heroically answered the call to save humanity from the shit storm that is coming. Well, you are fucking delusional if you truly think you have stopped anything. Logan is not dead. If he were dead, I wouldn't still be linked to the Nequam and I wouldn't be able to feel his rage and lust for blood. He is majorly pissed, and he is coming for you. The army haven't prevented anything. In fact, all they have done is act as a catalyst for the Apocalypse that is coming. It is just around the corner and there is not a damn thing you or they can do about it.'

'Now that is a bit over-dramatic, don't you think?' replied Doug. 'The Apocalypse? We will purge this town of every werewolf so that the so-called Apocalypse never happens. Humans will go back to their everyday lives and forget all about the existence of werewolves.'

'You are too late. You could wipe out every last werewolf tomorrow, but it will not make any difference to the fate of this world,' replied Ash. 'You want to know who Cerridwen is? Well, she is a demon that has been waiting, along with thousands of other flesh-eating demons, to once again walk this earth. All she needs is for the Nequam to take a thousand souls and those numbers are soon within his reach. Once the Nequam has his quota, he will resume his old form and open the portal to the next world, bringing all manner of demons into our dimension. It will happen on the next blood moon and unless he can be stopped, we are all fucked.'

'He's right,' said Paige, looking up from her iPad. 'I found an old prophecy that warns of the end times and we are already experiencing some of the signs. Listen to this: *"When the waters doth turn crimson and the earth haemorrhages its precious life blood, mankind will tremble in the light of a new dawn of death and destruction of which they have never seen before. The Goddess will walk the earth with her brothers and sisters and the faithful will bask in her glory and in her mercy"*.'

'Can't you see? You are fighting the wrong battle. We need to find a way to expel the Nequam from Logan and stop anyone else from dying or the Apocalypse will happen,' Ash said.

'No, we kill Logan and the Nequam disappears to wherever it came from,' Doug replied.

'It won't stop if you kill its host. You are making a huge mistake. As Logan's brother, I am the only one that can get close to him, we just need more time to come up with a plan,' Ash replied wearily, struggling to keep his eyes open.

'There is no way in hell that I am going to trust you. This is all bullshit and part of your plan to distract us,' Doug responded, angrily shaking his head. 'Mark my words, Wakehurst, the end of your kind is near. We will end this tomorrow by killing your brother and once we have finished with you, you will meet the same fate.'

Chapter 11

Captain Lawrence exited his tent at the sound of approaching vehicles and pulled his coat on. Bracing against the chilly evening air, he strode towards the first jeep and watched as the soldiers dismounted and stood at attention.

'Private Banks, where is the Lieutenant?' he said gruffly.

The Private lowered his head, unwilling to meet the captains eyes as he pointed to the truck behind him. With a stern look, Captain Lawrence dismissed the Private and made his way behind the truck and pulled open the canvas flap. Quickly covering over his mouth and nose, he took a step back and turned to the group of soldiers.

'What the fuck is that?' he demanded, singling out Private Banks once again.

'The remains of Lieutenant Sommers, Ronnins, Crickshank, Davies, Lotta and Guerero, sir,' Private Banks replied. 'They were ambushed by a lone werewolf and taken out.'

'Taken out? One of them looks like a fucking skinned rabbit!' he roared.

'That, sir, was the lieutenant. He was skinned alive before we could get to him. We could hear him screaming and it was most God-awful sound I have ever heard in my entire life and definitely not something I ever want to hear again,' choked Private Banks.

'It had to be Smythe. You heard what he and his brother did to the chief of police. We need to find that fucker and destroy him. If he is capable of doing something like this against highly trained soldiers, what is he capable of doing to innocent civilians,' the captain declared, pulling the canvas flap back down. 'Did you kill the rest of the survivors?'

'Affirmative, sir. We believe we killed them all. We only found half a dozen or so that were still alive, the rest had been close to the warehouse when the missile struck and there wasn't much left of them,' Private Banks explained.

'We need to be on high alert. He will come after us soon, but first he will want to refill his ranks and my guess is that he will go looking for his brother. Get a hold of Doug, we need to warn him,' the captain ordered.

Private Banks saluted the captain and turned on his heels, walking a few paces before slowly spinning back around to face him. His mouth suddenly contorted, and a look of confusion swept across his face as he shakily reached for his rifle and aimed it at the captain before firing and hitting him in the arm.

Shouts broke out around them and the private was knocked to the ground. More disturbances could be heard from within the compound and guns began to fire from various positions around the base. The captain dashed for cover under the truck while bullets ricocheted off the hood and chassis. A few yards away, he watched in horror as two soldiers shot each other in the face point blank, dropping to the ground in perfect unison. One after the other, in something akin to a ripple effect, the soldiers open fire on their comrades and fell to the ground.

Minutes later, when the firing finally ceased, Captain Lawrence crawled out from beneath the truck and cautiously poked his head up over the side of the hood, his hands shaking as he took in the carnage around him. The entire base was eerily silent except for a muffled sobbing sound emanating from somewhere behind the mess tent. He quickly raced to the source of the sound and found a sole soldier, sitting by the side of one of his fallen friends. As the captain approached him, the soldier looked up and shook his head slowly, his face streaked with tears and blood. He got to his feet and held one of his hands out to the captain. His fist slowly unfurled revealing a small metal pin nestled in his palm. The captain only had a split second to register his surprise before a grenade exploded, killing them both and scattering the nearby ground with their eviscerated bowels and limbs.

****

A rumble from deep within the earth sent a mild shockwave that rippled through the burning town and surrounding forest. Lillian watched from her balcony, smiling as the decking beneath her bare feet shook and the trees around her mansion swayed momentarily as the shockwave passed.

'It is happening!' she said excitedly, gripping Bernard's arm. 'The quota has been filled!'

'Look at the skyline!' Alexa said, standing beside her.

Over the horizon, the sun was dutifully setting, filling the sky with a warm red hue as it gradually darkened. The trio watched as the moon became brighter and took on a pink and orange glow as it shone brightly in the sky.

Lillian reached for Alexa and Bernard's hands and beamed at them both.

'Once the moon turns red, it will begin. We must get to the lake and welcome Cerridwen as she is reborn. Bow before her and you will both be spared the fate of all those who remain alive. You can serve her by my side, and we will live under her protection for all eternity,' she gushed.

'What about Logan?' Alexa replied. 'What will happen to him once the Nequam manifests and leaves his body?'

'You cannot be worrying about Logan. His fate is his own. You, my dear, are destined for bigger and better things now that the Gods are returning,' Lillian replied, walking back inside the house. 'Come with us, your destiny awaits you.'

Reluctantly, Alexa followed Lillian and Bernard, hastily grabbing an overcoat as they made their way towards Bernard's Rolls Royce and headed into town.

****

The underground laboratory shook violently, sending equipment and vials smashing to the ground and shattering an overhead light. Paige and Tash screamed and ducked under the examination table as shards of glass rained down on everyone in the room. Holding each other for comfort, they watched as the men struggled to keep their feet and hung onto anything that remained upright.

A loud siren sounded from outside and Doug swore, staggering like a drunk as he tried to reach the laboratory door.

Stu had already opened the latch and was on his way out as the rumbling suddenly ceased.

'I will check on the house, you had better see to our patient,' he said as he quickly closed the door behind him.

'What the hell was that?' whispered Nate, bending down to pick up a stainless-steel bowl at his feet.

'I don't know, but it can't be good,' Doug replied, dusting glass off his shoulder. 'Is everyone alright?' he asked, pulling the girls to their feet.

Tash and Paige nodded as they checked on Ash, brushing glass off his chest. He was still heavily sedated and had not stirred throughout the tremors despite several large shards of glass becoming embedded in his thigh and side. With Paige's help, Tash pulled out the glass and his wounds healed instantly, leaving no trace of them ever being there. Jonno and Nate had not fared as well with each of them sporting cuts on their arms and faces and Doug immediately went to their aid.

The lab door suddenly beeped and opened allowing Stu back in. Judging by the grim look on his face, Doug suspected the news was not going to be favourable. Accompanying Stu was Joe and one of the soldiers that had stayed behind to offer additional security.

'Doug, the army base has been compromised. Private Sainsbury has not been able to reach anyone for the past thirty minutes,' Joe exclaimed. 'And that is not the only problem, some weird shit is happening at the lake.'

'Private, are you sure your equipment is still working properly,' Doug said, addressing the soldier.

'Affirmative, sir. I have been in constant contact with the base throughout the day, but at 1700 hours, the lines all went quiet,' Private Sainsbury replied.

'How many of your squad have remained to guard the compound?' Doug enquired.

'There are ten of us remaining here and up to a dozen men still on patrol. The rest, including the sergeant, returned to the base to prepare for the attack on the werewolf hideout.'

'Get the other squad on the line and bring them in. We are going to need all the help we can get to take out Smythe when he comes. The base will have to wait until later,' Doug ordered. 'Joe, what is happening at the lake?'

'The CCTV footage is picking up unusual vibrations within the lake. It looks like the water is boiling and has changed colour,' Joe replied.

'We will check it out. First, we need to get the compound secured and the alarms switched back on,' Doug replied. 'Stu, did the house hold up alright?'

'Yeah, I think we fared worse having been underground. The house is intact, and no major damage has been done. I will reset the alarms and the motion sensors. Nothing and nobody will get near this place without us knowing,' Stu declared earnestly.

'Good. We will wait for the soldiers to arrive and then we will head out to the lake,' Doug replied.

'Hey guys, you might want to come and have a look at this!' Paige yelled from the other side of the room. Doug raced over to the examination table and stood next to Paige while she pointed to the side of Ash's neck. A series of black lines spread out like a spider web and multiplied as they began to cover his shoulders and chest.

'Nate, what do you think it is?' he asked as Nate bent down to examine the mystery black substance.

'It is not on the surface of his skin. It must be in his veins. I will try and get a sample,' Nate replied, carefully scraping Ash's neck with a scalpel.

Ash's eyes suddenly sprung open and he began to convulse, his body jerking violently against his restraints.

As his eyes rolled back into his head and turned black, he stopped convulsing and began to laugh softly. He continued to laugh and turned his head to look at Doug.

'*You fool*,' a raspy voice sounded from deep within Ash's throat. '*He tried to warn you, but now it is too late. As the moon bathes in blood, we will be reborn, and you and all your kind will be obliterated. Nothing will remain but the dust from your bones as we walk this earth for all eternity.*'

'Who are you?' demanded Doug, leaning in closer.

'*I am the Nequam,*' the voice rasped as the blackness crept back up Ash's body and disappeared.

Ash woke up and his eyes returned to normal. Frantically, he thrashed at his restraints and cried out in pain.

'Let me go! He is calling me. Please! You have to let me go!' he pleaded, groaning in pain.

'You are not going anywhere, Wakehurst, we are not finished with you yet,' Doug replied, looking across at Nate. 'Give him another shot.'

'No!' Ash bellowed as Nate approached him. 'Don't do this. I can't fight him for much longer. If I turn, you will all be torn apart! Let me go and I will stop him. You have to let me go!'

'Sorry buddy, it ain't gonna happen,' Nate replied, trying to jab Ash's arm.

The room began to shake again, and objects levitated from the counter and shelves, spinning around the ceiling and sending everyone ducking for cover. The syringe in Nate's hand began to vibrate and he quickly dropped it onto the floor. It spun around in circles and then shot through the air, stopping millimetres from Paige's left eye.

'Let me go or I will kill her,' Ash warned, his chest heaving with exertion. 'Undo my restraints and I will walk out of here without harming anyone. You have my word.'

Jonno strode towards him and held his rifle to Ash's forehead.

'You will not touch a single hair on her head, or I will FUCK you up beyond recognition. Get that fucking needle away from her. Do it now or I will shoot!' Jonno seethed through clenched teeth.

Ash shook his head. 'If you kill me, you will all die. I am your only hope at taking down the Nequam and you know it!'

'How can we possibly know that? The Nequam is inside you and can control whatever you do,' Doug replied, edging cautiously towards his niece. 'Please don't hurt her, she is an innocent girl!'

'I may have the Nequam controlling me, but somewhere deep inside me is the Triune. I awakened it once and I can do it again, but you have to let me go or I am of no use to anyone,' Ash replied, his eyes glazing over in pain. 'Please! This is agony trying to hold him off. I can't resist for much longer.'

'I can't take the risk of having you turn the minute we set you free. Drop the needle Wakehurst or I will order Jonno to put a bullet in your brain,' Doug ordered.

A wave of pain surged through Ash's body and he cried out in agony, losing his control over the spinning objects and sending them clattering to the ground. The syringe also dropped, smashing on the hard floor at Paige's feet. Seizing her opportunity for freedom, Paige rushed to her uncle's side and buried her head in his chest, sobbing hysterically.

Ash writhed in pain as his body began to transform. Fur began sprouting across his body and his jawline extended with an audible crack.

'Run!' he screamed at the stunned group and the girls both scrambled for the door.

'Just say the words, Doug, let me put this bastard down,' Jonno shouted as he kept his rifle trained on Ash's head.

Doug shook his head and held his hand up. 'Not yet, I want to see him transform,' he replied.

'You can't be fucking serious! What if the restraints don't hold? He will tear us apart,' Jonno said incredulously.

Ash roared and emitted a deep guttural growl that sent shivers down their spines. Pulling against his restraints, he snapped his right hand, breaking it in several places. Slowly he pulled his mangled hand through the metal cuff and freed it.

'Fuck!' Doug and Jonno said in unison, taking a step backwards as Ash's hand instantly healed itself and ripped the electrodes from his chest.

'I think you had better shoot him now,' Doug said frantically.

'It's about fucking time,' Jonno replied, re-positioning himself for the shot.

'Stop!' a loud voice called, startling them both and Doug looked back at the door to see Leila Merrin step into the lab. 'I can cure him!' she yelled as two other women, including Anya, joined her.

Jonno lowered the rifle and looked to Doug. 'Can I shoot him now or what?'

'No! Don't you fucking dare!' Anya stormed, pushing Jonno in the chest. 'We have a cure and we know it works.'

Jonno and Doug shrugged their shoulders and stepped aside allowing the three women to approach Ash as he continued to transition. Another group of people walked in and Doug stared in disbelief at a dreadlocked man who stood at the back.

'You used to be a werewolf. I saw you with my own eyes. How is this possible?' Doug asked intrigued.

'She cured me, and she can cure Ash too,' the man replied.

Anya raced around the other side of the table and placed her hand on Ash's arm. 'Help me hold him still,' she yelled at Jonno and he obligingly rushed to her side. Evelyn and Giana also joined them, holding each other's hands as they waited patiently.

As Jonno and Anya struggled to hold him down, Leila pulled out the crystal shard and plunged it deep into Ash's chest.

'*As we speak these words, we cast you out. He who lingers in shadows and in the depths of this man's soul. We command you leave from whence you came. Your influence is void, and he will no longer be your vessel for destruction. Liberation ab intra. Liberatio ab intra,*' the women chanted in unison.

Ash's chest heaved, and the room pulsated as the crystal syphoned the darkness from Ash's veins, turning the crystal jet black in colour. When Leila removed the crystal, he slumped back on the table and began to resume his human form. The fur covering his body was quickly replaced with smooth skin and his jawline returned to normal.

Anya leaned over his chest and placed her cheek near his open mouth.

'He's not breathing,' she said in a state of panic. 'Why isn't he breathing?'

Evelyn stepped forward and touched Anya's arm gently.

'Give him time, Anya. He will come around,' she said reassuringly.

Anya nodded dumbly, her face blanched white with worry as she ran her fingers through Ash's tousled hair. He flinched slightly at her touch and suddenly sat up, scanning the room in confusion. Sobbing with relief, Anya kissed him and pulled him into a strong embrace as the other women also gathered around him.

'Oh baby, I thought I had lost you all over again,' Anya gushed.

'You could never lose me, Anya. Not even the Nequam could keep us apart,' he said, looking across at Evelyn, Giana and Leila.

'Thank you,' he said earnestly 'The Nequam has gone and no longer has any control over me. I know what his next move will be, and we will need to move fast if I am to have any chance at stopping him.'

'That is what we are now counting on,' Doug replied, removing the remaining cuffs from his feet and left hand. 'We fear the army base may have come under attack. If what you have told me previously is true, then you are our only hope.'

'I wish it wasn't so, but every word I said was true. The Nequam is bringing his army of demons to Rockdale with the dawn of a blood moon. We need to get to the lake before the moon is at its fullest,' Ash replied, jumping down from the table. Looking across the room towards the doorway, his eyes locked on Morgan and then did a double take as Will stepped into view. He gently pushed his way past Doug and Jonno and strode towards Will. After hesitating for a few seconds, he embraced him and slapped his back affectionately.

'You have no idea how good it is to see you, buddy. I am so fucking glad, you are back to normal,' he gushed. 'This cure will work on Logan and Matt too, I just know it.'

'Ash,' Will said softly, lowering his gaze, 'Matt didn't survive the blast at the warehouse. Only Logan and I made it out.'

Ash's jaw clenched and he nodded sadly, placing his hand on Will's shoulder. 'We will grieve for him properly later. Right now, I have to stop Logan,' he said. 'You and Morgan need to stay here with Giana, you will be safer here.'

Evelyn grabbed Ash's arm and spun him around gently. 'Ash, we need to move. Your reunion with Will is going to have to wait until later,' she said firmly. 'Do you have control over the Triune?'

'Yes, for now. It might be a different story once we get to the lake, but we will have to cross that bridge when we get to it,' he replied, reaching for Anya's hand and following Evelyn out the door.

Doug waited until most of the others were out the door before turning to Paige and gripping her arm. 'I need you to stay here with Tash and the others,' he said gently. 'Nate will keep an eye on you both.'

'But I want to come with you. I can help!'

'No, not this time, Paige. I need you to help protect the compound and keep the lines of communication open,' he said. 'If anything happens to me, this place is all yours and I need to know that you will carry on my legacy.'

Paige nodded and held open the door for her uncle. 'Yes, Uncle Doug, you can count on me. Just make sure you all come back to me in one piece!' she added pulling him into a strong embrace.

'That is the plan,' he said with a grin as he closed the door behind him.

As Ash and Anya climbed the steps, he leant over to Anya. 'Please tell me my bike is still okay,' he whispered.

'If by okay you mean that it now resembles a post-modern sculpture of twisted metal, then I can definitely tell you it is okay,' she replied.

'I figured as much, but thought it was worth asking all the same. It looks like I will need to find another mode of transport.'

'If we all survive this, I will get you a new motorbike,' she said, placing her arm around his waist, 'although I think I might have to buy you a new shirt first.'

'I thought you liked me with my shirt off,' he joked, climbing into the backseat of Leila's car.

'I certainly do, but I can't vouch for your mother and her friends,' she replied.

'Trust me, they won't mind. I am wearing a lot more than I was the last time they saw me,' he said as the car began to speed off.

****

The incessant beep of a car horn sounded through the empty streets as a car teetered on the edge of a ditch, its back wheel still spinning despite its impact with a large tree. Thick smoke snaked out of various gaps from within the crumpled hood and began to fill the car, rolling over the slumped form of Logan Smythe as if caressing his back. Logan groaned and lifted his head from the steering wheel, bringing an instant end to the relentless beeping. He rubbed his head and began to cough as the acrid smoke became thicker. Grabbing the door handle, he pushed it hard and nearly fell out onto the road with the exertion it took to force it open.

Crawling out, he dropped onto the wet grass, his chest heaving with rasping coughs as he tried to expel the toxic smoke from his lungs. He looked around the crash site in confusion, trying to recall what had happened to make him lose control of the car. Spotting a large form on the road behind the car, he staggered towards it, pulling a large piece of glass from his neck and arm. By the time he reached the misshapen mass on the road, his body had completely healed and the car behind him was well alight. Bending down to examine the dead creature, he recoiled as his boots came into contact with a pool of black blood and intestines.

His men had told him about the mutant werewolves that scavenged through the town, but this was the first time he had seen one in the flesh. It was a gruesome looking creature which looked remarkedly like a large sloth with its long front limbs. The resemblance ended there, however, as the creature from all reports, was surprisingly fast and aggressive. The Nequam could exert control over a portion of the creatures; those that had mutated after direct exposure to Nequam blood, but the ones that had been turned after being bitten by the mutants could not be controlled. They were rogue creatures that infected humans and werewolves alike, turning them into ruthless killing machines and killing indiscriminately without mercy or hesitation. Logan had ordered that any rogues be brought in, but so far, they had proven to be an elusive prey. Dave, along with a small group of werewolves, had ventured into the forest to try and capture one alive, but they had not yet returned.

Kicking the dead creature over with his foot, Logan saw something glint amongst the fur on its mangled wrist. Bending down, he ran his fingers through the matted fur, finding the smooth surface of a watch face. Turning his face away in revulsion, he peeled the watch from the fur with a sickening tearing sound and flicked several clinging chunks of flesh from underneath. He turned the watch over and read the inscription: *To my dearest David, Happy 15th Anniversary, All my love, Doreen.*

'What the fuck happened to you, Dave?' he said aloud, wiping the watch on his jeans.

A sharp pain suddenly tore through his head, forcing him to drop the watch and sink to his knees. Holding his head with both hands, he cried out in agony.

'*It will soon be time,*' the Nequam bellowed from deep within him. '*We must go to the lake to greet my brothers and sisters for the moon is full and red.*'

As the pain finally subsided, Logan got to his feet and began to remove his clothes. In one fluid motion, he instantly transformed and padded off down the street in the direction of Rockdale Lake. The car exploded behind him, setting off the alarm and sending a single, smoking tyre rolling down the empty street.

****

The air thrummed with a static energy that seemed to energise the tall reeds growing by the side of the lake. They undulated with each vibration, giving the effect of a Mexican wave as they swayed in unison around the lake foreshore.

The night was deathly quiet as a group of people approached, their footsteps light on the dewy grass as they reached the jetty that jutted out from the shore. Several kayaks were tethered to the wooden structure; their fibre cast hulls gently knocking together with the motion of the water. Breaking off from the rest of the group, Lillian, Bernard and Alexa stepped onto the jetty. Making their way to the end, they stopped and stared across the water. Below the trio, the lake shimmered and rippled, reflecting the crimson glow of the Blood Moon as it cast out its light across the lakes surface.

'Isn't it beautiful?' whispered Lillian as she admired the red hues of the cliffs behind the lake. Turning to Bernard, her eyes lit up with excitement and she reached for his arm and pulled him towards her.

'My love, I can't believe this day has finally come,' she said, gushing like a school girl. 'We will soon meet Cerridwen, it won't be long now.'

'But nothing appears to be happening,' replied Bernard, pressing up against the railing and peering out over the lake.

'The quota has not yet been met. There is still one more soul to offer to the goddess before she can be reborn on this plane,' Lillian replied, shooting a furtive glance at Alexa as she watched on in silence.

'Who did you have in mind?' Bernard queried, turning to look at her.

'It needs to be someone I love dearly and someone not human,' she replied, touching his face tenderly.

A look of realisation spread across Bernard's dark features and he vehemently shook his head.

'Me? You want to sacrifice me after everything I have done for you. You can't be serious!' he replied incredulously, backing away from Lillian.

'Please don't be like that, my love. This is a great honour, and I have saved it for the one I love the most. Your death will herald the arrival of the most powerful gods the world has ever seen. This will be your greatest legacy, Bernard. Embrace it,' she replied.

'No. I will not die for you, Lillian. Not you or anyone else,' he snapped, pushing her out of his way. He took one step towards the shore before freezing, his face contorting in shock as he realised Alexa had paralysed his body.

'No, no! Don't do this! Please Lillian, after everything I have done, I don't deserve to die like this,' he pleaded.

'Shh,' hushed Lillian as Alexa handed her a knife. 'Alexa will ensure that you do not feel any pain and I will make it quick.'

'Please accept my ultimate sacrifice to you, my beloved Goddess. Bathe in the blood of my lover and be reborn to us, once more,' Lillian whispered into the breeze.

Walking behind him, Lillian swiftly slashed the knife across his throat, leaving a gaping wound in its wake. Bernard spluttered and gasped for air as blood spurted down the front of his shirt and spilled onto the planks at his feet. Collapsing onto his knees, his hands scrabbled at his throat as life blood ebbed from his open jugular and pooled beneath him. Alexa approached and knelt down before him, pulling his head up by his hair. Reaching into his chest, she wrenched out his still beating heart and threw it into the lake before letting his lifeless body drop onto the dock. A thick pool of blood quickly spread out from his body and began to drip into the glassy water below.

The ground instantly began to shake, and the two women struggled to keep their feet, hastily grabbing each other for support. With each rumble, the jetty began to disintegrate around them, and they ran for the shore, making it moments before the jetty collapsed and disappeared beneath the broiling surface of the lake.

An ear-piercing screech split the night air and the group of women covered their ears, huddling together against the trunk of a tree as they watched the lakes surface. It rippled and bubbled, its surface now resembling blood as the moon overhead turned a darker shade of red.

Another shriek sounded, and the ground shook violently, sending the women and girls ducking for cover as trees fell around them. They ran for the car park, but a four-metre crack opened up between the footpath and the lake, encircling them and trapping the group where they stood. Alexa screamed as a large vine tendril shot up through the earth and grabbed her leg, drawing blood as its sharp thorns dug in. Around her, more vines emerged from the sodden ground and the girls screamed in terror as they were dragged into the mud by their ankles or legs.

'*Incenderunt*!' shouted Lillian and the exposed tendrils burst into flames and let go of their grip.

Helping the girls to their feet, Alexa and Lillian herded them into the centre and stood protectively in front of them.

More tendrils appeared and snaked their way across the grass towards the group.

'We have to get out of here!' Alexa cried, backing away and scanning the area for an escape route.

'Alexa!' a male voice shouted, and she looked up to see Ash standing on the other side of the crevice with a group of soldiers and civilians.

'Ash! Help us!' she screamed back.

Ash waved his hand and the vines shrunk away, their shrieks hurting his ears as they returned back to the mud. Quickly scanning the play equipment around him, he located a long seesaw and ripped it from its base, placing it over the crevice.

'Quick, get across before the crack gets any wider,' he shouted to the group and they quickly obliged, crossing the plank in single file. One of the group, a fifteen-year-old girl named Amy, was halfway across when she was snatched from the plank by a large vine and pulled into the darkness below. Her terrified screams were cut short by a sickening crunch and in a panic, the rest of the group surged forward.

'One at a time! Stop pushing each other or you will over balance the plank,' Ash shouted as one of the panic-stricken girls was shoved from behind and almost fell over the side. 'Nice and easy girls, just concentrate on reaching me.'

Several sharp vines slithered up over the side of the crevice and darted for the soldiers as they frantically opened fire. Ash jumped out of the way, narrowly avoiding a razor-sharp vine that had aimed for his head. He instinctively reached out to the soldier next to him, grabbing him by the jacket. The soldier didn't move, and Ash looked across to see Private Sainsbury frozen in fear as two vines snaked up his legs. Before Ash could utter a word, the private was impaled through both eyes and dragged into the abyss below along with several other unfortunate soldiers. Jonno stepped forward with a flamethrower and let loose on the remaining vines, their tendrils writhing as they shrunk back into the abyss.

The earth rumbled again and a loud whooshing sound emanated from the centre of the lake as a large vortex opened up. The seesaw plank shifted and threatened to topple the remaining girls as they crossed. Ash grabbed the end of the plank and shouted at Alexa to do the same on her side. Between them they managed to get the remaining girls and Lillian safely to the other side.

'Your turn, Alexa. You will need to run fast. The crack is getting wider,' he shouted.

'What if one of those things grabs me,' she replied, nervously looking around her.

'You will make it, I promise. Just run and don't look down,' he said, holding out his hand.

Alexa ran, her eyes focused on Ash's as she made her way across. The ground shook again, just as she had nearly reached the end and the plank slipped and began to fall beneath her. Ash reached for her hand as she fell and caught her by the wrist, quickly hoisting her back up over the side as the plank disappeared below.

Hugging him, she sobbed in his arms, her body trembling with relief.

'Thank-you, Ash,' she sniffed. 'I know I didn't deserve your help after what I did to you, but I am so grateful you decided to save me.'

Ash stiffened and pushed her away, holding her at arm's length.

'Don't mistake my help for forgiveness, Alexa. We are a long way from that point,' he said turning back to the others.

Watching him intently, Anya pushed through the group of survivors and grabbed Alexa's arm.

'You should thank your lucky stars that it was him on the other end of that plank and not me, because I would have let you die,' Anya said. 'You are lucky that Ash is still a decent guy, despite your best efforts to turn him into a monster,' she snapped.

'Anya, now is not the time,' Ash said softly.

'No, that is where you are wrong. Now is the perfect time,' she seethed. 'Look around you Ash, look at what she has done! She has doomed us all!'

'Oh, enough of the dramatics, Detective,' replied Lillian as she approached the trio. 'It is not all doom and gloom, well, at least for some of us. There are a chosen few who will advantage from the Goddess's arrival. Bow to them and you will fall under their protection.'

'Bow to this, you fucking, psycho bitch,' replied Anya, punching her in the face before storming off towards Doug and the rest of the survivors.

Lillian cried out and held her nose as blood poured between her fingers.

'What is coming out of the ground next, Lillian?' Ash said, gently touching her nose and uttering a healing spell.

'Worse, so much worse,' she replied. 'Dozens upon dozens of flesh-eating demons are coming through the vortex as we speak.'

'I can stop them, just like I stopped you,' he replied. 'I am not afraid anymore. I know my purpose and I will destroy every last one of them.'

Lillian laughed and shook her head.

'What is it about you young people today? You honestly think you know it all and that you are indestructible. You know nothing about what is to come, and you will not survive this night. Cerridwen is coming for you and she will devour everyone you hold dear. Enjoy your last moments on this earth, my dear grandson, for they will be fleeting,' she said turning away.

Ash shook his head and joined the others as they retreated towards the relative safety of the carpark.

'You should have killed her, Ash, that bitch does not deserve to live after everything she has done,' Anya admonished.

'Yeah, you are probably right, but that would make me just like her and trust me, the only thing we have in common is our bloodline,' Ash replied. 'Besides, I don't have time to exact justice on anyone right now. According to her, we are about to face something much worse than killer vines. We need to get the civilians to safety and locate Logan. He is key to all that is happening right now.'

A sudden burst of energy hit Ash in the chest and sent him flying backwards into a parked car, temporarily winding him.

'Looks like I found him,' said Ash as he struggled to his feet and began to run back towards the lake.

Chapter 12

Logan stood beyond the tree line, one hundred metres from the assembled group of survivors, watching as the events unfolded. Although his subconscious screamed at him to try and help Alexa, the Nequam's hold over him was too strong and he watched helplessly as she fought to survive. Walking to the water's edge, he held his arms up and slowly waved them over the lake in front of him. A huge vortex opened up in the centre and the water level dropped dramatically as it was sucked it into its churning centre.

'*Veni foras*, my brothers and sisters. Come forth and walk this earth with me,' he shouted across the swirling waters before dropping to his knees.

The ground rumbled, and another deep crack opened behind him, cutting him off from the rest of the park. A strong breeze whipped around him as a strange mist began to form on top of the lake, slowly rolling across the surface. Hearing gunfire, his focus shifted back to the group of people as several soldiers opened fire into the sinkhole. Logan watched as they fought off the killer vines and made a hasty retreat to the car park behind them. Alexa was now safely on the other side of the large sinkhole and a mixture of jealousy and relief surged through him as he watched her embrace Ash in gratitude.

Logan stood up; his face distorted in anger as he glared at his brother. He knew he was losing control; that he was letting the Nequam take over, but he couldn't curb the surge within him, and searing pain tore through his body as he relinquished it completely. Everything went black as he retreated into the recesses of his mind. The Nequam was in charge, once again and everyone was at his mercy.

'Time to end this once and for all,' the Nequam said aloud in a guttural voice; shifting the energy from the vortex back to his hands and shooting it straight towards Ash; the impact knocking Logan's brother backwards.

As Ash spotted him and began to run towards him, the Nequam waved his other hand and felled several large pine trees. One of them hit the ground at Ash's feet with a splintering crack, narrowly missing him. Another fell awkwardly across the widening ravine, providing a makeshift bridge between him and Ash. Leaping up onto its sturdy trunk, the Nequam coolly walked its length, intercepting Ash halfway across.

'It is good to see you, Ashton,' it said with a sneer. 'Have you come to join me or beg for mercy?'

'Neither,' Ash replied slowing his steps as he stepped up onto the log. 'No, I came here to end you, once and for all.'

The Nequam laughed and rested his hands on his knees. 'Oh, the delusions of mortals,' it said, shaking his head. 'There will be an end, of that I can assure you, but it will not be the one you are imagining. You are too late. Nothing can save your precious humans now. My brothers and sisters are already here,' the Nequam hissed. 'See for yourself.'

Ash looked over the Nequam's shoulder, his heart rate quickening as he saw the first of the demons emerge from the vortex and wade towards the water's edge. The eyeless creature sniffed the air and darted its tongue between two circular rows of razor-sharp teeth as if it was tasting the wind. Its head shot around in Ash's direction and it keened shrilly, forcing Ash to cover his ears.

'That is a mud demon, but don't worry, he won't harm you while I am here. Join me, deny the Triune and I will spare you the agonising death that the others will soon experience.'

'No. That will never happen,' Ash declared, standing nose to nose with the Nequam, his eyes flashing in anger.

'That's a real shame because now your mother is going to witness the demise of her favourite son,' the Nequam sneered, pushing him hard in the chest. 'First I will dispose of you and then I will destroy everything that is left of your brother.'

'Not if I can help it!' replied Ash, swinging his fist and connecting with the Nequam's jaw, the impact almost knocking him off his feet.

The Nequam coolly snapped his jaw back into place and swung back, his fist connecting in quick succession with Ash's sternum and doubling him over. Grabbing him by his head, he brought his knee up to Ash's nose with a sickening crunch. Crying out, Ash scrambled away from him, blood pouring through his fingers as he tried to stem the flow of blood from his broken nose. Before he had the chance to recover, the Nequam launched itself at Ash, knocking him over and pinning him to the trunk.

'Is this what you really want, Ashton? You can't beat me, especially now that you no longer have wolf blood in your veins,' the Nequam mocked. 'I gave you a gift and you refused it. You will regret that decision. Before I finish you, I need to know how you purged your body of my blood?'

'The same way we got rid of the blood in Will. We have a cure,' Ash retorted.

'No, that is not possible,' the Nequam replied, shaking his head.

'It is true, I have seen it with my own eyes. Will is no longer a werewolf,' Ash replied as he repositioned his leg and catapulted the Nequam over his head and onto the tree trunk, causing the whole trunk to shudder beneath them. Ash leapt to his feet and turned to face the Nequam, deftly sidestepping two balls of energy that shot past his face. A third hit him in his chest, sending him hurtling back across the tree trunk and over the side. As he fell, he caught hold of a branch with his left hand and heaved himself back onto the trunk, quickly sending a pulsating ring of blue light in the Nequam's direction.

Clapping his hands mockingly, the Nequam sneered at Ash as he stepped off the trunk and onto the ground.

'Bravo, Ashton, you have proven to be a worthy adversary. It will break your brother's heart to see you die, but he should have had the balls to kill you ages ago,' the Nequam said, stroking the tree trunk and setting it on fire. 'You may have been able to fight back against me, but you are no match for Cerridwen. You belong to her now.'

Flames quickly shot along the base of the fallen tree and Ash was forced to turn around and run for the other side. The tree crackled and split in two, falling into the deep crevice below and trapping Ash on the lake side of the ravine.

'You fucking coward, come over here and fight me. I am not finished with you yet!' Ash shouted.

'No, but I am finished with you,' the Nequam shouted back, turning towards the carpark. 'It is time I became reacquainted with the lovely detective. She looks like she has a bit of fight in her. I find that very attractive in a woman I am about to kill.'

'You son of a bitch! Keep your fucking hands off her!' Ash shouted in vain.

'You should have embraced the Triune when you had the chance. Now you are both doomed,' the Nequam replied, disappearing into the fog.

Hearing a squelching sound behind him, he spun around to find several mud demons slithering towards him, their legless bodies moving with ease through the mud. His eyes flashed, and the creatures screamed in fury as their bodies instantly blistered. Quickly shedding their burnt outer skins, the demons crawled out and stood at full height to face him. Their keening so shrill that Ash was forced to his knees as he tried to block out the sound. As the first demon reached him, it slashed out with its scaly talons and left a deep gash across his chest. Another demon took a swipe at him, but Ash managed to scramble to his feet and stagger away towards the water's edge. Breathing hard he turned to face them, holding his arms up and bringing them together in an arc shape before sending a brilliant ball of flame hurtling towards them. It exploded on impact and the creatures were blown apart, scattering chunks of charred flesh for several metres around him.

'Ashton, my love,' came a voice from behind and he spun around to find a beautiful blonde-haired woman standing in front of him. She was completely naked and surrounded by writhing tendrils that eddied around her as she stepped closer to him.

'Rana?' Ash said, taking a step forward.

'I can be whomever you want me to be,' the woman whispered as a shimmer ran down her body and she changed her form to resemble Anya. 'I hear you have a thing for redheads too.'

Ash shook his head and instinctively took a step backwards, holding his hands up in front of him.

'Stay back!' he shouted as two balls of fire formed in his hands.

The woman laughed, and her eyes flashed red with anger.

'Ashton, my love. I have waited a long time for this. You were promised to me by your grandmother and I will have you,' she affirmed, as two of her vines shot out and secured his wrists. 'Give yourself to me willingly and it will be a lot less painful for you. We will be together for all eternity.'

Ash tried to free his hands, but his efforts were in vain. His body incapable of movement as several more vines slowly wrapped around his legs and crept sensuously up his thighs. The woman's intense green eyes held his gaze and her lips parted, revealing a row of sharp teeth.

'No,' Ash replied, shaking his head stubbornly, 'I will never be yours.'

'You already are,' she said, running her serpentine tongue up his throat and pulling him into her arms.

Slowly edging backwards, she stepped into the water and Ash began to sink with her, unable to extricate himself from the web of tendrils that enveloped his body.

****

Doug pointed his rifle skyward and opened fire on the winged creature that reached for him with its sharp talons. Screeching in pain, it flapped its webbed wings backward and retreated into the safety of the trees.

'Jonno! How many rounds do we have left?' he shouted across the carpark to where Jonno was positioned alongside their truck.

'Not many, Dougie. I don't know how much longer we can hold them off,' Jonno replied scanning the skyline.

'We will need to improvise. They don't like fire so let's make a ring around us to keep them out. Use the gas cans on the back of the truck,' Doug ordered.

'It will only be a temporary fix, Doug, but it might buy us some more time,' Jonno agreed, reaching into the back of the truck for a jerry can.

A terrified scream reverberated through the air and the two men looked up to see one of the creatures carrying off a girl. As it flew, it tore her head off and her body dropped onto the ground with a sickening thud nearby.

'Jesus!' swore Doug. 'We need to get that group over here now. They are being picked off like fish in a barrel!' he shouted.

'We tried. They won't leave the Russell woman,' Jonno despaired.

Doug looked across at the fledgling group of women with Lillian positioned at the centre. She had her arms raised skywards and was chanting something in Latin. The group of girls around her were holding hands in a circle and bowing their heads as they awaited their fates.

'Crazy bitches!' Doug muttered under his breath. 'How is that fire going, Jonno?'

'Nearly ready, just making sure that no cars are in the way. I don't think we will benefit from blowing ourselves up,' he replied.

'Did you find the other women?' Doug shouted.

'No, I don't know where they went or if they are still alive. Nate said they took off towards the trees when Ashton spotted his brother, but with this damn fog, I can't see shit anymore. They could be anywhere,' Jonno replied, lighting the gasoline. 'I feel a Johnny Cash song coming along, Dougie. Feel free to join in when you get the urge,' he shouted, belting out a rather bad rendition of "Ring of Fire" as he ducked back under the truck.

Shaking his head, Doug returned his focus to the sky as a thick fog rolled in around them.

****

'Evelyn, I can't see them anymore, the fog is too thick,' despaired Anya as she scanned the shore.

'We need to get closer if we are to have any chance of stabbing Logan with the crystal,' replied Evelyn.

'Are you serious? You want us to get close to those things? We can't even see two feet in front of us,' Anya replied incredulously.

'Do you want to stop Logan or stand back and watch the world end around us?' Evelyn sniped.

'Well, when you put it like that, I guess we don't have a choice,' Anya replied sheepishly.

Leila looked across at her and touched her arm reassuringly. 'Evelyn has this covered. We are not going to let anything happen to you,' she said.

Anya had watched in terror as the creatures first began to emerge from Lake Rockdale, some dragging their hideous bodies through the mud, others taking to the air and flapping their enormous wings. She had wanted desperately to run to Ash's side and help him fight off Logan, but she knew her sudden appearance would make Ash vulnerable. A stern look from Evelyn had affirmed this and she resorted to waiting until both her and Leila judged it was safe to approach. As the fog began to roll in, they knew they had to act fast and they had quickly made their way to the tree line in the hope that Ash would manage to restrain Logan.

The trio stopped suddenly, and Evelyn waved her hands in front of her, dissipating the fog and revealing a small group of demons as they crouched in wait. Leila lunged at them, taking out the first two with a well-aimed swipe that removed their heads from their scaly shoulders. Anya instinctively reached for her side arm, but Evelyn grabbed her arm.

'No! We cannot risk making any noise and alerting Logan to our presence. Leila can handle them on her own, we need to keep moving,' Evelyn insisted, pulling her along.

Moving silently across the grass, Anya and Evelyn finally reached the line of trees. They could barely make out the shapes of Ash and Logan as they fought each other only a few feet ahead of them. A flash of blue light suddenly pierced through the fog and impacted with the tree beside them, causing both women to duck for cover. The tree crackled and groaned before disintegrating and sending shards of splintered wood in all directions.

'Jesus Christ,' muttered Anya as she got to her feet, 'What the hell are they doing over there?'

'Hopefully sorting out their differences,' Evelyn replied.

'It doesn't look as though they are making much progress on that front!' Anya remarked. 'Why doesn't he just let the Triune take over. He could end this once and for all.'

'He doesn't want to lose control again. He is afraid of what would happen to Logan if he does,' Evelyn explained.

A loud whooshing sound reverberated through the mist and the ground ahead of them lit up as a fallen tree trunk caught fire. Anya held her breath as she watched Ash leap from the burning trunk and land safely on the other side. Feeling Evelyn's fingers gripping her arm, she ducked down behind the tree and waited as Logan headed towards the car park.

'Do you think he saw us?' Anya mouthed silently to Evelyn. Evelyn shook her head and pointed to her amulet on her chest. Remembering that she was still wearing a cloaking charm, Anya nodded with obvious relief and remained perfectly still.

All of a sudden, Leila appeared at Anya's side causing her to jump in fright.

Clutching her chest, Anya reeled on Leila. 'Was that absolutely necessary?' she seethed, brushing pine needles from her pants and getting to her feet.

'We have to go now. There are demons everywhere and they are coming ashore,' Leila replied, ignoring Anya's retort.

'No, not without Ash. I am not leaving him here all alone,' Anya insisted.

'I agree. He is strong, but he could still use our help,' Evelyn replied, waving her hands across in front of her and clearing the fog. 'There he is, down by the shoreline,' she said pointing across the fissure.

The women looked down towards the shore, Anya's heart hammering in her chest as she watched a female demon pull him into the water.

'Nooo!' Anya screamed, trying to break free from Leila's firm grip. 'We have to help him!' she despaired.

'There is no way to get to him in time. Trust me, if there was anything I could do, I would do it to try and save him,' Evelyn said tearfully. 'He is on his own now and so are we.'

****

Paige scanned the area around the compound from her vantage point on the water tower before passing her binoculars to Tash. She had seen enough to know that the compound would soon be compromised, and she needed to warn the others. Fumbling for her radio receiver, she pressed the transmit button and called for Nate.

'They are everywhere, Nate, get the others to the lab, Tash and I will do what we can to keep them away,' she said.

'How many are there?' Nate replied.

'Dozens at least. They are coming in from town and heading towards the lake and we are in their direct path,' she replied, watching as the horde of creepers quickly approached. 'Get the civilians to safety now, they will be here within minutes.'

'Stay safe, Paige. Doug will never forgive me if anything happens to you,' Nate's voice crackled before cutting off.

'You too,' Paige whispered sadly, reaching for her rifle.

The intruder sirens suddenly blared and erratic machine gun fire broke out below her amidst the shouts of the five remaining soldiers.

'Get ready to kick some ass, Tash,' she announced positioning her gun against her shoulder and firing.

As the electrified fence claimed its first victims, the creepers began to screech, and reluctantly pulled back. The soldiers took out a few more and the horde simultaneously attacked the fence, using the bodies of their fallen friends as a bridge. Tumbling over each other, they easily scaled the electrified fence and breeched the compound within seconds, sending the soldiers running for cover.

Paige and Tash shot at the horde, their bullets finding their targets each time, but the horde kept coming. Several creepers began to scale the water tower and the girls picked them off, one by one. Once again, the bodies began to pile up and the remaining creepers used the mound of bodies to launch themselves into the air at the tower.

'Holy shit!' swore Tash as she put a bullet between the eyes of a creeper. 'They are much smarter than we thought.'

'Yes, and they seem to know where everyone is hiding,' Paige said pointing towards the lab. 'They are going after Nate and the others.'

Several creepers were throwing themselves at the lab door like a battle ram and Paige wondered how much longer the door could hold. With Will no longer a werewolf, the group inside the lab would be completely defenceless if the door was breached.

'We have to help them!' she said grabbing her crossbow and attaching an incendiary to the arrow shaft. Aiming towards the lab, she shot the arrow directly into the horde of creepers, obliterating them on contact.

'Good shot!' shouted Tash, picking off several more with her gun.

'Don't celebrate just yet, there are a lot more coming,' Paige said, scanning the nearby hill. 'And they are coming fast!'

****

Morgan and Giana huddled together against the far wall of the lab; their hands firmly covering their ears as the screeching outside the door intensified. The heavy, bolted door jolted again, and Morgan caught Will's panicked glance at Nate as they tried to reinforce the door with furniture from the lab.

The door shuddered again, and Morgan was sure she had heard something crack, but to her relief, the door held, and their safety was assured again for at least a few more moments.

She glanced up at the small CCTV screen that jutted out from the wall in the opposite corner of the room, involuntarily holding her breath as she watched the horror unfolding outside. The screen was divided into four separate areas within the compound, one of which clearly showed the creepers outside the lab door and their efforts to gain access. Giana had obviously seen it too as she was now gripping Morgan's arm with renewed vigour.

'They won't get in,' assured Will as if reading their minds and Morgan turned her head to see him watching her intently. She saw the strain on his face, despite his best efforts to mask his own terror, and she wondered if these would be the last words he spoke to her before the lab was breached.

'Who are you trying to convince? Me or you?' she said, looking back at the screen.

Will did not have time to respond as the door suddenly jolted again and a distinct dent appeared at the top of the door frame. Will and Nate backed away from the barricaded door, raising their rifles in preparation for the breach. They both knew they wouldn't survive if any creepers got in, but they were not going down without a fight.

A deafening bang sounded outside the lab and the group all jumped in alarm. A series of ear-piercing shrieks quickly followed forcing them to cover their ears until the noises subsided. The lights overhead flickered sporadically, and the television screen went blank for a few moments before coming back on. Morgan stared at the screen in disbelief, finally getting up from her position on the floor and walking towards it.

'They are all dead. Something blew them to pieces,' she said staring at the screens grainy images.

'It looks as though the rest are leaving too. I wonder what is drawing them away?' Nate replied, staring at the screen with unfeigned interest.

'Whatever it was, it just saved our asses,' said Will as he strode across to Morgan and wrapped her in a strong embrace. Looking across at Giana, he noticed how pale she was as she stood mutely, transfixed by the screen. 'Are you okay, Giana?'

She nodded and crossed herself profusely, her hands visibly shaking with each motion. 'Thank the Lord,' she said kissing a silver pendant that hung from her neck.

'The Lord may have had a hand in preserving us, but I think we can credit our survival to Paige and Tash's shooting skills,' interjected Nate. 'If it wasn't for them, I doubt the door would have held out for much longer. Will, give us a hand moving this stuff out of the way. Hopefully, this door can still be opened from the inside.'

****

As the fire gradually died down around them, Doug bolstered his defence, repositioning himself alongside the remaining men. Most of the custodians had survived the initial onslaught, including Jonno and Stu, but the soldiers had suffered considerable losses. Of the dozen men who had accompanied them to the lake, only three remained and one of them was severely wounded. The winged demons had picked off most of them before an attack could be coordinated and although the fire had kept most of them at bay, it would not have deterred the land demons who could be heard screeching in the distance. They now remained in a huddle with an army jeep at their backs.

Stu had managed to save several of the coven girls after Lillian and Alexa had walked off into the fog and left them, but it had been to the detriment of his ammo supply.

'I've got nothing left,' Stu despaired, throwing his rifle to the ground. 'We might as well face it. We are all sitting ducks out here!'

'Now is not the time to throw in the towel, Stu. We still have these,' Doug admonished, holding up his bare hands. 'I can't speak for you, but I do not intend to go down without a fight. If I must die, then I plan on taking as many fuckers with me as I can.'

Jonno grinned and slapped Doug across his shoulders. 'Now that's the spirit, Dougie!' he said reaching down to his ankle and pulling out a hunting knife. 'This is my weapon of choice when all else fails and she hasn't let me down yet. I have a spare one if anyone needs it.'

Private Dominic Simms, one of the surviving soldiers, crawled over to Doug and removed his headpiece. 'Good news, Doug! Private James has got us back online and radioed for help. The general is sending us some air support at 2100 hours. We just need to hold them off until then,' he said earnestly.

'That only gives us twenty minutes to find the others and get them to safety. We need more ammo,' Doug said, shaking his head. 'Dom, what do you and Jack have left? Can we pool it?'

'Jack is down to one round, but I still have a full clip and I might be able to scavenge for more. Give me two minutes and I will bring you everything I can find,' Private Sims replied, cautiously crawling around the jeep.

'What are you planning, Doug? You can't go out there alone, that would be suicidal!' Jonno warned.

'I don't have a choice. If I don't find them, they will all be killed when the air support gets here. I have to at least give them a chance,' Doug replied.

'This wouldn't have anything to do with a certain old flame now, would it? You are not usually the reckless type, Doug,' Jonno teased.

Doug looked past him and shook his head. 'I just don't want you to be the one who gets all the glory when we take these fuckers down and save the world,' he said with a grin.

'That is never going to happen. Besides, I am coming with you. I would rather die out there trying to save civilians than sitting here scratching my balls,' he said.

'Great, I could definitely use your help,' Doug said slapping Jonno's back. 'Guys,' he said addressing the rest of the group, 'I need to you to hold this position for as long as you can. We are cut off so there can be no retreat by foot. We have no choice but to wait for air rescue to get here. Until that time, I am counting on you all to stay alive and look after each other,' he said, spotting Private Simms as he emerged from the front of the jeep carrying two more rifles. 'If I don't return, I want you to know how proud I am of you all. It has been an absolute pleasure fighting by your side and I consider you all as family,' he choked.

'For fuck's sake, Doug, wipe your eyes with your hanky and let's get the fuck out of here before you make me cry in front of all my friends. I have a reputation to protect!' Jonno joked, pulling Doug away from the group.

After some quick embraces and affirmations of friendship, the pair waved good-bye, and jumped across the waning ring of fire, disappearing into the fog.

****

The cold water swirled and rushed around him as he was pulled under the water. The surface above him resembling a shimmering glass ceiling as it became more distant and impossibly out of reach. Water probed its way into his mouth and nose, callously invading his lungs and evicting the last remaining air bubbles. His chest felt like it would explode as the bubbles spewed from his mouth and hurried to the beckoning surface.

'Stop fighting me, my love, death is nothing to be afraid of. It is a release from everything and everyone that has ever

caused you pain,' a voice sounded in his head as a single tendril crept up his chest.

Cerridwen placed her hands around the back of his head and pulled him closer, guiding his mouth to hers. Kissing him hungrily, her serpentine tongue darted into his mouth in search of his own. He tried to pull away, but she held on firmly, running a hand down his body and fumbling with the clasp on his jeans.

Ash's resolve was quickly diminishing and a part of him wanted her desperately, but thoughts of Anya clouded his mind. He had to break free from her before it was too late.

In one last desperate surge for freedom, he tried to kick his legs, but Cerridwen quickly grabbed him by the throat.

'There is no escape. You are mine!' her voiced screamed in his head as her grip tightened.

His eyes, wide with shock and desperation, fixed on Cerridwen's as he felt his body go limp in resignation. He no longer felt any pain, but a sense of peace washed over him and warmed his cold skin. As his eyes fluttered shut, he felt a surge within him and his body jolted, seemingly energized by an unseen force. Everything seemed to slip away; his consciousness, his senses and his control as the Triune reawakened within him.

Cerridwen's facial expression suddenly changed and she hastily began to unravel her tendrils as she backed away from him. His eyes snapped open and he reached for her throat, clasping his hand tightly and pulling her towards him.

'*No! He was promised to me! You cannot have him!'* her voice screamed in his head.

Ash's eyes flashed blue and Cerridwen let out a garbled scream as her skin began to blister and blacken beneath his hands. She struck at him with sharp talons, sloughing skin from the side of his face and shoulder in a frenzied attack. Ash only squeezed her throat harder and she clawed at his hand in desperation; her eyes bulging and filling with blood as the capillaries in her eyes burst. Her tendrils thrashed around, churning the water in her desperate struggle to break free.

'Please, don't do this! I will let him go, I swear!' she begged.

Ash maintained his grip and began to squeeze, slowly constricting her throat until the delicate bones in her neck suddenly snapped. With one effortless twist of his hand, her head was separated from her shoulders and her body left to sink to the bottom.

With a firm grasp on the trophy head, he kicked his feet and propelled through the bloodied water to the surface above, his thoughts consumed by one driving force; the destruction of the Nequam and anyone else who got in his way.

****

Lillian watched the trio of women carefully, knowing that she would need to confront her daughter eventually, but for now she needed to remain unseen. Alexa stood solemnly by her side, her thoughts obviously elsewhere as she surveyed the lake for signs of Logan.

'He will be alright, Alexa. Ash won't defeat him, not without the Triune,' Lillian declared.

'How do you know for sure that the Triune won't resurface? How do you know anything for certain?' Alexa whispered. 'I have followed you blindly because you said I would be spared. You told the girls that too and look what happened to them. None of this feels right anymore, Lillian. I feel like I have picked the wrong side and now it is too late to turn back.'

'There is no turning back now,' Lillian snapped. 'The girls died because they were not worthy. They didn't make the sacrifices that I did. They didn't have to make the choices that I have made. Cerridwen is waiting for us and we will be her vessels. If you turn back now, you will die along with the rest of them. Prove you are worthy of Cerridwen's mercy and she will spare you, Alexa.'

Alexa looked down at her feet and shook her head.

'No, I don't think any of us will be spared, Lillian. She needed us so she could be reborn, but now that she has succeeded, we will not be of any further use to her.'

Lillian grabbed her by the shoulder and spun her around. 'Don't you say that! Don't you EVER say that!' she said furiously. 'Cerridwen would never betray us; she is the reason you are still alive! It was her that spoke to me all those years ago when your bitch of a mother lay bleeding in the gutter. She guided me to you so that I could save your life and keep you safe until she needed to be reborn. Everything you have done and ever will do is because of her mercy and you stand there and throw it back in her face like it means nothing!'

'It does mean nothing! I have killed hundreds of people in her name and what will I have to show for it in the end? I won't even have Logan. You know as well as I do that the Nequam will dispose of him once he takes his true form. What sort of life will I have without him?' Alexa despaired. 'The only hope I have now is that Evelyn and Leila's plan works.'

'What plan?' Lillian demanded angrily. 'What plan have you kept hidden from me?'

'They have a cure for the werewolf toxin and if they use it on Logan, he will be free of the Nequam,' Alexa replied.

'Why didn't you tell me this before?' Lillian seethed, grabbing Alexa's arm. 'What are they planning to do?'

Alexa had been able to read Anya's mind for the briefest of moments and their plan had manifested itself clearly in her own head in a series of visions. Alexa explained the power of the ancient Selenite crystal and how it had freed Will and Ash already by absorbing the Nequam blood.

'This changes everything! If they have the means to remove the Nequam and contain it, then I now have a means to control it. I will be even more powerful than Cerridwen herself.'

'That is what I am afraid of. You are so hungry for power that you are willing to sacrifice anyone who gets in your way; your daughters, your grandsons, your lover and no doubt, even me. When will it ever end, Lillian? When you are surrounded by demons and every single person you have ever known is dust? Will you be satisfied then?' Alexa replied angrily. 'We are about to be wiped off the face of the earth by a horde of demons that we both brought here and all you can think about is your next power trip.'

'Don't be so dramatic, Alexa. You are not an innocent in any of this. You knew what you were doing when you killed all those men, you didn't hesitate to do what had to be done. You cannot tell me that you didn't enjoy the power you exerted over each and every one of your victims,' Lillian retorted.

'It was fun at first, I will admit that, but it doesn't feel good anymore,' Alexa replied. 'I thought I was going to die, Lillian. I thought about everything I had done up to that point and all I could feel was shame and regret for the decisions I had made. Despite everything I have done to Ash, he still chose to save me because he thought I was worthy of saving. I doubt Cerridwen will feel the same.'

'You will find out soon enough, but for now, you don't have any choice but to stick with me and I have a plan to free Logan. I will need your help though, Alexa, so now is not a good time to be having second thoughts,' Lillian said.

'If it means helping Logan, then I will help you, but this is the final time,' she said firmly.

'If you help me, I promise I will never ask anything of you ever again,' Lillian said, glancing across at the women. 'Now all we need to do is ensure their plan works.'

****

The Nequam stopped and stood perfectly still; its eyes closed as it tried to hone in on Anya's location. The air around it was thick with static energy and it focused on the different waves of colour that pinpointed the positions of every human around him, each carrying their own heat signature. It knew that Anya would be close by, but her energy signal was muffled, and it couldn't sense her exact location. Holding its hands up, it reopened its eyes and shouted "Videor", instantly clearing the fog.

A flapping sound overhead momentarily broke its focus and it looked up to see a winged demon circling above, its eyes on a group of survivors huddled together in the carpark.

'Ut imperium!' the Nequam whispered, and it instantly found itself looking through the eyes of the creature as it flew across the park in search of more victims. With its keen sense of hearing, the Nequam could hear the heartbeats of the survivors rise in panic with each sweep. As the creature honed in on a pair that had separated from the main group and began to make its descent, the Nequam heard a voice coming from the tree line.

'Anya, you sly minx!' it whispered, a smile spreading across its face. 'You were watching me the whole time!'

Quickly resuming control over the winged demon, the Nequam forced it to change direction and fly towards the area where it had heard her voice. It hovered and circled a stand of singed and burning trees before it finally spotted footprints in the mud. Footprints that were leading straight towards where it now stood.

'She is cloaked!' the Nequam said with a mixture of respect and amazement. 'And she is not alone,' it added, quickly returning to its body and spinning around.

'*Te mihi revelare!*' it shouted, and the trio of women suddenly materialised in front of him.

Leila was the first to act. She swiftly lunged, swinging her arm up in a stabbing motion towards the Nequam's chest, but it grabbed her wrist and stopped her mid-flight.

'You are going to have to do better than that, you bloodsucking bitch!' it sneered, twisting her wrist until it snapped with a sickening crunch.

Leila screamed in agony and dropped to the ground, her broken wrist dangling like a wooden marionette's limb. The crystal blade landed in the mud at the Nequam's feet and it stomped on it before delivering a jaw crushing kick to Leila's face and knocking her out cold.

'Did you really think you could stop me?' it asked incredulously, glaring at the two remaining women. 'I am the Nequam!'

'We were sure as hell going to try,' said Anya defiantly, quickly averting her eyes from its nakedness.

For Christ's sake, does this man ever wear clothing? she thought.

Interrupting her thoughts, Evelyn pushed forward and stood in front of the Nequam. 'We are only trying to help you, Logan, no one wants to see you get hurt,' she said earnestly.

'Speak for yourself,' muttered Anya as she glared back at him.

'Logan can't hear you! He will never hear your whining voice again,' the Nequam seethed. 'This crusade of yours to save your sons has been an epic failure and you now have nothing. Ashton is gone, and soon everything you know will be dust,' it added, grabbing her by the throat and squeezing hard as she began to slip into unconsciousness.

'You son of a bitch!' shouted Anya, pulling out her gun and shooting the Nequam repeatedly in the chest. Its body jerked back, and it released his grip on Evelyn, but it now turned on Anya.

'There's my girl!' it sneered, grabbing her by the back of her head and pulling her towards it. 'Feisty to the very end. I can see why Ashton fell for you. I think he liked the challenge. For me personally, I prefer my women to be a lot more compliant,' it said, forcibly holding her head in the crook of his arm as she struggled. 'Rana fought me until her dying breath too, but she still died screaming and now you will as well.'

'Logan! Stop!' came a shout from behind him and the Nequam spun around to see Alexa with Lillian.

'That is not Logan!' Anya said, her voice raspy and desperate as she tried to extricate herself from the Nequam's vice-like grip.

Ignoring Anya, Alexa approached the Nequam. 'Logan, I know you are in there somewhere,' she said, stroking its face tenderly. 'Come back to me.'

She kissed him tenderly and it let go of Anya. Returning her kiss, it ran its hands up her back and through her hair. Its body suddenly jolted, and it pulled away from Alexa in shock, looking down to see a shard of crystal protruding from its side. Anya's hands were on the hilt and she pushed it in deeper, defiantly glaring at him.

'Men are so fucking stupid!' she said, helping Evelyn and Leila to their feet.

Chanting the words *"liberation ab intra",* the women joined forces and surrounded the Nequam. It groaned in pain as it dropped to its knees and tried to pull the shard out. The women chanted louder, and the Nequam began to convulse on the ground, the skin on its side turning black as its blood was gradually siphoned from its body. Alexa held its head on her lap, stroking Logan's hair as he finally stopped shaking and his body became limp. The shard slid from his side and landed in the mud, the white crystal now a dull black hue.

'He's not breathing,' Alexa fretted, looking to Evelyn for help.

'Give him time, Alexa, it might take a few minutes,' Evelyn assured her, kneeling beside them both and applying pressure to his wound. 'Come on, Logan, don't give up now,' she added, removing her jacket and placing it over his nakedness.

'He is losing a lot of blood,' said Leila, her fangs involuntarily protracting at the sight of his blood soaking into the ground beneath him. 'I think we need to get him out of here, Evelyn, the blood is attracting the demons.'

Evelyn scanned the area around them, horrified to see dozens of mud demons cautiously inching towards them, their scaly bodies easily moving through the mud.

'*Manere retrorsum*!' she shouted sweeping her arm across in front of her, 'Stay back!'

The mud demons snarled and shrieked, but didn't move any closer, their keening hurting their ears as the women tried to move Logan.

'We are going to need help, Leila. We won't make the distance to the carpark on our own,' Evelyn shouted, helping Alexa pull Logan into a sitting position. 'Can you find Doug? We may need his surgical skills to stitch up Logan,' she added.

'Sure, he shouldn't be too hard to find now that the fog has cleared. I will be right back with some help,' she said racing off in the direction of the carpark.

'I hope he is still alive! I haven't heard any gun shots for a while now,' said Evelyn, looking across at Anya. 'I can't stop the bleeding, I think he may have been stabbed too deep.'

'No, I stabbed him to the hilt, the same as Ash. Shit! Shit!' fretted Anya, suddenly dropping to her knees and searching the ground. 'It's gone. The crystal has gone. I swear it was right in front of me. Did anyone pick it up?'

'No, I thought you still had it,' Evelyn said, joining the search. 'Perhaps Leila took it with her?'

'No, I don't think so, she never went anywhere near it.'

'I didn't see her take it either,' said Alexa peering around her. 'Did anyone see where Lillian went?'

'No, but if she is gone too, I am betting that she has taken the crystal with her,' Anya said, her brow furrowing in concern. 'Why would she want it? It is of no use to her.'

'If she has it, then I can guarantee she has a use for it,' Alexa replied. 'Is it possible to put the Nequam into another body?'

'No, the Nequam must choose its vessel and it must be someone with the right bloodline,' she replied.

'The same bloodline as Logan, by any chance?' Alexa replied. 'Logan is a Russell by blood.'

'Oh, my God,' Evelyn replied. 'She is going to use it on herself. We have to stop her. If she becomes the Nequam's next vessel, there will be no end to her cruelty. The whole world will suffer!'

Anya opened her mouth to respond but was suddenly knocked off her feet and sent sliding through the mud. She screamed as a large creeper pounced on top of her and snapped at her face, its putrid breath making her stomach heave in disgust. Momentarily knocking it off balance as she lifted her knee into its side, she deftly pulled her sidearm from her waistband and fired four rounds into the creature's chest infuriating it even further. It let out a guttural roar of fury and swiped at her, slicing open her chest with its razor-sharp claws.

A shot rang out and the creeper's body jolted, shifting its focus from Anya to the men behind it. Jonno and Doug opened fire, decimating the creatures head with a volley of bullets. It made a gurgling sound before slumping to the ground and pinning Anya underneath.

Pulling Anya's semi-conscious body from beneath the creeper, Jonno swung her into his arms and began to run back towards the carpark.

'We have to move now!' he shouted to the others. 'This place is about to be lit up like the fourth of fucking July.'

Leila and Doug quickly picked Logan up and began to follow Jonno. The distant drone of a plane quickly approaching, sending them into a panicked run.

'Holy Fuck!' Jonno exclaimed, coming to an abrupt halt in front of Doug. 'Where did they all come from?'

The group stopped and fearfully glanced around them. They were completely surrounded by dozens of creepers that awkwardly ambled towards them, cutting off any possible escape routes.

'We are all officially fucked,' Jonno declared, gently placing Anya on the ground and raising his rifle.

Doug looked across at Leila, his face unable to hide his despair. Shaking his head, he pulled out a grenade and held it to his chest.

'I am not going to become one of them,' he said, looking at each of their pale faces. 'We may as well take out a few of them at the same time.'

'Yeah, I'm with you, Dougie,' Jonno replied. 'There is no way I am going down without a fight. Let's take as many of these bastards with us as we possibly can.' He opened fire on the nearest creepers.

Leila, Alexa and Evelyn held hands and moved closer to the two men, crouching down over the inert forms of Logan and Anya and waiting for it all to end.

A piercing whistling sound followed by a brilliant flash of blue light filled the air around them and the group looked up to see the silhouette of a man walking towards them with his arms outstretched. A ring of blue light emanated from his body and pulsed through the throng of creepers, disintegrating them on contact. He was surrounded by a brilliant white aura of light and they watched in astonishment as the light spread out, manifesting into the shape of a large pair of wings. Each translucent wing had a span of at least three metres and the man knelt before them on one knee, covering the entire group in a protective glow of light.

A plane engine sounded overhead, and the women screamed as a deafening blast and orange flash engulfed the lake shore and surrounding park.

Chapter 13

Lillian moved quickly towards the shoreline; the crystal blade held out in front of her in the hope it would deter any possible attack from the hundreds of demons that amassed around the shore. She had planned on stealing the blade once the Nequam had been vanquished, but she hadn't expected the theft to prove so easy. With the other women focused on Logan's deteriorating condition, she had easily picked up the crystal and slipped away unnoticed. The next part of her plan was not going to be as trouble free, however, as she now needed Cerridwen to allow the embodiment of the Nequam and start the ritual.

The plan had manifested in her head after realising that she was losing Alexa's loyalty. Alexa was corrupted by her feelings for Logan and Lillian knew she would do anything to keep him safe, even if that meant betraying her.

They always betray me in the end, she thought bitterly as she finally reached the shore.

Blood red water lapped at her feet and she quickly removed her shoes, relishing the feel of the soft mud beneath her toes. Looking out across the water, she could see that the vortex had now closed and the last of the demons were making their way ashore. They ignored her for the most part and she continued up the shore, buoyed in her faith that she would be protected as a chosen one.

As she neared a large group of keening mud demons, her blood suddenly ran cold. The demons were amassed around an upright post that had been placed in the mud and they appeared to be in mourning.

'*Manere retrorsum*!' she shouted, waving the crystal as she pushed her way through.

Lillian cried out in dismay and dropped to her knees at the base of the post, her hand covering her mouth as she openly wept.

'Cerridwen, my beautiful Goddess, what has he done to you?' she wailed, looking up into the bloodied eyes of Cerridwen's disembodied head. Yanking the head from the post, she cradled it in her lap and wailed along with the demons.

'He will pay for this! I will embody the Nequam and tear Ashton apart, limb by limb. He will suffer, I promise you, my Goddess, you will be avenged!' Lillian shouted, plunging the crystal blade into her chest. '*Me Involvunt.* I give you my body and soul,' she whispered before slumping to the ground and passing out.

****

As the pilot dropped his pay load onto the park below, he whooped with delight, instantly radioing in his success.

'This is Eagle Number 2. We have a direct hit on the target. I repeat, we have a direct hit on the target. I will do another sweep to secure the area before the Hawkes set down. Over and out.'

'Roger that, Eagle 2, please advise of any surviving hostiles. Over and out,' relayed the static voice through his earpiece.

Pulling sharply to the left, the pilot dropped altitude and flew across the blackened park, opening the missile hatch in preparation. As he neared the drop zone, he felt the left engine shudder and stall, followed quickly by the second one.

'What the fuck?' he muttered, frantically pushing several buttons on the instrument panel.

'Mayday, mayday! I have multiple engine failure and I am going down,' he shouted into his mouthpiece.

Emergency beepers sounded, and the plane began to lose altitude as the pilot struggled to keep the nose up. Realising he had to bail, he pressed the ejection switch and the roof opened up, spewing him out into the cold air. He crossed himself with relief as the parachute deployed and he began to descend gently, watching as his abandoned plane continued on its collision course. It crashed into the lake moments later, sinking almost immediately after hitting the surface.

As the pilot descended, he surveyed the decimation below him. The park resembled a blackened crater and twisted and charred bodies littered the ground. He could see pockets of survivors within the untouched carpark but was surprised to see another group several yards away, in the epicentre of the blast. A ring of scorched grass surrounded them, but the small area they now stood in appeared to be intact. Puzzled, but relieved that they had somehow survived the blast, he shifted his weight and headed down towards them. Some of them were waving their arms and shouting at him, but he couldn't hear what they were saying. He waved back just as an impact from his right knocked the wind out of him. Startled, he turned his head and screamed in terror as a large, winged creature grabbed his head and crushed it like a watermelon before ripping it from his shoulders. The creature flew off with its trophy, leaving the pilot's lifeless body to continue its graceful descent to the charred earth below.

****

Evelyn clung desperately to Leila and Alexa, her hands covering her ears as the missile struck the park around them. Cocooned in their halo of light, they were protected from the force of the blast, but they were not spared the deafening roar or the subsequent ringing that persisted in their ear drums.

Feeling disorientated, Evelyn looked towards their saviour as he stood up and helped her to her feet. The glow around his body slowly dissipated and she gasped in relief as she finally made out his features.

'Ash!' she cried, reaching for his face. 'You're alive!' she sobbed.

Ash's eyes flashed from blue back to deep brown and he embraced Evelyn.

'I'm fine,' he replied, kissing her forehead, 'but Logan and Anya are not,' he said motioning to the prone forms at Leila and Alexa's feet. 'What happened to them?'

'We expelled the Nequam from Logan, but he should have recovered by now. Will did almost immediately when we used the crystal on him,' Evelyn replied. 'Anya is in a bad way too.

She was attacked by a creeper and if we don't get her help soon, she may not make it.'

Kneeling beside Logan, Ash extended his arms over his body and lowered his head, softly chanting as his hand hovered over Logan's wound. His hands began to glow, and a brilliant flash of light pulsated from them, entering Logan's body and bringing instant colour back to his pallid skin. He repeated the same process for Anya, and she sat bolt upright and threw her arms around him with relief.

The sound of another approaching plane droned overhead, and they all looked skyward as the plane suddenly went silent and began to plummet to the ground. Moments later the pilot ejected himself and was now falling slowly towards them, his parachute having successfully deployed. Jonno suddenly swore and began waving and shouting frantically at the pilot. The pilot merely waved back, oblivious to the danger that was quickly approaching him from behind. He suddenly realised at the last moment and screamed as a large, winged creature tore his head off and flew away.

Horrified, the survivors looked away, cringing as the headless body impacted with the ground with a sickening thud. Anya buried her head into Ash's shoulder, and he ran his hand up her back protectively.

'I have to go, Anya,' he said, gently pulling away. 'I have to finish this now, once and for all. I will be back for you, I promise,' he said, kissing her before turning his back and walking away.

Anya began to follow him, her eyes brimming with tears, but Evelyn placed a hand on her shoulder and whispered in her ear.

'Let him go, Anya. He has to do this, it is his destiny,' she said softly. 'He has awakened the Triune once again and he will now stop at nothing to defeat the Nequam. Once he has done what he came to do, Ash will be back, and you can be together again.'

Shaking her head sadly, Anya watched as he disappeared into the smoke haze and headed for the lake.

'But he needs our help,' Anya insisted. 'What if he can't defeat the Nequam on his own?'

'If he can't defeat him, then no one can and we are all doomed,' Evelyn replied. 'In the meantime, we need to get you and Logan out of here. Logan is human now and no match for any demons that may have survived the blast. The sooner you are both evacuated, the better.'

Logan suddenly groaned and opened his eyes, looking up at Alexa.

'What happened?' he said groggily.

'The Nequam is gone. He can no longer control you,' replied Alexa as tears of relief ran down her cheeks.

'It's gone? Are you sure?' he replied, struggling to sit up. 'But how?'

'The crystal from the caves allowed us to siphon it out once Anya stabbed you with it. The Nequam is now trapped in the crystal,' she replied. 'How are you feeling, Logan?'

'I'm fine,' he said looking across at Anya. 'Shit! We have to find Ash. If Cerridwen gets him…'

'Ash is fine, no thanks to you,' Anya snapped. 'In fact, he just saved your miserable life.'

'Anya, it wasn't Logan's fault,' admonished Evelyn. 'He was being controlled and…'

'I don't care! I look at him and all I can see is a monster that has taken countless innocent lives. Everything that has happened and is yet to happen is because of him and his psychopath girlfriend,' Anya interrupted. 'Evelyn, whether you think Logan is responsible or not, I can't even begin to forgive him. And quite frankly, I can't believe that you are so quick to forget what he has done,' she added, glaring at her.

'He is my son and I will love him no matter what. You will understand that one day when you have kids of your own. A mother's love knows no boundaries and I know in my heart that Logan is a good man who under normal circumstances would be incapable of hurting anyone and I am certain that Ash will feel the same way,' she said helping Logan to his feet.

'Ladies, we don't have time for this right now, we need to get you all to the evacuation point before more of those things decide to turn up for an "all you can eat" buffet,' declared Doug motioning to the lake side. 'We don't know for sure that they have all been destroyed.'

'I am not going anywhere without Ash. You do what you need to do, but I am not leaving him again,' retorted Anya defiantly.

'Anya, you need to get out of here. You will be of no use to Ash if you are injured again,' replied Evelyn.

'I can't sit back and do nothing and none of you are going to stop me!'

'Okay, okay. I will come with you. A cloaking spell should keep us safe from any stray demons. Leila, we could use your help too,' replied Evelyn.

'I told you, Dougie, women are bat shit crazy,' remarked Jonno, shaking his head.

Shooting him a look of unbridled disdain, Anya approached him, standing mere centimetres from his face.

'Crazy hey? Well I would rather be considered crazy than a fucking coward!' she snapped. 'This isn't over until every last one of those demons is destroyed and until that happens, we can't evacuate. You run along, by all means, but I am staying here to fight.'

'I hate to say it, Jonno, but she might have a point,' Doug replied, looking across at Jonno's sheepish face. 'It is our job to ensure these creatures are put down and now is the only opportunity we may have. Besides, the army may be reluctant to send a helicopter now for a while, once they realise what has happened to their pilot.'

'Well, I guess we have some free time on our hands after all. Count me in,' Jonno said with his trademark grin.

'I want to help too,' remarked Logan, wincing as he got to his feet.

'Not a chance,' chided Alexa. 'You can hardly stand up on your own. We are going back to the carpark,' she said dismissively, leading him away from the group.

'Logan,' Evelyn called after him, waiting as he spun around. 'It is good to have you back. I am so glad you are okay.'

Nodding, he shot her a hesitant smile before looking down at his bare feet. Running his hands nervously through his hair, he lifted his head and looked across at her. 'Look, Evelyn, I'm sorry if I have done or said anything to hurt you. That wasn't me,' he said. 'I know what you have done to try and save both Ash and I and I just hope that it is not too late to help him as well.'

Nodding, Evelyn smiled back. 'You know I will do whatever I can to protect you both. I will not come back without your brother. We will see you again soon, I promise,' she said.

'I am counting on that. Bring my brother back in one piece,' he said, turning his head and limping away with Alexa.

****

The ground rumbled beneath the water tower and the support struts swayed briefly, threatening to topple the girls off the side.

'What the hell was that?' said Paige looking towards the lake. 'It looks like someone dropped a fricking bomb!'

'I think someone did!' replied Tash, repositioning herself on the narrow ledge and peering through the binoculars. They hadn't heard any planes due to the constant gunfire, but Tash could clearly make out the shape of a plane as it flew over the lake.

Paige cast a worried look at Tash before reloading her gun and robotically firing at individual creepers on the ground below. She couldn't allow herself to entertain the very real possibility that her uncle had been caught up in the fray. That was not what he would want, and she could hear his voice prompting her to stay focused on the task at hand. '*Lesson number two: never take your eyes off your enemy because they will be watching you for any sign of weakness,*' he had said in her first week of training.

She had made the mistake of becoming complacent around their werewolf captive, a few weeks earlier; turning her back to the cage when she thought he had been adequately sedated. He had not, and she had come within mere millimetres of being swiped by his razor-sharp claws. It was a lesson well learnt and she now continued to fire upon the creatures below without any hesitation or further thought for her uncle's fate. Most of the creepers had left the compound earlier, heading in the direction of the lake. Their movements through the trees ahead had seemed choreographed and Paige couldn't help but marvel at the strange sight of them moving in perfect synchrony as though an invisible conductor was directing their every move.

Tash shot an injured creeper with her crossbow and it screamed before crashing to the ground in an undignified heap. Confident that it had been the last one, the girls cautiously dropped the rope ladder and began to climb down. They carefully made their way around the inert corpses and ran to the back door of the house. The door creaked open and Paige called out to Private James. Hearing a faint voice coming from the armoury, she rushed in to find him sitting in her uncle's favourite armchair. The room had been destroyed and Paige stared in disbelief at the upturned chairs and smashed glass that littered the carpet. Private James sat rigid in shock, his hands visibly shaking as he tried to wipe blood from them. At his feet lay the dead body of a large creeper; its face drawn in a grotesque grimace as its lifeless eyes stared at the ceiling.

Paige gently placed her hand on the soldier's arm, and he flinched at her touch but didn't make any attempt to move.

'It's over, Private, they have all gone,' she said gently. 'Do you know where the others are?'

He took a deep breath and slowly turned his head to look at her. A single tear slid down his cheek, cleaving a pale, neat line down his blood-soaked face.

'They're all dead,' he choked. 'I saw them get torn apart with my own eyes.'

Paige bit her lip and glanced across at Tash, hoping her friend would be able to intercept the unspoken thoughts that now flitted through her mind. To her relief, Tash was already moving towards Private James, her eyes full of understanding and empathy as she took his hand in hers. Tash was no stranger to trauma of this nature, having witnessed the massacre of her entire dorm at the hands of Logan and his werewolf pack. A calmness appeared to have taken over her as she spoke with the private and pulled him into a strong embrace.

Leaving Tash to provide what comfort she could, Paige headed out the door, deliberately averting her eyes away from the mutilated body of one of the fallen soldiers who lay awkwardly across the top step. Taking a deep breath, she radioed Nate.

'It's safe to come out, Nate, the creepers have moved on. I will clear the steps for you, but it ain't pretty out here. There are blood and guts everywhere!' she said.

'I would rather it looked like that out there than in here,' Nate replied, yanking back the latch and grinning as Paige's smiling face came into view. 'I don't ever think I have been happier to see someone in my entire life.'

'I have that effect on people, or so I am told,' she said. 'Now give me a hand, these suckers are heavy,' she added, dragging a charred torso from the steps.

****

Lillian awoke to find herself buried by charred bodies. Pushing them away from her, she struggled to stand up, slipping in the mud and gore that lapped against her bare feet. She surveyed the area around her with a feeling of anger and despair at the destruction of so many demons. Crying out in anger, she felt a ripple of power surge through her and exit her fingertips in an arc of white energy. Examining her hands, she began to laugh.

'It worked!' she said aloud, turning to retrieve Cerridwen's head from the mud and holding it aloft. 'It worked and now I can avenge you,' she vowed, gently placing the head back in the mud.

Turning to face the lake, she waved her hands and the choppy waters began to swirl, gradually reopening the vortex. 'Come my brothers and sisters. Join me and we shall make this earth ours,' she shouted.

'That is not going to happen,' a male voice interrupted from behind her.

Quickly spinning around, her eyes bulged in fury at the sight of her grandson standing before her.

'Wakehurst!' she spat. 'You, pathetic little cocksucker! You will pay for killing Cerridwen, you and everyone you care about!'

'You can't embody the Nequam. It will destroy you. Give me the crystal before it is too late,' Ash replied calmly.

Lillian began to laugh and took a few steps closer to him.

'It is already too late. I have embodied the Nequam and now I am going to crush you like a fucking cockroach,' she seethed, reaching for his throat.

'You need to listen to me, Lillian. You can't contain the Nequam, it is too strong. If you try and turn, it will tear you apart. Give me the crystal and I can reverse the spell,' Ash pleaded.

'Never! What makes you think I would ever listen to you? You nearly killed me once, but I won't ever be that weak again,' she replied. 'I am stronger than you now and I am going to make you pay for everything you have done,' she said, lunging at him.

Grabbing him, she threw him onto the ground with such force, that the ground cracked beneath him. Shaking his head, he quickly jumped to his feet, ducking as she swung a post at his head. Before she could take another swing, he reached up and gripped her throat, tossing her like a ragdoll into a nearby streetlamp. The pole snapped on impact and the top half toppled onto the ground leaving its sharp base dangerously exposed.

Lillian roared with fury, sending out beams of energy from her hands into Ash's chest, knocking him off balance. She pinned him to the ground and spread her fingers across his face, trying to gouge his eyes out with her sharp fingernails. Ash screamed as her fingers dug in, unable to extricate himself from her firm grip.

Lillian's head suddenly jolted forward as something impacted her head, and she swore, letting go of Ash's head and twisting around to confront a person behind her.

Evelyn stood tall; a wooden post gripped firmly in her hand.

'Get your fucking hands off my son,' she muttered through gritted teeth, readying the post above her head.

'You little bitch!' Lillian screamed, launching herself at Evelyn and knocking her to the ground. 'I should have suffocated you in your sleep as an infant. You have brought me nothing but trouble your whole miserable life!' she screeched, pinning Evelyn down.

'I am surprised you didn't. You seem to have a knack for killing defenceless babies,' Evelyn replied, struggling to push her off.

'Yes, I have killed many times and before I squeeze the life from your useless body, I want you to know something,' she whispered. 'I killed your precious Harry. It was me that tampered with the brakes in his car and I have never regretted it, not once. I just wish that you and your pathetic brat had perished along with him!' she added, squeezing Evelyn's throat.

Ash grabbed Lillian from behind and threw her off his mother, facing off with her once again.

'It is not too late, Lillian. You have to get rid of the Nequam or it will destroy you!' Ash warned.

Lillian laughed and lunged for him, pushing him backwards with a bolt of energy that struck him square in the chest. Pursuing him, she struck again, but this time he raised his arm and deflected the blow. Infuriated, her eyes flashed red and turned to face Evelyn and the others. *'Displodo,'* she hissed as a shockwave left her hands and rippled through the small group, knocking them all off their feet.

Anya quickly jumped to her feet and fired her gun, hitting Lillian between the eyes. Lillian sneered at her as the bullet dislodged from the wound and hovered in the air in front of her face.

'You will have to do better than that!' Lillian said, sending the bullet flying back at Anya, only stopping short when Ash plucked it from the air and crushed it in his hand.

'Enough!' Ash shouted, glaring at Lillian. 'Your issue is with me and if it's a fight you want, then it's a fight you will get.'

'Finally!' Lillian said rolling her eyes. 'I was wondering when you would finally grow a set of balls!' she mocked. 'Say good-bye to your slut of a girlfriend, once I am finished with you, she will be...'

Ash stepped in front of her and punched her hard in the face, smashing her nose with his fist and sending her reeling backwards. Anya followed Ash, cracking a steel pole across Lillian's forehead and leaving a gaping wound. Before her injuries could begin to heal, Jonno and Doug stepped forward, spraying her chest with a volley of bullets until the barrels of their guns clicked over empty.

'You, fools!' she screamed. 'You can't kill me! I am immortal!' a voice thundered from within her body as she began to tear off her clothes.

Dropping to her knees, she began to transform, screaming as her bones cracked and bulged in their sockets. Her spine rippled and arced, her skin tearing apart and exposing the sinews and muscles in her back. Screaming in agony, she rolled onto her side, convulsing as her body tried to transition. As her ribcage bulged within her chest, her skin stretched impossibly tight and exploded, showering the horrified group with chunks of flesh and bone. The screaming stopped, and Ash approached Lillian's limp body, turning his head in revulsion at the sight of her mutilated torso. Her ribcage looked as though it had been prised open from the inside out and it now resembled a twisted and broken mess. Her remaining internal organs were scattered around her while her ruptured intestines oozed their vile contents onto the ground by her side. Prodding her lifeless body with his foot, Ash jumped back as a thick black mass emerged from her open mouth and dissipated into the air above their heads, hissing as it eddied and disappeared from view.

Retching sounds alerted Ash to the others and he spun around to see Jonno squatting and heaving the contents of his stomach into the slimy mud. Anya stood white-faced, glancing towards the spot where his mother lay on the ground with her head in Leila's lap.

'Mum?' Ash said, quickly making his way towards Evelyn. 'Oh God, Mum, what happened?' he said frantically.

Evelyn's shirt was soaked through with blood and she moved her hand shakily to show Ash the gaping wound in her side that a sharp pole now protruded from. She opened her mouth to speak but began coughing up blood.

'She was impaled on the base of the lamp post when she was thrown backwards. I don't know if we should try and move her, she could bleed to death,' she fretted.

'She'll die anyway if we don't. We need to get her to safety,' Ash said, gently lifting Evelyn up from the pole.

'Hang in there, Mum, you are going to be okay,' Ash replied, holding his hand over her wound and chanting gently.

She smiled weakly, her eyes glazing over as his hands filled with blue light.

'Ash, we have trouble!' Doug shouted across to him, pulling out his knife.

'In a minute, Doug, Mum needs my help first,' Ash replied, hastily continuing his healing ritual.

'You don't have a minute,' Doug retorted pointing towards the shoreline. 'The Nequam is not finished with us yet.'

Ash spun around and swore at the sight before him. A large black mass was manifesting on the shoreline and absorbing the bodies of dead demons as it made its way towards them, increasing in size upon its approach. It emitted a droning buzzing sound and Ash swatted at a stray fly that flew at his face. Several more followed and Ash turned to the others.

'Fuck, I need more time,' he said in desperation. 'Leila and Anya, get my mum to safety, I will deal with this and then find you.'

'Ash, I don't think she will last much longer,' Leila said sadly, picking Evelyn up in her arms.

'Just get her out of here! Do what you can to save her, none of us are going to last much longer if I don't stop the Nequam now,' he snapped, standing up and striding towards the mass.

'Ash! You can't face it on your own!' Anya yelled after him.

'I won't be on my own, Anya,' he said spinning around to face her. 'I have the Triune,' he said as his eyes flashed blue and he ran into the swirling mass of flies.

****

The pilot carefully set the Black Hawke down and several soldiers jumped out onto the tarmac of the Liberty Park carpark. Raising their rifles, they scoured the area and began to spread out in their search for the survivors.

Rounding the side of a nearby jeep, Lieutenant Monty Sullivan swore, covering his mouth with his hand in revulsion at the sight of a dead teenaged girl propped against the wheel. She had been disembowelled and her head hung at an unnatural angle as her blank eyes stared at the ground.

'Jesus Christ,' he muttered, signalling to the others before continuing on his way. Confronted by several more bodies in different locations, he was relieved to finally find a surviving girl hiding inside a vehicle. She was inconsolable and clearly suffering with shock as he tried to coax her out. Realising his efforts were futile, he reached in and picked her up, cradling her gently as her whole body shook. Another soldier approached with a blanket and she was quickly whisked away to the safety of the helicopter.

Hearing voices, he raised his gun and watched as a small group of people, including two soldiers limped towards him.

'Boy, are we glad to see you!' said the first soldier, introducing himself as Private Sims. 'We thought there for a while that no one was coming.'

'We nearly weren't, especially when we lost contact with our bird,' Lieutenant Sullivan replied. 'Do you know what happened to it?'

'It crashed into the lake after it was attacked by a demon,' replied Doug, straight-faced.

'A demon? You can't be serious,' scoffed the lieutenant.

'Mate, I wish I wasn't, but this place was crawling with them until your man dropped a missile right up their asses,' replied Doug. 'We have been under siege for hours and they have been picking us off, one by one. There are hardly any of us left.'

'Where's the pilot? Did he have time to eject?' Lieutenant Sullivan enquired.

'He didn't make it. His body is somewhere over there,' Private Sims interjected, pointing towards the darkened park. 'We need to get out of here, some serious shit is going down over by the lake shore.'

Private Sims walked past the stunned lieutenant, carrying an injured soldier with Nate's help. Stu quickly followed, supporting a teenage girl as she limped unsteadily.

'How many more survivors are there?' Lieutenant Sullivan asked, eyeing Logan as Alexa stopped to wipe his face. The tall man was naked – save for a strategically placed jacket – and covered in blood. He kept looking back towards the lake and seemed reluctant to leave.

'We still have four more out there. We need to give them some more time,' Doug replied, turning back towards the lake.

'I have orders to evacuate everyone from this area within the next fifteen minutes. I cannot allow you to go back for anyone else,' the lieutenant replied.

'Listen mate,' said Jonno, pushing past Doug. 'I don't give a rat's ass about your orders. We are not leaving without them. Give us more ammo and we will return with them quicker than you can shake your dick.'

'I am not giving you ammo. You are a civilian!' retorted the flustered lieutenant.

'On the contrary,' interjected Alexa as she sauntered towards him. 'You will give these good men the ammo they need, you will also send back another helicopter to pick them up when they return,' she said, touching the lieutenant's shirt, suggestively. 'And you will give Logan your clothes.'

'Give them what they need, Private,' he said, addressing the nearest soldier. 'We need to get that bird in the air and radio in for another one,' he ordered, quickly removing his pants and shirt before handing them to Logan. Pulling his socks and boots off, and leaving them on the ground at Logan's feet, he sullenly headed back towards the helicopter wearing nothing but his jocks and singlet.

Logan quickly dressed and pulled Alexa towards him, planting a kiss on her forehead.

'Thanks, baby, I don't know what I would do without you,' he said with a grin. 'Listen, Alexa. I'm going to go with Doug and Jonno. I can't leave knowing Ash and Evelyn are still out there.'

'You know I can now use my whispering powers on you too, don't you,' Alexa warned, stroking his face.

'Yes, I am very aware of that, but I have to try and help my brother. He would do the same for me,' Logan replied.

'Yes, I think you are right, Logan, he would do anything to save you,' she replied earnestly. 'But there is no way you are leaving me behind, I am coming too,' she said grabbing a gun from a passing soldier.

****

Ash felt himself being flung around, spinning in the vortex of darkness that engulfed him. His skin crawled with masses of flies, thousands of Calliphoridae clamouring to gain access to his nostrils and mouth as they poured over his face. Gagging as the persistent creatures invaded his airways, he summoned the energy from within and a blue light rippled through his body, shrouding him from the flies.

A deep guttural sound rumbled around him, and he was knocked to the ground, gasping as he felt the crushing weight of the mass upon his chest. Once again, the flies swarmed, their microscopic mandibles gnawing at his skin as they amassed by the thousands. Struggling to free himself, he cried out as the bones in his body began to crack under the tremendous weight atop him. Flies swarmed into his open mouth, filling his mouth and throat and blocking his airway.

As he gasped in vain for breath, he fell in and out of consciousness, his body frantically trying to heal as it slowly began to shut down. He suddenly felt a wave of peace wash over him and his mind was transported to another dimension. Opening his eyes, he squinted as brilliant light filtered through the clouds above him and peppered the verdant countryside in which he now stood.

A woman dressed entirely in white began to approach him, her face concealed by a veil that hung down to her slender waist. By her side, walked a small child, her chubby fingers clutching the fabric of her mother's gown as she toddled along. The woman stopped a few feet ahead of Ash and removed her veil, tossing her long auburn hair over her bare shoulders. Her long strapless gown clung to her body, accentuating the curve of her waist and her perfect cleavage as she glanced sadly towards him. '*Anya!*' Ash called out and he willed himself to move his legs, but they felt like they belonged to somebody else and wouldn't cooperate.

Anya stood serenely, her hair blowing around her as the breeze began to pick up. The grass beneath her bare feet began to blacken and rot as it shrunk back into the ground and was replaced by a slick black substance. She remained expressionless and turned her head to look behind her as a dark figure approached.

The sky unexpectantly began to darken and Ash felt his heart thumping within the confines of his chest as he frantically willed his body to move. He cried out to her again, but she didn't respond, her gaze was firmly fixed on the approaching form.

Finally turning back around, she looked towards Ash and pulled the child closer to her thigh, a single tear cascading down her cheek. A large human-like demon began to circle her, touching her face and hair with its scaly fingers. Its putrid breath panted on her skin as it lasciviously ran its slimy tongue across her cheek. The demon turned to look at Ash and opened its mouth wide, revealing several rows of impossibly long canines. The child began to whimper by her side and Anya screamed, reaching out her arms out to Ash.

'Ash! Please help us! Wake up! Ash!' she pleaded, jolting him back into his mind and his unconscious body.

A rush of adrenaline filled him, and a brilliant surge of light escaped his hands and eyes, filling the space around him. The light intensified and shone as bright as the sun as it burst from his body and inundated the mass atop of him. An ear-splitting shriek emanated from the churning mass before it exploded with a hiss and dissipated into millions of tiny pieces of obsidian rock. The rock fell from the sky like volcanic ash, littering the entire lake and burying Ash beneath it.

Chapter 14

Anya struggled to support Evelyn's weight, even with Leila's help as they headed towards the carpark. Leila was weakening by the minute and she staggered in her efforts to hold Evelyn up. Eventually slipping in the mud, she collapsed and let go of Evelyn.

'You need blood, Leila,' Anya said, noting Leila's pallid complexion. 'You are going to have to feed from me.'

'No,' Leila insisted, shaking her head. 'I haven't fed directly from a human in over a decade. I don't think I would be able to control myself.'

'Leila, you have to feed. Evelyn needs you!' Anya insisted, holding out her wrist. 'Do it. It's okay. It's not like I haven't been fed off before,' she said blushing at the memory of Ash biting her during sex.

'I do not want to know the details of that particular story,' Leila said, reaching for her wrist and hesitating before sinking her teeth into her tender flesh.

'Ouch!' cried Anya, 'it doesn't hurt when Ash does it!' she said as Leila continued to feed.

Feeling faint she tried to pull away her hand, but Leila gripped her wrist tighter.

'Leila, that's enough, I think I am going to pass out,' she said, struggling to free her wrist.

Leila ignored her and continued to drink greedily from her veins.

'Leila! Stop! You're hurting me!' Anya begged desperately.

A loud explosion sounded behind them forcing Leila to momentarily let go of Anya's arm. A light mist of ash particles began to float down from the sky, dotting the two women's faces and clothes with tiny black specks.

Leila's black eyes narrowed, and she hungrily looked across at Anya, lunging for her throat.

'Leila, stop! You need to control yourself. This is not you,' shouted Doug as he raced over to the women.

'Stay away from me,' Leila shrieked, quickly shielding her face before running away from the group.

'Leila! Wait! It is not safe out there on your own!' Doug pleaded to her fast retreating back.

Shaking his head, he reached out his hand to Anya and pulled her to her feet.

'Are you okay, Anya?' Doug enquired, inspecting her wrist wound.

'I'll be okay, I just feel very weak,' she said staggering on her feet and falling sideways into Jonno's arms.

'I knew you'd fall for me one day,' Jonno joked, supporting her weight.

'Oh please! That will never happen!' Anya sniped, pushing him away and standing beside Evelyn. 'She is fading fast. We have to get her some help!'

Logan was quickly by her side, holding Evelyn's limp hand.

'I might be able to help,' he said, rubbing her hand and lowering his head. Muttering something in Latin, he ran his hand up her arm and cradled her head gently.

A slight blush crept across her skin and she jolted awake, staring with obvious surprise into Logan's face.

'Logan? Is that really you?' she said incredulously, reaching out to wipe the soot from his blackened face. 'You can heal too?'

'It looks like being having a witch bloodline can have its benefits after all,' he said with a grin.

'Oh Logan, your father had the same gift for healing and now it has been passed on to you and your brother. I can't believe it,' she said shaking her head.

'Speaking of Ash, we need to go back and help him,' Anya stated, turning to face the group.

'Yes, we should keep moving,' Doug agreed, motioning for the others to move ahead. Grabbing Anya's arm, he spun her around and whispered in her ear. 'Why I am I picking up a supernatural vibe from you?'

'I don't know what you are talking about,' said Anya dismissively, shaking her arm from his grip and quickly joining the others.

Shaking his head, Doug glanced at Jonno and began to follow the group towards the lake shore.

'We need to keep an eye on her. There is something she is not telling us,' Doug said solemnly.

'Good luck cracking that egg,' Jonno replied, 'She is a closed book.'

'Well, it is a good thing that I like to read,' Doug replied, quickly picking up his pace.

As the group neared the lake, the soggy ground underfoot was replaced by small stones that crunched beneath their feet. The shoreline and lake were completely blackened; the stones blanketing the lake and park over a one hundred metre radius. The only indication that they were still at the lake were the tops of the park benches that poked through the rocky surface and the twisted playground equipment.

'Where the hell is he?' Anya said, desperately scanning the various rock mounds around them. Kicking the nearest one, the top layer of stones rolled away revealing the lifeless body of a mud demon, its face drawn in a final snarl.

'Shit! Ash could be buried underneath the stones! Help me find him!' she pleaded, racing to the nearest mound and unearthing another demon's body.

The group spread out, digging through the rocks with their bare hands in the hope that one of the mounds would contain Ash.

'I've found him!' shouted Jonno, pulling Ash's lifeless body from beneath the rock debris. 'He's not breathing!' he said, rolling him onto his side.

Anya raced over to help, quickly clearing his mouth of debris before rolling him over onto his back. Jonno began chest compressions as Anya desperately performed mouth to mouth resuscitation. As Jonno began to tire, Logan took over, muttering the healing incantation as he thumped Ash's chest in frustration.

'Come on Ash! Breathe goddamn it!' he muttered.

'Don't you dare give up on him,' Anya snapped. 'He is in there somewhere, I know it!'

'It's not working, I can't heal him!' Logan replied.

After a while, Doug stepped forward and gently placed his hand on Anya's shoulder.

'It has been over ten minutes and we don't know how long he had been buried under the stone before that. It is time to let him go,' Doug said softly.

'No! He is still a vampire; he can't die like this! He will come back to life, I know it!' she said.

'Anya, sweetie. There was always the chance that this would happen once the Triune was expelled. I prayed he would be okay, but it was too much for anyone to endure,' Evelyn said, choking up. 'I don't think he is going to come back from this.'

'No! It's not fair! Not after everything he has gone through,' Anya sobbed, cradling Ash's head in her lap. 'He can't be gone!'

Evelyn crouched down beside Anya, and robotically stroked Ash's face as her tears silently fell onto his soot covered skin. Placing her arms around Anya's heaving shoulders, she pulled her into a strong embrace and the pair sobbed quietly, each lost in their own grief. Logan sat back on his haunches, holding his head in his hands as he stared at his brother's lifeless body.

'The odds were stacked against him, but he went in anyway,' Logan said solemnly, looking across at the rest of the group. 'He knew it would probably cost him his life, but he wanted to give us a chance to live. It should be me lying there, not him. He didn't deserve to fucking die!' Logan said, openly weeping as Alexa comforted him.

'None of this is your fault, Logan. Ash did what he had to do. What he was destined to do. He didn't just save us, he saved all of mankind with his actions tonight,' Alexa said, stroking Logan's back.

'It wasn't his destiny to die! He was meant to live and be with me and all those he loved,' Anya snapped. 'I didn't even get to tell him that he was going to be a…' she faltered before bursting into fresh tears.

'A father?' Alexa said. 'You're pregnant with his child?'

'Is that true, Anya? Are you pregnant?' Evelyn probed urgently.

'What difference does it make if I am? He won't ever get to see the child that we made together and now my child will have to grow up without a father. I can't do this on my own, especially if the child is…different,' Anya replied.

Doug stepped forward and knelt in front of Anya.

'The supernatural signature I was getting from you earlier, that's what it was, wasn't it? Your baby. But how is this even possible? He was a vampire and to my knowledge, vampires can't breed,' Doug said.

'So, what are you suggesting, Doug? That maybe Ash isn't the father? Are you fucking serious? I haven't been with anyone else,' Anya fumed.

'That's not what I was suggesting, Anya. I know Ash was special and a lot about him didn't fit the norm in regard to vampire abilities and behaviour. What I do know is this. If that baby inside you is really his, then it is also special and has most likely inherited his unique abilities. It is giving off a similar read to him.' Doug replied.

'So, do you think that Anya's baby also might have the gift for healing?' Logan interjected. 'It won't help. I have the same gift and it didn't make any difference. Trust me, I tried everything.'

'No, the baby's abilities are much greater than yours. I can feel it,' Doug replied.

Suddenly Anya's eyes rolled back in her head so that only the whites were showing. She began muttering incoherently and her head lolled backwards.

'Anya, are you okay?' Doug said, grabbing her shoulders and gently shaking her.

Anya's head rolled forward, and she fixed her milky eyes on Doug.

'I am fine, now get out of my way,' she said, pushing past him and robotically placing her hands upon Ash's chest.

Logan stared at her in confusion and then shot an accusatory glance at Alexa.

'Alexa! What are you doing to her?' Logan shouted.

'What I must do to save your brother,' she replied, her eyes focussed on Anya. 'I owe him my life and trust me, this is his only chance.'

Anya began to chant, swaying backwards and forth as she ran her hands along Ash's chest. The air around them began to buzz with static energy and gradually a soft white light radiated from Anya's fingertips. As the light intensified, Anya's nose began to bleed and her whole body shuddered.

'Alexa, you are hurting her!' Logan shouted, trying to break her concentration.

A pulse of energy suddenly shot out of Anya's hands, piercing Ash's heart and sending a shockwave through his entire body.

Ash instantly jolted awake, coughing and spluttering before doubling over and retching a vile black substance onto the ground beside him. Doug rushed to his side with a canteen of water and helped him to his feet. After taking a deep swill of the water, he shakily wiped his mouth with the back of his hand and looked around for Anya. She was sitting on the ground nearby, looking very confused as she examined her hands. Reaching her in one stride, Ash pulled her into his arms and pressed his forehead to hers. She looked wearily into his eyes and reached up to touch his stubbled jaw.

'Is it really you? You've come back to me?' she whispered, stroking his face.

Nodding, Ash grinned. 'Yes, it's really me. I heard your voice calling for me.'

She raised her head and pressed her lips to his, wrapping her arms around his neck.

Evelyn raced over and, after helping Anya to her feet, hugged them both with unabashed emotion.

'It's over, Ash, you destroyed the Nequam,' Evelyn said in between hugs. 'It is gone for good and so is the Triune. You and Logan are now free to live your lives,' she gushed.

Logan stepped into view, cautiously eying his brother as he moved to stand in front of him.

'It's good to see you're okay, buddy,' he said, sheepishly. 'Listen, I feel like absolute shit knowing what I put you through. I will completely understand if you want nothing to do with me now, but I really hope you will find it in your heart to forgive me one day. You have no idea how much I have fucking missed you, Ash!'

Ash nodded and placed his hand on Logan's shoulder.

'I have missed you too, Logan. It was so hard not having you by my side through all of this,' he replied. 'But a lot has happened, and I need time to process everything before I can move forward, as does Anya. Let's just take it one day at a time.'

'Whatever you need, you only have to ask,' Logan replied.

Ash scanned the relieved and weary faces of the people around him 'Did everyone make it? Where's Leila?'

'We don't know,' Evelyn replied. 'Anya let her feed from her to give her some strength back, but she lost control. She has now become Aphotic again.'

'What the hell does that mean?' Anya said.

'It is when a vampire goes dark,' Evelyn explained. 'A vampire who feeds straight from the veins and completely drains a person of their blood is at risk of losing their humanity. They cannot feel empathy and the light essentially leaves their soul. Because Leila was originally Aphotic, before meeting Doug, she automatically reverted back when she began feeding from you. She hasn't fed on fresh human blood in over a decade, but it still affected her,' Evelyn explained. 'It is like an addiction.'

'When I met her, she was a killer,' Doug interjected. 'After months of captivity, I was able to wean her off the blood and rid her of her Aphotic urges. She became a completely different person and we even became a couple there for a while.'

'Rana fed from me all the time and it didn't affect her. I have drunk human blood too,' replied Ash, casting a quick glance in Anya's direction.

'Small amounts of blood won't affect most vampires, but if Rana had taken your life, there is a good chance she would have gone down the same path as Leila. Every vampire is affected differently. Some can drink small amounts straight from the source and some can't tolerate any, such as Leila,' Doug explained.

'You have had the Triune spirit to keep you centred. Now that it has gone, if you drank blood now, you could potentially become an Aphotic vampire as well,' warned Evelyn. 'You will need to be careful in future, Ash, especially now that Anya is…'

'What will happen to Leila now?' Anya interrupted, shooting Evelyn a warning look.

'Don't worry about Leila. I will find her and get her back to her normal self. I won't harm her in any way, you have my word on that,' Doug replied earnestly.

'Good. That is good to know,' Anya replied, distractedly biting her nails. 'Maybe we should all head back to the carpark now. That helicopter should arrive soon.'

Looking across at Ash, she caught him staring at her with suspicion and quickly averted her eyes, pretending to concentrate on the hole in her shirt. The sound of a helicopter approaching, ignited the group and they quickly turned to head back to the car park. Grabbing Ash's hand, Anya dropped back behind the rest of the group and turned to face him.

'Ash, there is something I really need to tell you, but I am scared of how you will react,' Anya said warily.

'What is it? You know you can talk to me about anything,' Ash replied, furrowing his brow in concern.

Anya looked down at her feet, her hands trembling as she finally found the courage to look at him.

'I'm pregnant, Ash,' she blurted before bursting into tears.

Ash stared back at her for a moment, his mouth opened as though he wanted to speak, but no sound escaped. Instead a huge grin lit up his face and he pulled Anya into his arms, kissing her feverishly.

'Oh, Anya, you couldn't possibly make me any happier than you just have,' he gushed, wiping the tears from her face. 'How long have you known?'

'For a week now,' she replied. 'With everything that has been happening, I didn't know how I was going to tell you. I honestly thought you would run for the hills.'

'Why would you think that, Anya? Have I ever given you a reason not to trust me?' Ash said softly. 'There is no way I could ever leave you, Anya. I am so in love with you.'

Anya smiled weakly and buried her head into his chest; her body shaking as she struggled to hold back the torrent of tears that welled within her.

Sensing her anguish, Ash gently lifted her head and cradled her face.

'What's wrong, baby? What are you not telling me?' he gently probed.

'I am terrified that the baby might not be human and that I might give birth to something evil,' Anya said bluntly. 'The baby has powers and those powers are what brought you back to life,' she added tearfully.

'Anya, how can something that gives life be evil?' Ash reasoned, placing his hand on her stomach. 'This baby is a gift, and I don't care what he or she looks like when it is born, I will love and protect them with everything I have,' he said.

Anya smiled and placed her hand over his, her watery eyes finding his.

'I know you will. I should never have doubted that,' she said, wiping her eyes. 'I fucking love you, Ashton Wakehurst, don't you ever forget that.'

'Always so eloquent, Anya, one of the many things I love about you,' Ash joked, kissing her forehead. 'Let's catch up with the others; we can talk more along the way,' he said, wrapping his arm across her shoulders.

'Yes, I would love to hear about all the other things you love about me. I believe we have at least ten minutes up our sleeve,' Anya replied, matching his stride.

'I will need more than ten minutes. It would take me a whole lifetime to list everything,' Ash replied with a grin. 'Could you put up with me that long?'

'I honestly think I could,' Anya smiled, leaning in for a kiss.

As the group of survivors reached the carpark, the sun was rising, flickering its soft beams of light through the scorched trees and blackened park benches. They came to a stop at the large fountain which once stood proudly in the centre of the park. Its centrepiece, a large brass bell, was now lying on its side in the stagnant pool at its base. The cracked and blackened tiles defiantly holding together, steadfast in their duty to contain the water within.

The group turned around to bear final witness to the demise of the once thriving park. The landscape around them was almost unrecognisable beneath the soft morning haze that had begun its slow trek across the charred earth. Holding hands in memory for all those who had lost their lives, the survivors each bowed their heads, thankful to be still counted among the living. The melodic thrum of the waiting helicopter beckoned like a beacon and the group turned back towards the carpark and their certain liberation.